A
SUPERIOR
WAY TO DIE

A
SUPERIOR
WAY TO DIE

A KARIN NIEMI MYSTERY

LINDA W. FITZGERALD

LEVEL
BEST BOOKS

First published by Level Best Books 2025

Copyright © 2025 by Linda W. Fitzgerald

This novel is entirely a work of fiction. The names, characters and incidents portrayed in it are the work of the author's imagination. Any resemblance to actual persons, living or dead, events or localities is entirely coincidental.

Linda W. Fitzgerald asserts the moral right to be identified as the author of this work.

Author Photo Credit: Universal Church Directories

First edition

ISBN: 978-1-68512-956-9

Cover art by Level Best Designs

This book was professionally typeset on Reedsy.
Find out more at reedsy.com

For Tom

"My actions are my only true belongings:
I cannot escape their consequences."

— THICH NHAT HANN

Preface

This book is a work of fiction. Except for familiar landmarks in Michigan's Upper Peninsula (commonly referred to by state residents as the UP or, occasionally, The Yoop) as well as various restaurants in Munising and Marquette, all names, locales and incidents are products of the author's imagination. Likewise, all characters in this book are entirely fictional, and any resemblance to actual persons, living or dead, is mere coincidence.

Chapter One

Benjamin Roberts died on a star-spangled summer night while soaking in a hot tub on his private stretch of Lake Superior shoreline and sharing a bottle of wine—a Rioja Gran Reserva as I would later learn—with his occasional business partner and longtime bed partner, Meredith Wood.

It's exactly what those of us who knew him would have expected.

What I for one *wouldn't* have expected was that Ben would shuttle off his mortal coil less than a mile from my own rustic beach rental on the shores of the National Pictured Rocks Lakeshore in Michigan's Upper Peninsula. Or that I would learn about his passing at seven a.m. on a perfect July day while sipping the morning's first cup of coffee and listening to a homegrown newscaster from the Channel Six studios in nearby Marquette.

The woman staffing the news desk this morning had changed surprisingly little since the bygone days when we'd passed gossipy notes to each other in English class and lusted after unattainable football players in the lunchroom. Except for a few additional pounds, some barely noticeable wrinkles, and the usual traces of grief and wariness that time etches on every adult face, Sandy Heikkola looked much the same now as she did back in our days at Munising High.

Coffee mug in hand, I studied her face, trying to see it for the first time as if I were a fresh-eyed stranger. It's a little game I play with myself every now and then to shake off lazy habits of mind. Something Ben taught me when I was one of his menials. He insisted it would make me a better copywriter—more alert, more objective, more clear-sighted and clear-minded. Maybe it did. All I know is that it's helpful when I need to put some distance between me and an emotionally charged situation.

Looking at Sandy, I ticked off the details: Scandinavian blonde hair that just grazed her shoulders. Intelligent, don't-mess-with-me blue eyes. Broad face. Soaring cheekbones. A mouth that had to be reminded to smile. And skin that was still the texture of satin, unless the station's makeup consultant was working overtime. I made a mental note to call her and schedule a catch-up lunch. Maybe at Doncker's in Marquette.

Donckers. The very thought of D's old-fashioned soda fountain meals set off food fantasies. Of course, these days the place was always filled beyond capacity with pushy tourists from who-knows-where, all knees and elbows, waving their credit cards like tiny flags and using their outdoor voices to place orders. Still, most of them never get beyond the candy counter, circa 1920, on the first floor.

In my mind's eye, I dodged around the crowd, climbed the creaking steps to the second floor, and made my way through a hodge-podge of painted wooden tables jammed with root beer floats, milk shakes, steaming coffees, and Melmac plates buried under small mountains of chicken salad, five-inch-high Reuben sandwiches, deluxe cheeseburgers, potato chips, and homemade pickles.

"Once again, our top story this morning." Sandy's voice broke through my daydream. Like most lifelong residents of the UP, she made no effort to camouflage her slight but unmistakable Finnish lilt, if she even noticed it anymore.

"Shortly after ten p.m., Marquette Police responding to an emergency call from the Sand Point area of Munising discovered the body of well-known businessman and real estate investor Benjamin Roberts in an outdoor hot tub at his home. According to police, a preliminary medical examination conducted by emergency techs at the scene revealed a violent rash and a bluish tinge to the skin which, along with a medical alert bracelet noting an allergy to penicillin, could indicate death by anaphylactic shock. Based on details provided by Roberts' longtime companion Meredith Wood, who was with him at the time and who placed the nine-one-one call, the two had been sharing a bottle of wine. An investigation is underway, and an expedited coroner's report will be released within the coming week. In a few minutes, we'll be taking you to the scene for a more detailed report by our own Ken Balducci, including, we hope, a brief interview with Munising Police Chief Chuck Sallinen. But right now, let's check in with Pat Koski for a recap of last night's contentious meeting of the Alger County Board of Commissioners, which included another surprising and troubling accusation by local leaders of the Sault Tribe of Chippewa Indians regarding a proposed multi-unit residential development on National Pictured Rocks Lakeshore property."

I walked over to the ancient microwave, slid in my lukewarm cup of coffee, and pressed the start button. Turning to face the picture window—easily the best feature of my funky little lakeside getaway—I let myself be lulled by the whitecaps sweeping in from Munising Bay. Today, the Big Lake was a vibrating cobalt blue that borrowed its color from the sky.

As the microwave began pinging away the seconds, I tried to get my head around the fact that Ben Roberts was gone. Forever gone. And that he'd died less than a mile from where I was standing, his life surrendered to what could have been anaphylactic shock.

But how was that possible? The Ben I knew was a force of nature, ferociously alive, a seemingly permanent fixture in the world, immune to failure and grief and death and all the other inevitable tragedies this world doles out. He was also a bon vivant of the first order, eating and drinking his way through life with abandon. He used to brag that the only thing he couldn't tolerate was penicillin, which was easy to avoid. Or, given recent events, maybe not.

I let out a long, slow sigh.

Somehow, I would have expected Ben to take his leave with more panache. Claimed by a freak accident at some remote archaeological site in Greece or Peru. Drowned during the annual Chicago Yacht Club Race to Mackinac. Wrapped around a tree while driving his cardinal red Porsche under the influence.

Well, at least Ben could take consolation from the fact that he was true to his brand, as he liked to call it, right to the end. In his usual sybaritic style, he had played out the final scene in unapologetic luxury, with a little sex thrown in for good measure.

Granted, being suffocated by your own throat muscles was a wretched way to go. Assuming, of course, that the cause of death was allergic shock. But there are worse ways to die and worse places to do it than the shores of Lake Superior on a soft summer night. In any case, Ben was now beyond all earthly suffering, and his ever restless soul was having its first taste of real peace. Or so they always told us in Sunday School.

But if that was true, and I wanted to believe it was, why did I feel this growing sense of unease? Why this prickling in my spine? Why this feeling of agitation? Was it mild shock? Low-level grief? Or something else, something more elusive and harder to name?

I reclaimed my cup from the microwave, blew gently on the steamy surface, and tried to still my brain. For a minute or so, I struggled to focus on the summer light and willed myself to remember bits from an NPR feature on mindfulness I'd half-listened to on the drive up north. But it was no use. The internal monologue continued.

Desperate for distraction, I walked over to the sun-bleached coffee table, shifted a stack of Nero Wolfe mysteries, and picked up *Death of a Demon*. That's what I wanted right now, to immerse myself in the far-away, long-ago world of Nero Wolfe. The brilliant, eccentric, egoistic, everlastingly logical, astonishingly rude, and relentlessly truthful Nero Wolfe.

Gripping the book, I told myself there was no reason why Ben's death should intrude on my well-deserved vacation. No reason why I couldn't go back to lazy days of sightseeing and agate searching and beach reading. No reason whatever.

Was there?

From somewhere in the depths of my brain, I swear I could hear the voice of Nero Wolfe himself: *"Oh come now, my dear. Don't be disingenuous. Given how well you knew Ben, you also know the very obvious answer to that question."*

Chapter Two

As I watched the breakers lapping at my rented beachfront, I thought back to my one and only visit to Ben's up-north oasis. It was early August of last year. By some odd quirk of fate, the invitation to his open house had coincided with my annual summer trek home to Munising, on Michigan's northernmost coast.

At the time, I had considered all my reasons for not going. God knows there were a lot, based on our long and often acrimonious relationship. But, as usual, curiosity won out over caution, and I showed up dutifully at Ben's open house along with about a hundred other guests, a bottle of grocery store wine in hand, a twitchy feeling in the general vicinity of my stomach, and a small chip on my shoulder.

I'd expected to be greeted by some good-looking lackey rented for the occasion and decked out in a white shirt and black bow tie. Ben always liked to surround himself with underlings. I should know. Instead, he opened the massive double doors himself, flashed that Big Bad Wolf smile of his, and kissed me on the mouth hard before I realized what was happening. Obviously, my reflexes weren't what they had been back in my agency days.

Ben's amorous display drew considerable attention, especially since he wasn't in any hurry to let me go despite my struggling and squirming. A few feet away, I could hear a group of his cronies speculating as to whether I was his latest side piece.

But that wasn't the end of it. Ben loved a captive audience. So, of course, he insisted on taking his former wage slave on a guided tour, making sure to share every exquisitely expensive detail of what he called his beach shack—all four thousand square feet of it, as he kept reminding me.

Fortunately, I had long ago mastered the art of tuning out Ben's monologues, a talent which allowed me to focus on whatever interested me most. Things like the wrap-around second-floor balcony and the fireplace made of locally quarried stone and sized for roasting wildebeests. True, the mirrored walls in the master bedroom were clichéd even for Ben. But that predictable lapse in taste was offset by the window-wall and its panoramic view of Sand Point harbor. In the background, Ben was droning on ad nauseam about his latest project, a luxury condo development less than half a mile north of where we were standing.

As our tour continued, I lingered on the stone terrace that stepped down to a blinding white sand beach—private, of course. Standing there, gazing out at the largest freshwater lake in the world, I decided that California had it right, requiring public access to every stretch of ocean-front property on its shores. Nobody should ever own a piece of Lake Superior all to themselves. For one thing, it was impossible to possess anything that wild and vast. For another, it seemed immoral even to try.

Clutching my coffee mug as if it were some kind of talisman against dark thoughts, I glanced around at the living room of my summer retreat. The inventory included one boxy couch in avocado green that dared anyone to get comfortable on it. One overstuffed recliner upholstered in a sun-faded brown plaid. Two identical maple end tables scarred with scratches and cigarette burns. A coffee table in the same condition. A surprisingly comfortable wooden rocker. Two reading lamps prone to short circuits. Three large glass ashtrays sporting painted images of local wildlife. And one smoke-stained fireplace. Above it all, the mounted heads of elk and deer stared back from split log walls shiny with varnish.

Granted, it wasn't much. The place was a relic of the past, scheduled for demolition in late fall to make way for three mini beach house rentals. But for the next eighteen days, it was mine and mine alone, a reward for having completed two seemingly endless, anxiety-inducing, brain-bending annual reports for which I had been overpaid. An unusual occurrence in my world of freelance marketing communications.

Actually, the place wasn't *all* mine, a fact I was reminded of when the door of the second bedroom opened and a tall blonde female shuffled into the living room. Except for her soaring height, Bixie Murray would be a perfect casting choice for Ophelia in any production of *Hamlet*. Even in a sleep-dazed state, when most of us dread the prospect of gazing into a bathroom mirror at our swollen eyes and dented hair, Bixie managed to look beautiful. The kind of beautiful that compels strangers to look twice. Her hair, white-blonde right down to the roots, flared around her shoulders in a way that would make a photo stylist swoon. Her violet—not blue, violet—eyes squinted into the strong northern light that drenched the room. Completing the picture, the neckline of her vintage nightgown had slipped just enough to recall a recent Ralph Lauren ad.

Glancing down at my faded yoga pants and frayed Henley, I promised myself that I'd buy new nightwear. Someday.

"Morning," I offered, raising my coffee cup. Bixie answered with a slow blink.

While she got her bearings, I turned my attention to the news. Today's lead story was back, and Sandy was dwarfed by a giant close-up of Ben on the video screen behind her. It was a face familiar in every detail. The haircut borrowed from Lord Byron, dark auburn waves fading to grey at the temples. The broad boy-next-door smile, so at odds with those predatory ice green eyes. There he was, my former employer, mentor, teacher, bully, exploiter, occasional ally, once-in-a-while friend, and perpetual tormenter.

The sight of Ben's face jolted Bixie out of her muzzy state. She made a failed attempt to capture the wayward curls that tumbled across her forehead. "Oh my God. Is that Ben? It is, isn't it? It's him." Her bare feet moved closer to the TV screen. "What's he doing on the Marquette news? Another big real estate deal? Or did he get pulled over for a DUI?"

"No danger of either of those happening anymore," I answered, also moving closer to the screen and giving the volume button a couple of taps. "He's dead."

"Dead?" Bixie's eyes seemed to double in size. "Ben? How? When?"

"Last night. Possibly anaphylactic shock. The police are still rooting around." I pointed to the screen. As I did, the camera panned to the well-groomed face of Ken Balducci, the UP's answer to Anderson Cooper both in terms of good looks and dogged journalism.

Right now, Ken was on the scene, just a pleasant trek from where we stood. Behind him, emergency vehicles filled the screen and nearly blocked out the familiar outline of Grand Island floating in the quiet lake waters. The deceptively quiet waters.

In a voice that strayed occasionally into the operatic range, he recapped the sudden passing of former downstate ad agency executive-turned-local entrepreneur Benjamin Roberts. There was brief mention of a panicky phone call in the late hours of yesterday evening made by the victim's longtime friend and colleague, Meredith Wood. Then, an account of police arriving on the scene at Roberts' Sand Point mini-mansion and discovering Ben's dead body in the hot tub. Exact cause of death was still unknown.

Cut to Munising's sheriff, who offered a few short sentences noting the community's shock at this loss and adding that criminal investigators were working closely with the coroner and state pathologists to determine the exact cause of death. This was followed by an almost identical statement from a female state trooper. Which in turn was followed by Ken Balducci's promise of more details to come, along with a quick mention that police had begun questioning friends and acquaintances of the victim.

That last sentence stuck in my brain. The idea of interrogating people who knew Ben didn't make much sense. Unless—I switched into what I like to think of as my Dorothy Sayers mode—unless, that is, Ben's death wasn't quite so natural as it seemed. Unless the police knew more, or suspected more, than they were telling.

I did a quick calculation. Bixie and I were less than a mile south of Ben's place, so it was possible that the police might cast their net in our direction. If they did, they would discover that the two downstate women renting the Donahue cottage shared some history with Ben. And they might also discover that one of the neighbors had happened to see a tall, slender woman walking north along Sand Point Road last night in the moonlight.

But how could I have resisted a solitary ramble on such a perfect Upper

Peninsula night? Especially with the promise of the Northern Lights being dangled by local forecasters. Especially when that same walk had been a favorite route for Terry and me, and one that seemed to bridge the gap between then and now, between life with him and life without him. If you could call it a life.

And besides, how could I have known that death was traveling up that same road, in the same direction, at approximately the same time?

Chapter Three

The cameras shifted to a fresh-faced young thing in a snug dress and a smile so bright white it hurt my eyes. I found myself wondering if all TV weather people frequented the same dentists. As she began her litany of temperatures and tides, my brain slipped into time travel mode.

Amazing how memories can take you out of the moment, can block out the here-and-now and shift you into a kind of parallel reality, a second world. Suddenly, I saw Ben leaning on the wall of my cubicle in that proprietary way of his, heard his gravelly baritone making its way around the unlit cigarette in his mouth. He leaned toward me, leering. "You know, Karin, you and I have a love-hate relationship." I braced for the punch line. "Heavily weighted towards hate." A burst of laughter. Then off he swaggered down the hall, in a random search for his next victim.

Ben Roberts. Impossible to please? Generally. Selfish? Definitely. Crazy? Possibly. Sadistic? Occasionally. Mercurial? Absolutely. Prone to rampages? Certainly.

With Ben, collateral damage was inevitable. Yet there was no one I'd rather brainstorm with. No one I trusted more to carry the day in a presentation. No one who had a keener instinct for strategy and messaging. No one who ever taught me more about spot-on headlines, or solid copy, or perfect graphics, or failsafe techniques for managing a difficult client. To give Ben his due, he was a true pro, a brilliant ad man and, in spite of himself, if your skin was thick enough, a damn good teacher.

"Karin, did you hear what I said?" Bixie's voice found its way into my fugue state. "I want to drive up to Ben's place and see what's happening. I mean, after all, he was our…"

The logical word at this point would be "friend." But being a pathological truth teller, at least about some things, Bixie couldn't bring herself to offer even a white lie in Ben's honor. "Our employer."

I knew from the slight frown on her face that a homily was on the way. Sure enough. "He gave us our start in this business," she said, then waited. I held fire. "We both owe our careers to him." Such as they were.

I thought about the death scene—which turned out to be a crime scene—that Bixie and I had visited ten months earlier. It was completely inadvertent on our part, a matter of sheer coincidence. Something that Bixie, of course, adamantly refuses to believe in. Feeling desperate and overwhelmed by widow's grief, I had finally given in to her well-intentioned nagging and made an appointment with Dana Lewis, a local psychic who also happened to be a friend of hers.

I'd expected nothing more than a harmless diversion. And as I kept telling myself, one wasted hour was a small price to pay for ending Bixie's constant harangues. Besides, truth be told, I was curious as to what a professional psychic actually did. How she worked. And whether maybe, just maybe, she could ease the searing pain that had taken up permanent residence in my heart.

Who could have predicted that we'd stumble onto a murder scene?

"Karin!" Bixie's voice jerked me back into the present moment. "Where were you just now? What were you thinking about?"

"I was thinking about our excellent adventure in tracking down Dana's killer." As I spoke, my stomach gave a lurch, and I cringed at the memories that flooded in.

In a collective, colossal lapse of judgment, Bixie and I, along with our friend Paul, decided to do a little investigating on our own. Our goal was to help exonerate Dana's daughter, who seemed to be the suspect of choice. And to be fair, we did turn up some stunning evidence—a fact that the police steadfastly refused to acknowledge, even after appropriating said evidence and using it as the centerpiece of their case.

But that evidence came at a high cost. In the melee that followed, I nearly got myself killed by a psychopath masquerading as a trophy wife. And Bixie's relationship with her hunky brother, Andrew, who happened to be heading up the murder investigation for the Ann Arbor Police, had been strained ever since. The same could be said of my own relationship with Andrew, but for different reasons entirely. Reasons that made me uncomfortable to think about since, whenever I did, I felt guilt tugging at the corners of my conscience and saw Terry's face gazing at me from distant vistas.

Terry had been gone now for—how long was it? I did some quick math. Nineteen months, almost to the day. Time was, I always knew precisely how many weeks, days, even hours had gone by since the love of my life disappeared into death.

My eyes began to burn, and I gave my head a hard, quick shake to ward off the emotional ambush I knew was coming. Grief is like that. It's a monster, a treacherous beast that seems to withdraw but only feigns defeat. It lies in wait, everlastingly patient. Then, at the most unexpected moment, seemingly out of nowhere, it attacks. Defense is useless. No matter how much time has passed, no matter how thick and gnarled the scar tissue has become, grief breaks through. And with it come the flashbacks and the heart-bruising truth that you are alone. Always and ever alone. The person you loved most in the world, the person who was your world, who defined your world, is gone. Dead. And you are here. Still here. A living ghost moving through a familiar daily landscape that has become completely alien. And you wonder, day after day, how can everything be the same and yet utterly different?

I took a couple of shaky breaths and waited until I could trust my voice.

"Bixie, think back a minute. The last time we visited a police scene, things didn't exactly turn out well." Talk about a gross understatement. "Remember the hours we spent at police headquarters? That cozy interrogation room? The questions they kept lobbing at us? The veiled threats? That battery acid they tried to pass off as coffee? The expensive lawyer? Oh, and let's not forget Detective Sergeant Moses Caldwell." Who still haunted my dreams.

"And," I pressed on into dangerous territory, "can you honestly say that things between you and Andrew are all better now? That he trusts you?" Or me?

Unfortunately, Bixie was in one of her do-or-die moods. Her voice hardened. "Oh, come on, Karin. No one is using the word 'murder' this time. All we know is that Ben died suddenly and unexpectedly, and that he may have come into contact with penicillin. Supposedly the only thing he was allergic to." Her voice hardened, and she straightened her spine. Never a good sign. "Besides, Ben was a big part of our lives. We worked for him." Slaved for him would be more accurate. "And you still work for him from time to time."

"Purely on a freelance basis," I reminded her. "Only now and then." When I'm desperate for projects and my cash flow has bottomed out. "And always on my terms." Bixie might be allergic to white lies, but I've never been troubled that way. The fact was, no one ever worked for Ben on any terms but his.

"Whatever." Bixie's arm traced a dismissive wave in my direction. "Look, I know the man could be impossible. But even so, he was part of our lives. I think we owe it to him to go to the place where he died and just be there for a while."

"And I think that's an incredibly bad idea," I countered. "In fact, it's beyond bad. It's crazy, even for you, especially given the fallout from our last little foray. We need to stay out of it this time. Entirely." If the police would allow it.

Bixie picked up the cup of green tea she'd been brewing. "Fine!" Chin high, she began striding resolutely in the general direction of her room, oblivious to the trail of splashes and spatters she left in her wake. "I'll go without you." The scene reminded me of Vivian Leigh at the end of *Gone with the Wind*, when she does her valiant tomorrow-is-another-day shtick. Watching Bixie stride past me, ramrod straight, blonde hair bouncing, I was temporarily mesmerized.

The spell was broken when she veered abruptly off course to grab a banana from a chipped bowl on the kitchen counter. Before resuming her march, she looked over at me with big, earnest eyes. "Karin, I know you don't believe it, but Ben needs us right now. He's disoriented and confused. His spirit, I mean. It's still hovering around there. Can't you feel it?"

The thought of Ben's ectoplasm floating nearby made me shudder, but there was no stopping Bixie once she got into her woo-woo frame of mind. "Besides which," she switched into rational mode, "everybody in this town who doesn't have a straight job is probably swarming around the place by now. And don't forget the tourists. They'll be mobbing the scene and taking photos like mad. No one will even notice us." Right. Famous last words.

She turned her purple-blue gaze on me full force. After holding out for maybe ten seconds, I sighed. "Alright. For the sake of damage control, I'll go with you. But only for a few minutes."

I put down my coffee cup on one of the wobbly end tables. "After all," I said, more to myself than Bixie, "what harm could it possibly do?"

Of course, I should have known better than to utter those eight innocent, hopeful words. I should have realized that I was tempting fate. And I should have guessed that the answer to my question was likely to be very unpleasant.

Chapter Four

I was wrestling with my favorite T-shirt, which had shrunk after an unfortunate experience in a dryer, and had just discovered that I'd been trying to shove my head through one of the armholes when my cell phone gave that nerve-jangling brrrring I hate so much.

Yes, I know, I know. In this year of our Lord 2007, cell phones are as necessary as air. An indispensable human appendage. Proof that cyberspace is the true realm of miracles. At this very moment, hordes of early adopters were queuing up outside their nearest Apple store, clutching credit cards in their sweaty hands, chatting excitedly with roving reporters, and working out their battle plans for reaching the sales counter, where they would lay down hundreds of dollars for Steve Job's latest, greatest techno-bauble, something he called the iPhone.

Granted, like everyone else, I couldn't live without a cell phone. But that didn't mean I had to like it. In fact, I'm not sure what I dislike most: the tyranny of being constantly accessible to anyone who happens to have my number or the fact that even a proud troglodyte like me responds to its signals as predictably as a rat in a Skinner Box.

Mark my words. Three or four or maybe five generations from now, when you and I are slowly turning into topsoil, human beings will be very different creatures. Darwin will prevail. In thrall to their precious devices, our progeny will have huge frontal lobes to better absorb the endless streams of data being spewed out by bots. Their eyes will be monstrously large to take in all that their screens can offer. Their tiny noses and mouths will be perfectly adapted to filter the polluted air. Their long, spindly fingers will dance compulsively across ever-shrinking keyboards. And you and I will be responsible for starting the whole ugly, irreversible process.

Case in point. Here I was, struggling to get dressed in order to face a tragedy of yet-unknown proportions and keep a friend from making said tragedy even worse than it needed to be. And what's at the top of my mind at this very moment? Making the ringtone stop.

Yanking off the hopelessly twisted T-shirt, I snatched my phone from the nightstand and barked out an exasperated "Yes?"

"Darlin' girl! I can't believe it. You actually picked up the call. And here I was, thinkin' you'd leave me to the mercies of your voicemail. Which, as we all know, is the equivalent of being consigned to a black hole."

"Roger?" There was no disguising the dread in my voice.

"Yes indeed, darlin'. Who else? Unless you happen to know another extremely good-looking reporter with an ever-so-slight Irish brogue and a Southeast Michigan area code."

I took a breath. "Look, you caught me at a bad time. I'm in a rush right now, so..."

"Ah, yes, I thought you might be. Heading over to Ben's house, are you?"

Did that gasp come from me? If so, I was too stunned to notice. Or speak.

"How did I know that, you're wondering. Well, it's no secret I happen to be the best journalist ever to bless the Ann Arbor News staff. In fact, I'm so good it took me only two phone calls to track you down. And Bixie's with you, I believe. Quite a time you picked to take a sentimental journey, isn't it? Just imagine, Ben Roberts dying in that very same little town where you happen to be. Talk about coincidence."

So that was it. Leave it to that hyper-ambitious newshound to sniff out a story. Poor Ben. Being turned into media fodder before his corpse was even cold. But then Roger would cheerfully walk over any number of bodies for a byline.

I felt a surge of contempt, which generally happens whenever I talk with Roger. But along with the contempt came a small tug of anxiety at the ironic way he said *coincidence*.

I finally found my voice. "Am I correct in assuming that one of those phone calls was made to my next-door neighbor?" As if I didn't know. Paul could be such a snitch. He loved being the keeper of secrets. The only thing he loved more was doling them out to impress people. Still, he knew perfectly well how I felt about Roger. Or Badger, as I preferred to call him.

"Ah, Karin, it always lifts my spirits to hear your lovely voice. So when are we going out for dinner? Don't say when hell freezes over, which is what you told me last time and, if memory serves, the time before that. Surely, you don't want to break my poor adoring heart yet again."

"Was it Paul?"

"You know I never give up my sources." Why did I find that accent of his so aggravating? Probably wasn't the accent at all. Probably had more to do with his tiresome attentions. I mean, how many times would a normal man ask a woman out, knowing she found him loathsome? "Protect all sources. That's my code. Which means you can tell me everything you learn about Ben's death, with no fear that your name will ever cross my lips. Especially in any dealings I may have with the police."

"Police?" I echoed, hoping he hadn't caught the slight edge of panic in my voice. "You better recheck your news feed. All I know is what I heard on the Marquette channel. And all they seem to know right now is that Ben may have died from anaphylactic shock."

"Ah, dear girl, don't be so naïve." Did I mention that Roger has the most annoying chuckle? "A man with as many enemies as Ben, and as many likely heirs, rarely has the luxury of dying from natural causes. Even if it appears otherwise. And speaking of enemies, you and he weren't exactly fast friends, were you?"

"Look, Roger, as much as I'd love to continue this fascinating conversation, I really do have to go."

"Can't resist returning to the scene of the crime, hmmm?"

"Actually, I'm on my way to breakfast. With a man. We've been seeing each other for a while now. I assumed you knew. But I guess there are some things even your highly reliable sources can't help you with."

There it was, that annoying chuckle again. "Karin, Karin. Did I ever tell you what a charming but completely unconvincing liar you are? Not for lack of trying, though, I'll give you that. I know very well that once you get over the worst of your grieving, I'm at the top of the list."

"You…" I spluttered, then gave up on the rest of the sentence. The outrageous thing is that, given Roger's outsized ego and the self-referential universe he inhabits, he probably believed what he just said.

"Roger," I tried again, in a calmer voice. "For the record. You've stumbled on a dry hole this time. There's no story here, unless you count the new man in my life."

"My instincts tell me you're wrong, darlin'. There's a story, alright. My editor will be all over this once I've made my pitch. In fact, it's too good to hand over to one of our stringers. I may just pop up there and check things out for myself. Perfect weather for a road trip. Besides, I've never been north of the bridge. And what better incentive than a dead body and a gorgeous tour guide to show me around her home turf? Bye, darlin'. I'll be in touch."

I stood where I was, frozen in place, mouth open, staring at the phone in my hand. How could a day go so wrong, so fast? It wasn't even eight o'clock yet, and here I was. Caffeine deprived. No breakfast. Barely any clothes on. Dealing with a dead employer and a live pain in the butt, who would probably be heading my way before the week was up.

With a sigh, I yanked the wayward T-shirt over my head and marched into the living room with the intention of trying, one last time, to talk Bixie out of her latest bad idea. A fool's errand, of course, but I had to try.

Turns out her brother had the same idea. Her brand new cell phone—she always has a brand new cell phone—was propped up on one of the coffee tables. At the moment, she was dividing her attention between forcing her curly blonde tresses into a scrunchie and attending to Andrew, whose voice was blaring over the speakerphone and who had evidently heard the news about Ben through the police grapevine.

"So we're agreed then, right? You are not going near the murder scene."

Bixie tightened the scrunchie. One long blonde curl escaped and cascaded down her cheek. "Not near it," she said. No, I thought, not *near* the scene. She's going directly *to* the scene. I had to admire her ability to split hairs.

"By the way, Sergeant Caldwell asked me to pass on a message to Karin. Tell her, for him, to stay out of trouble for a change." He paused. "Although I suspect it's too late for that."

"Gotta go, Andrew." Bixie picked up the phone, ready to end the conversation. "We haven't had breakfast yet, and I'm famished. Thanks for calling." She looked at me and rolled her eyes. "I'll be sure to give Karin the message. And tell Sergeant Caldwell not to worry. How could we possibly get into any trouble up here, in God's country?"

Chapter Five

Bixie was right about one thing. The ghouls and gawkers were out in full force. Despite the early hour, news of Ben's death had traveled fast. Vehicles of every description lined both sides of the road, and curiosity seekers walked along what was left of the asphalt, like eager pilgrims in cut-offs and khakis making their way to a shrine. We'd barely driven half a mile before I was forced to pull over.

As I began inching toward the right, Bixie clutched the rim of her open window and let out a high-pitched shriek. "Karin, what in God's name are you doing? There's a ravine down there."

"It's not a ravine," I corrected her, pushing down a sigh. "It's an overgrown ditch."

Fact is, Sand Point Road is just that. A road. A generic Up North thruway. No thrills. No perils. Nothing like nearby Alger Heights Road, which is basically a strip of asphalt clinging to steep curves and perched on a long gorge that, ironically, is the main route to the town cemetery. With no guard rails along the drop-offs on either side, the road is wonderfully picturesque. But it does claim a few lives every year.

I edged my aging Malibu—Amelia by name—as far right as I dared. Far enough that Bixie was forced to squirm across the console and exit from the driver's side. The sight of a tall, willowy blonde slithering feet-first out of my dusty car wasn't quite enough to stop the parade, although most of the males passing by did pause and allow themselves a long, lustful look before resuming their march up the hill. Death trumps beauty every time.

Bixie finally managed to squeeze the last part of herself over the gear shift and out the door. As she stood up, I started walking. "Not a single complaint from you," I warned, tossing the words over my shoulder. "Don't forget whose idea this was."

Most of our companions were in no hurry this morning. Gripping cameras, phones, travel mugs, and to-go coffee cups from the local Burger King, they chattered and sauntered up the slope. After two or three minutes of speed walking our way through the obstacle course of bodies, Bixie and I gave up, slowed our pace, and joined the procession.

"It's going to take us forever to get there at this rate," Bixie complained.

"What's the rush? Ben's not going anywhere. And besides," I reminded her, "we want to blend in with the crowd, right?"

Bixie looked around doubtfully. To the left of us, a cluster of high school girls, nearly identical in every detail except hair color, giggled and whispered. The middle-aged couple on our right looked vaguely familiar, though I couldn't place them. Just ahead of us, a group of twenty-something tourists outfitted in Eddie Bauer T-shirts and distressed jeans kidded around in a clubby way.

"Not much cover here," Bixie said. "And our size works against us."

"True," I agreed. "Although by size, I assume you mean height and not weight." I stopped, leaned against her for support, and dumped out the pebbles that had worked their way into my loafers.

Without answering, Bixie reached into her beach carryall and pulled out two crushed and faded Toledo Mud Hens baseball caps, one of which she handed to me. "Here, put this on. And get out your sunglasses."

Using the tips of two fingers, I held the cap at arm's length. "I don't even want to know where you got this. Do you really think these hideous things are going to disguise two women who look like the spawn of professional basketball players?" By an odd twist of fate, both Bixie and I are slightly taller than the average American male, who—as I discovered on Wikipedia—clocks in at five feet, nine inches.

We walked in silence for a few minutes, past modest ranch houses that had been built thirty or forty years ago when Sand Point was just a quiet rural road leading to Munising's favorite townie beach. Gradually, the lots got larger, the driveways got longer, the landscaping got fancier, and the ranches morphed into custom homes, mostly brick.

We weren't far from Ben's place now, maybe fifty yards or so. The civilian vehicles lining the road had been replaced by an ambulance, a couple of navy blue cruisers bearing the Alger County Sheriff insignia, a supersized SUV that belonged to the State Police, another one branded with a Marquette County logo, and a white van sporting a complicated antenna and emblazoned with the words "Channel Six News—Covering the UP."

Ahead of us, near the entry to Ben's gated driveway, a solid mass of humanity was pressed up against a waist-high band of yellow crime tape. What really held them back from the scene wasn't the tape but a line of uniformed police, five by my count. Just beyond the blue uniforms, I could see the outline of Ben's so-called beach shack.

Without warning, Bixie clamped a hand on my elbow and, somehow, don't ask me how, steered us through the crowd until we were closing in on the ragged line of onlookers pressed up against the yellow barrier.

"What are you doing?" I hissed, trying to wrestle my elbow out of her hand. "We're supposed to stay invisible, remember? Keep our distance?" I finally shook myself free of her grip. "What happened to blending in with the crowd? Can't you pick up on Ben's vibrations or whatever from a distance? I mean…"

"Karin? Karin Niemi?" The words came from a loud male voice. A voice that spoke with authority. I looked around for the source.

Rob Ketola. Correction. *Officer* Rob Ketola. The last time I'd seen him was two or three years ago. Terry and I were having a Friday fish fry with my Aunt Saimi at the Moose Lodge. Rob was in civvies that night, and if my aunt happened to mention that he was on the police force, I don't remember it.

"Karin." He moved our way wearing a grim, in-charge look. The onlookers pushing against us backed off slightly, possibly in deference to Rob or, more likely, to create a stage for whatever was about to happen. "I didn't know you were in town."

"Hey, Rob." I attempted a smile. "Yeah, I'm here for a few weeks. Just got in a couple of days ago." He turned to Bixie and waited. "So," I stretched out the word, hoping for a convenient distraction from the crowd. No such luck. "This is my friend Bixie Murray. Bixie, meet Rob Ketola. He and I knew each other in high school. Sort of. He was a couple of years ahead of me."

Rob nodded. "So what brings you here this morning?"

Stupidity. "Well, we were actually on our way to Miner's Castle," I ad-libbed. "Thought we'd see it early, before the hordes got there and then have breakfast somewhere." He wasn't buying this, I could tell. "Maybe the Dog Patch," I added, without much conviction. "But then we decided to take a detour and follow the crowd."

Amazing how fast law enforcement types can switch from semi-human to full-bore officer mode. Rob put on his cop face just as Lake Superior tossed up a cool gust of air. I shivered.

"Did you know Ben?" he asked. "He's from Ann Arbor, and you've been living there for a while now, no?"

The question hung there in the lake-chilled air. Bixie and I didn't dare even a quick glance at each other. Before I could say a word, she piped up.

"Yes, amazing as it is, we did know Ben." Bixie was using what I call her Vamp Voice, sort of a cross between Madonna and Marlene Dietrich. "In fact, we both worked for him years ago. At his ad agency. Before he got into real estate."

She slipped off her sunglasses. Rob seemed to weaken a bit, but managed to shake off the Bixie effect faster than most. "You worked for him. Interesting."

This was not going well. Suddenly, we weren't just accidental tourists. We were persons of interest. Roger's voice echoed in my head, like a perverted leprechaun: *Couldn't resist returning to the scene of the crime, hmmmm?* But of course there was absolutely no proof of a crime. Yet.

Bixie went on. I held my breath. "Oh, that was ages ago, when Karin and I were both starting out. And just for a few years. But when we heard the news this morning, we were stunned. And..."

Rob's deadpan baritone broke in. "And since you knew Ben, and since you were headed in this general direction anyway, you thought, why not stop and take a look."

Bixie nodded, dug out a sweet, slightly embarrassed smile, and made a point of surveying the crowd. "Looks like a lot of people had the same idea. I suppose this sort of thing doesn't happen too often in Munising."

"Depends on what you mean by this sort of thing."

"Well," Bixie began, then seemed to run out of words.

"It was such a sudden death," I jumped in. "Totally unexpected."

"People die sudden deaths all the time, Karin. Even up here." Rob scanned the crowd for a few long seconds. "Where are you staying?"

"In the Donahue cottage. The little one they rent out."

"Just down the way then." He made it sound more like an accusation than a fact.

"Right. The hotels are crazy expensive these days, with all the tourists. Anyway, we wanted to be on the lake if possible. And Eleanor gave us a good deal."

Rob nodded. "Okay." He flicked his gaze over to Bixie, then back to me. Like a lizard, I thought, scoping out the landscape for danger. Or prey. "Good talking to you, Karin." He pulled at the brim of his cap. Bixie and I were so still, we must have looked like a tableau vivant. "I'm sure we'll be seeing each other again before you head back downstate."

Chapter Six

Daisy Mae was lounging against a log. Pappy and Mammy were making moonshine. Li'l Abner, rifle in hand, was setting off to kill something for dinner. Joe what's-his-name was walking around under that perpetual rain cloud of his. Beneath the larger-than-life cartoon figures, tourists of every size, age, ethnicity, color, socioeconomic status, political persuasion, sexual orientation, and country of origin were waiting in line, pulling off their jackets, reading menus, placing orders, or chowing down.

I was staring at the fried eggs on my plate and counting to ten slowly. For the fifth time. Finally, grudgingly, I looked across the crowded table at Bixie. At that particular moment, she was holding up a small bowl filled with berries and melon chunks and frowning at the thing as if it were a lab specimen.

"The menu said fresh fruit."

I studied the wall murals for a few seconds and then said, in a voice that quivered only slightly, "It is fresh fruit. It's just not organic fresh fruit, which is what you mean." I let out an exasperated sigh. "In case you've forgotten, this is not Ann Arbor. You're not in Oz anymore, Dorothy. You're in the UP. You want organic fruit, go to the farm market down by the docks. Or drive out to the Seney Stretch and pick some wild blueberries. The Dog Patch doesn't do organic food. The Dog Patch does food. Everyday real people food."

Very slowly and deliberately, Bixie put down the offending fruit and stuck a spoon into her bowl of slowly congealing oatmeal. It stood straight up, like a little warning flag.

"What is the matter with you? You've barely said a word since we left Ben's house. In fact, the only time you've uttered a complete sentence was when you placed your order. Other than that, you've been sitting here in complete silence. You haven't responded to a single thing I've said. And now you're sniping at me. About fruit. What's going on? Talk to me."

"Talk to you? Sure. Why not? I'd love to." I slammed down my fork so hard it set off a small earthquake across the tabletop. The salt shaker toppled over and, without thinking, I picked up a few grains and tossed them over my left shoulder. In the din of the breakfast rush, no one noticed.

"You want to know what's the matter with me? With *me*? The question is not what's the matter with *me*. The question is what's the matter with *you*. What in God's name were you doing up there at Ben's house, pushing your way to the front of the crowd? What happened to our agreement about disappearing into the crowd? Do you ever stop to think? Or would that be too much to ask?"

I gripped the edge of the table, felt something sticky, dipped a paper napkin in my water glass, and proceeded to scrub off whatever it was with more force than necessary, talking as I scrubbed. "You did it again. Again. I can't believe I let it happen. But I did." From somewhere deep in my churning brain, a small, irritatingly sane voice struggled to the surface and told me to stop.

Bixie jumped into the silence. "What are you talking about? I did it again? Did what exactly?"

"Oh, for God's sake," I raised my eyes to the huge red ceiling beams that were supposed to make diners think they were in a barn. "Once again, you have dragged me—us—into a police investigation. Once again, there is a cop in my life. A cop who is now aware that you and I knew Ben. Not only that, but thanks to you, he also knows we worked for Ben. And not only that, he also knows that we just happened to arrive in Munising two days before Ben died. Unexpectedly. Suspiciously. Died."

"Suspiciously?" Bixie repeated, enunciating every syllable. "That's ridiculous. What's there to be suspicious about? Ben died from natural causes. If you can call life-threatening allergies natural."

I pushed my plate away. "That's not what Roger thinks. And much as I hate to admit it, the guy's got great instincts, at least when it comes to news."

"Roger? As in Roger Sullivan?"

"Who else?" I looked down, unclenched my fists, and began smoothing out the paper napkin I'd been throttling. "Can you think of any other Roger who would be among the first to hear about Ben's passing, from four hundred miles away?"

"Was he the one who called you this morning?" One thing I neglected to mention about our lakeside bungalow: the doors are even thinner than the walls.

"Yes. And the reason he called was because he'd heard the news about Ben and is totally convinced that foul play was involved. Somehow."

"Oh, come on, that's a reach even for Roger." Bixie took a sip of water, then another, and another. I did the same. The north coast of the UP is one of the few places on earth where I look forward to drinking from the tap. Lake Superior water is delicious beyond belief, especially if you've spent most of your life drinking city reservoir swill or downstate river dreck.

"Well, you'll have a chance to discuss that with him. In detail. As we speak, he's packing up. And he'll probably be heading our way within the next couple of hours."

Bixie's eyes popped at that piece of news. Then they swiveled to my right just as a familiar voice spoke my name. As I glanced up, a curtain of black hair brushed against my face, and two strong hands gave my shoulders a squeeze.

Chapter Seven

"Evelyn McGinty!" I stood up and realized I was smiling for the first time that day.

"Hey, kiddo. How's my favorite white girl?" Evelyn gave me a long hug, then stepped back and, holding my shoulders, ran her eyes over my face as if checking for wear and tear. She herself is one of those women who defy the ravages of time. Looking at her, I saw burnished skin, sky-high cheekbones, and almond eyes that could have belonged to a woman half her age.

"It's great to see you again," she said, giving my waist a squeeze. "Only I thought you weren't arriving 'til next week. Your last email said July fifteenth."

"Bixie and I decided to head north a few days early. Beat the weekend rush."

"Well, that's a relief." Evelyn threw a smile Bixie's way and winked at me. "I was afraid I'd been running on Indian time again. Losing track. Oh, and speaking of Indian time…." She turned slightly to the man at her side. "Do you know Charles Redbird? He works at the casino in Christmas. We decided to grab a coffee here before heading over to the Sioux for the tribal meeting."

She turned again to her companion. "Charles, you've heard me talk about Karin Niemi, my blood sister. And this is her friend, Bixie Murray."

Charles reached out his hand and engulfed mine in a warm, comforting grip. "Pleasure. I've heard a lot about you." I don't remember what I said at that moment, if anything, because my attention was entirely taken up by the baseball cap he wore. It was black with a silver-white thunderbird embroidered on the front and a cluster of what might have been eagle feathers attached to the side. It was quite possibly the most wonderful, the most beautiful hat I had ever seen. And I don't even like baseball caps.

Stretching across the table, he held Bixie's hand while they exchanged nice-to-meet-yous. Then he kept holding her hand for a few lingering seconds beyond that. No words. But from where I stood, their eyes seemed to be doing a fair amount of talking. I glanced at Evelyn, who grinned and arched a silky black eyebrow at me. This could be interesting. Although given Bixie's well-deserved Ice Queen reputation, maybe not.

Grateful for a diversion, especially this one, I pulled out a chair. "Sit down. Join us."

"We've already eaten," Evelyn began. "And we don't want to interrupt."

"Oh, please," I broke in. "Bixie and I can talk to each other anytime. And I haven't seen you in ages. Have a cup of coffee anyway. Besides," I shot Bixie a dark look, "you picked the perfect time to interrupt. Right now, anything short of a mass shooting would be welcome."

Wearing what might have been the start of a grin, Charles pulled out the chair I was holding and motioned to Evelyn. "I can always use another cup of coffee. Besides, we've got plenty of time to get to the meeting." While Evelyn seated herself and shrugged off her fringed deerskin jacket, he raised his hand, caught the eye of our beleaguered server, and held up two fingers. The server nodded, and Charles sat down.

"So," Evelyn put her hand on top of mine. "Tell me why you're so eager to be interrupted this morning. What's going on? What have you been up to? Don't tell me you're in trouble already." She leaned back in the battered captain's chair and crossed her arms. "Can't be much. You've only been in town a couple of days."

Even as a kid, I never could resist confiding in Evelyn and sharing my innermost thoughts, such as they were. She always listened in a deep way I wasn't used to. Quiet. Intent. And on the rare occasions when she gave advice, it was always spot-on.

"We were at Ben Roberts' place this morning," I said, in what I hoped was a casual voice. Eyes got wider. I kept my focus on Evelyn and Charles, pointedly avoiding Bixie. "You heard the news, right? That he's dead." They nodded.

"Well," I continued, "Bixie and I both know Ben. I mean, we knew Ben. Pretty well in fact. Back in the day, about a hundred years ago, we worked at his ad agency. So after we heard the news, we stupidly," I swung my eyes toward Bixie, "decided to drive up to his place and find out what we could."

"He ran an ad agency?" Charles asked, managing at the same time to smile up at the waitress who had just put two steaming cups of coffee on the table. "Didn't know that. I thought he'd always been a developer."

"Yeah," I went on, "he had an agency. A good one. In fact, he still has partial ownership of the business. The thing about Ben is, everything he did, he did well." I emptied three peel-back containers of chemical cream into the cup of coffee our waitress had just warmed up for me. "It sounds like you knew him. Were you friends?"

If the noise that came from Evelyn was a laugh, it was a bitter, hard one.

"Friends?" It was Charles who spoke. "Ben didn't have friends, at least not in this town. He had what the kids today call frenemies. And outright enemies, plenty of those. And employees. And other people, colleagues, I guess you'd call them. Business types. Wheelers and dealers who were useful to him." He paused and gave me a thoughtful look. "From what you were saying, there was some kind of problem this morning when you two were up at Ben's place."

Why does restaurant coffee taste so much better than the stuff I brew? I took another long sip before answering and considered whether or not to order one of the restaurant's legendary outsized sticky buns. "Yeah, I'd say it was a problem that Rob Ketola spotted me in the crowd and singled me out for a little chat. He seemed very interested in the fact that I was in town, and that we had decided to join the ghouls this morning to check out the scene." Another sip. "And then when Bixie told him that we both knew Ben—and had worked for him—he got even more interested."

"I don't get it," Evelyn said. "Ben died. Supposedly from some kind of allergic reaction. At least that's what they said on the news. You were curious, like everyone else. So?"

"So," I sighed, "for whatever reason, Rob seemed suspicious. More suspicious than he should have been. And stop rolling your eyes, Evelyn. I'm not being paranoid. Put yourself in my place. There I am, at the scene where Ben died just a few hours earlier." I glanced up just in time to catch the eye of our server and ask for one of the house cinnamon rolls, extra-large size.

I turned back to Evelyn. "So there I was, surrounded by police cars and yellow tape, being corralled by a member of Alger County's' finest. Who, if you recall, never liked me much. And who, even while we're talking, keeps giving me this slanty-eyed look as if he's trying to remember whether he's seen my face on an FBI poster. And then, right before we take off, he makes a point of telling me that he's sure we'll be seeing each other again before I go back to Ann Arbor."

"Oh geez. Come on, Karin," Evelyn shook her head. "Rob is just like that. Always has been. Always taking things too seriously ever since he was a kid. I swear, he'd ticket a five-year-old for jaywalking if he could. Which is probably why he's doing so well on the police force, at least from what I hear."

"But what if…" I hesitated as the server placed a warm, saucer-sized pastry in front of me, then breathed in the doughy cinnamon scent and, ignoring Bixie's squint-eyed look of disgust, pulled off the stretchy outer coil and tried not to drool. "What if the police know something we don't? What if they think Ben might have been murdered?"

Charles looked at me intently for a few seconds before he spoke. Amazing, I thought, how a man with his hair in braids could look so attractive. I suppose those broad shoulders and soulful, world-weary brown eyes had something to do with it. No wonder Bixie's pheromones were on high alert.

He gave his coffee a slow, thoughtful stir before speaking. "Actually, an unnatural death would be very natural for someone like Ben." He let that sink in for a moment. Long enough for me to recall that Roger had said something similar. Only when Charles said it, it sounded more believable.

He went on. "If the police think it's murder and you're worried about being a suspect, then take a ticket and get in line. You've got plenty of company.

Half the people in this town have a reason for wanting Ben Roberts dead." He took a long sip of coffee. "Me included."

Chapter Eight

The long silence that followed didn't seem to bother Evelyn or Charles one iota. In fact, they looked positively serene against the backdrop of boisterous customers and fleet-footed servers. Must be a Native American thing, that unflappable calm. Bixie and I, on the other hand, being the tightly wound Anglos that we are, fumbled for words to fill a quiet that was becoming more awkward by the second.

"Wow," I blurted out, relieved to be hearing a human voice even if it had to be mine. "So I was wrong in assuming that Ben mended his ways when he relocated up here." In an effort to appear only mildly interested in what I was about to say, I looked down at my plate and pulled off another gooey strip of pastry. "If you don't mind my asking, what exactly did he do to make so many people in this town hate him?" I looked up at Charles. "What did he do to you?"

Charles twisted his mouth into the kind of smile a Victorian novelist would describe as rueful. "It's not so much what he did to me. It's what he did, or what some of us are pretty sure he did, to the tribe." He glanced over at Evelyn, who gave him the look I knew so well from her days as my babysitter. It was a look that said, more eloquently than words ever could: don't do it, don't speak it, don't even think it.

Charles shrugged. "Let's just say that, in the two or three years he's been here, Ben has managed to stir up a lot of bad feelings in a lot of people. A lot. In my opinion, you and Bixie don't have much to worry about."

"Except Officer Ketola," I reminded him before turning my attention back to the sugary bliss in my hand.

Charles shrugged and glanced over at Evelyn. "We should probably get going." She nodded and freed the deerskin jacket from the back of her chair.

In one fluid movement, Charles stood up and put a crisp ten-dollar bill on the table next to his coffee cup. It was the kind of new, just minted bill that begs to be touched. Then, bending lower, he picked up his cap from the chair next to him.

"While you're waiting for Officer Ketola to make his next move, you two might as well enjoy yourselves." He smiled at both of us in turn, but let the smile settle on Bixie. Then he reached into his vest pocket, pulled out a business card, and put it on the table. "Stop by the casino sometime, and I'll show you around. Or better yet, I'll take you on a private tour of some local Indian sites." His smile faded. "Too bad so much of Grand Island is off limits, even to the Chippewa. That was our original home. Now we have restricted access, just like all the other visitors. Federal law."

"A tour sounds great. We'd love to." Bixie spoke in a voice I hadn't heard in quite a while, all eager and bright. I wondered where she'd been keeping it. "Is there any chance we could see some of the ceremonial sites? Are whites allowed?"

The smile Charles gave her set off a small spasm of envy in me. I've always considered envy to be the deadliest—and ugliest—of the seven deadly sins. But in my defense, it had been a long time since a man looked at me like that.

"Yes, it's allowed. Nice of you to ask, though. Most visitors don't bother." He adjusted his baseball cap, which I was coveting more by the second. "They just treat everything as if it were theirs and help themselves to whatever they want."

Noticing that my eyes were still glued to his cap, Charles took it off and handed it to me. "Like it?"

With one finger, I traced the raised embroidery of the thunderbird. "It's beautiful."

He nodded. "In Ojibwe legends, the thunderbird controls the upper world. And he battles the Great Serpent who runs the underworld." I turned the cap in my hands gently and touched the tuft of eagle feathers along the side.

"But his most important job is punishing humans who break the rules of basic decency."

A chill ran up my spine. I held the cap out to him, but he shook his head. "Keep it. It wants to stay with you. And who knows?" He winked. "You might need to call on the thunderbird someday. Evelyn tells me you're no stranger to trouble."

As she always does at moments like this, my dear, long-dead mother made a brief appearance to remind me of what "we" do in situations like this. And for once, my early home training held, just barely.

"Keep it? Oh, I couldn't do that." I held the cap out to him.

"Yes, you could." He pushed his chair back under the table. "It's yours."

Still holding the cap, I looked up at him with eyes that, to my everlasting embarrassment, were starting to tear up. All I could manage was a choked little "thank you."

Evelyn bent down and planted a warm, quick kiss on my cheek. "Charles is right. That hat wants to be with you. It must be good medicine." She straightened up and rearranged the buttery soft folds of her jacket. "I'll give you a call later today, and we can schedule a real visit. In the meantime, behave yourself. And steer clear of Rob Ketola."

They both turned to leave. For the next couple of minutes, I watched Bixie watch Charles work his way to the door, slowly and methodically breaking a path through the dense crowd of tourists with Evelyn in his wake, stopping to say hello to a friend or acquaintance every now and then.

My gaze strayed to the blurry mass of humanity around us. Just for something to do, I tried focusing on each individual face. Experts say it takes the average person roughly seven seconds to assess a stranger, get a fix on their status, create a storyline, and decide whether or not they're worth knowing. Of course, according to those same experts, that average person gets it wrong almost every time. I gave up and let the faces turn back into a homogeneous blob of "thems."

The sound of crockery and glassware crashing onto a tile floor made me jump. Somehow it failed to have that same effect on Bixie, who was still gazing at the front entrance with a dreamy look, as if considering far horizons and untapped, heretofore unimagined possibilities.

Time to take back the day.

Chapter Nine

"Pax."

"What?" Bixie didn't seem too thrilled at being drawn away from those romantic vistas and back to the grubby here-and-now.

"Pax," I repeated and spread my arms for emphasis.

"Karin, stop with the games, would you?" Every once in a while, Bixie reminds me of my kindergarten teacher, Miss Holmes, a grandmotherly harridan who believed that her chief task in life was to make sure every child learned to color inside the lines. Always. "Just tell me what you mean. But first, do something about those pastry crumbs on your left cheek." What did I tell you? Miss Holmes, through and through.

I scrubbed a paper napkin across my face. "Oh, come on, Bix. Don't tell me the daughter of a world-renowned classics scholar managed to get this far in life without ever hearing the word pax." I leaned in. "Pax. As in Pax Romana. Or pax vobiscum." I stopped there, having exhausted my supply of Latin phrases.

A light flicked on in Bixie's face, followed immediately by a narrowing of the eyes and a furrowing of the forehead. "Okay. So, what is this peace treaty going to cost me? An apology?"

I shook my head. "An apology would be nice, but not necessary. Besides, you and I both know you never apologize for anything." I began rummaging through my purse in search of the ancient wallet that my Aunt Saimi had been trying and failing to replace for the past several Christmases. Finally, my fingers closed around the warm, dog-eared cowhide. I pulled out three fives and began tapping them into a neat little pile next to my plate.

37

"Charles is right," I said, "we should enjoy ourselves while we can." I straightened the bills slightly. "So let's get out of town and head to Marquette. We can check out the new hammocks in Presque Isle Park. Maybe go to the lighthouse." Bixie's frown lines began to melt away. "Have lunch at Donckers." More melting. Now for the clincher. "And then stop in and see my Aunt Ilsa and Uncle Jalo. I think this is Ilsa's baking day."

"Perfect." Bixie picked up her purse and pushed back her chair. "That's one of the best ideas you've had in ages. What are we waiting for? Let's go. I'll drive."

"No!" The idea of Bixie driving instantly triggers my fight-or-flight response, which is why the word came out louder and faster than intended. "We'll take my car. That way, you can enjoy the scenery." And, I was tempted to add, we can avoid setting off a road rage incident. Or terrifying the local wildlife. Or, worst of all, collecting a big fat ticket from the State Police, who love nothing better than nailing anyone with out-of-town license plates.

As we made our way to the door, Bixie slung her hand over my shoulder. As usual, she seemed oblivious to the stares aimed her way, which ranged from mildly hostile to hot-and-heavy, depending on the gender of the person doing the staring. "Just think. At this very moment, your aunt might be pulling a loaf of her caraway rye out of the oven." We sighed in unison at the thought of little islands of butter melting into thick, steaming, fragrant slices.

"Yeah," I said. "Who knows, it might be the last treat we get for a while."

Bixie halted a few feet from the door and turned to me. "Because?"

"Because I seriously doubt they serve home-baked bread—or home-baked anything else—in the Alger County Jail."

As we tossed our jackets into the back seat and settled ourselves in the car, it occurred to me that this temporary escape was going to work only if we cut ourselves off from the mess Ben had unintentionally created. At least for the time being. "Just one thing," I announced. "We're only doing this if you agree to banish all cell phone contact for the next six hours."

"What? Are you serious?" From the look on Bixie's face, you'd think I had just asked her to take a job in a meat-packing plant.

"No exceptions. Full embargo on all incoming calls and text messages." I scrunched my shoulders, ready for a tirade.

Instead, after a few thoughtful seconds, she sighed, rolled her eyes, crossed her arms, sighed again and then surprised me by saying, "Oh, alright. I will not respond to any phone contact. But," she added, giving her seatbelt a brutal tug, "I am not turning my phone off. I'll just let it ring through."

Bixie managed to hold on to her pique for maybe ten miles, turning her head toward the open window to gaze at the deep blue water rimed with beach sand and dune grasses, and ruffled now by a gentle wind that felt more like a caress than a breeze. The morning air was so clear, so clean, so tangy with a mix of sweet grass and tamarack and wild leeks that I almost wanted to eat it instead of breathing it in.

Gradually, Lake Superior worked its magic. After a few idle comments about the weather, she leaned back against the headrest in contented silence. When we arrived at our first destination, she made no attempt to supervise my choice of a parking spot. And by the time we had walked the verdant trails of Presque Isle Park and lowered ourselves into a couple of lake-view hammocks, she was in full mellow mode. The hammocks were intended to serve as study hangouts, literally, for students from Northern Michigan University, which was just down the road. But there wasn't a student in sight, and, as an alum, I felt entitled to give them a test drive.

From there, it was on to lunch at Donckers—burger, hand-cut fries and coffee for me, turkey sandwich on gluten-free bread with iced tea for her. Then it was a short drive to NMU, where Bixie parked herself in the new library while I exchanged my loafers for a battered pair of Nikes and spent an hour chasing memories around campus and deciding whether to resent or admire the new buildings. Our next stop was the Marquette Food Co-op, where Bixie filled an entire shopping cart with virtuous items like kale and green tea and bone broth and almond milk. My purchases were more in the normal-human-being range: local cheese, fresh fruits, canned soup, potato chips, and crackers, plus three boxes of cookies and a dozen chocolate bars to assure a balanced diet.

Saving the best for last, we ended the afternoon at the kitchen table of my Aunt Ilsa and Uncle Jalo, where we chatted non-stop over coffee and freshly baked cardamom bread. Nothing of any note happens in Marquette County—or Alger County, for that matter—without Aunt Ilsa knowing about it, and the juiciest stories always end up as cheerful gossip at her kitchen table.

When the topic of Ben Roberts' death came up, as I knew it would, I shrugged it off as a freak accident in a way that seemed to convince both my aunt and uncle. Yes, I agreed, it was a strange coincidence, us being in town the night Ben died. Sure, it was a bit of a shock. But, as I reminded her, Ben wasn't a close friend, just a former employer. As a diversion, I piled on all the usual platitudes about how we never know what the future will hold and how death can come at any moment, in any form, for anyone. All of which seemed to quell my aunt's curiosity for the time being.

Except for that little hiccup, it was a perfect day. Made even more perfect by the ride back, during which we experienced the delicious, malicious, utterly human joy that comes from having a State Trooper emerge from out of nowhere, rev up his siren, switch on his bubblegum lights and swerve off in hot pursuit of a jackass driver. In this case, an idiot with New York plates who had just passed three cars, ours among them, doing seventy-five in a fifty-five-mile zone.

As I said, a perfect day. Of course, as Ben Roberts was fond of saying, the only problem with perfection is that you can't trust it.

Because it never lasts.

Chapter Ten

It is an unwritten law of the universe that every long, restless line of customers waiting to order a meal must contain at least one person with food issues. There can be no exceptions. In my experience, that person has always been Bixie. And today, she did not disappoint either me or the universe.

Lowering her violet gaze from the wall menu, she asked in a voice without much hope in it: "Do you have any organic pasties?"

I winced at the question, even though I knew it was coming. Up and down the line, the effect was immediate. Faces hardened, frowns sprouted, arms crossed, toes tapped, meaningful looks were exchanged. I'd seen it all before. Such are the perils of traveling with a clean food fanatic.

Fortunately, anticipating just such a scene, I had ordered first and then retreated to the far corner of the shop. There, clutching my neatly bagged beef pasty, I pretended to study the maple syrups on offer while keeping an eye on Bixie's antics at the cash register.

To his credit, the burly teenager behind the counter—a Huck Finn doppelgänger—kept a straight face. He didn't show any surprise, didn't roll his twinkly blue eyes or wrinkle his freckled nose, didn't give the slightest suggestion of a sigh. Of course, with so many outlanders swarming around these days, the kid had probably gotten used to food fetishes. Smile firmly in place, he shook his head and managed to look semi-apologetic.

"Sorry, ma'am." He pointed to the old-fashioned blackboard that filled most of the wall behind him. Under the words MULDOON'S PASTIES was a message in multi-colored chalk that read: Get Your Bigfoot Bait Here!

Below that, someone had scrawled out the day's menu in handwriting that would have made an elementary school teacher weep.

"Everything we have is listed right here. Nothing strictly organic. But we do have a veggie pasty. No meat, just onions, potatoes, rutabagas, and carrots. It's really good." He grinned, Huck-style. "Actually, everything here is really good."

He spoke the truth. I should know, having spent hours of my life standing at the counter in this funky old clapboard house, former abode of the Muldoon clan and now their corporate headquarters. A few years back, the Muldoons opened a trendy little storefront in town to capture the tourist trade, but most locals still prefer to get their pasty fix at the original location in Brown's Addition, just west of Munising. I breathed in the savory smells of meat and vegetables cooking inside their buttery crusts and wondered, for the hundredth time, who Brown was and what he'd done to get this little backwater named after him.

Oblivious to the foot shuffling and throat-clearing behind her, Bixie gave the matter some slow, serious thought. "Okay. I'll take a veggie pasty." At least she pronounced it correctly, the way I'd taught her, making the word rhyme with "nasty." The frustrated customers stopped fidgeting, and I heard sighs of relief, or maybe exasperation.

While Bixie settled up, I threaded a path through the crowd and waited for her at the door. Making our way down the paint-starved wooden steps to the parking lot, we stowed our dinners in Amelia's back seat next to a grocery bag filled with cardamom rolls, oatmeal cookies, and fresh rye bread, all lovingly wrapped in aluminum foil by Aunt Ilsa.

The afternoon breeze that kicked up waves in the navy-blue waters felt delicious after the stuffy warmth of the shop. I leaned my head back and gazed skyward just in time to spot a flock of Canadian geese slanting across the sky in a ragged arrowhead design.

"How many?" Bixie asked.

"How do you know I counted?"

"Because you always do. And then you get upset if there's an odd number. So how many?"

"Eleven." I pulled out my cell phone and punched the on button. "And I don't get upset, just thoughtful. They mate for life, you know. And the loners stay with the flock." Eager to change the subject, I waved my phone at her. "Aren't you going to check your calls? You must be feeling withdrawal pains by now."

Sunglasses deployed, Bixie and I leaned against my sun-warmed car and stared at our phones. Geeky by nature and easily distracted by bright, shiny objects, she had shelled out a small fortune for the new gotta-have-it miracle touchscreen. But it was a sure bet that in a matter of weeks, she'd abandon her new toy in favor of an iPhone. Being a confirmed Luddite myself, I was sticking with my old flip-top for the time being. I began tapping away at my tiny keypad.

"Damn!"

The word slipped out before I realized it. A few curious faces turned in my direction, and one indignant young mother stopped wrestling with her toddler's car seat long enough to send me a disapproving glance.

"What now?" Bixie kept tapping her screen as she spoke.

"Two messages from Roger." I pulled off my sunglasses and rubbed the spot on my forehead that Bixie refers to as the third eye, but which now seemed to be the launching pad for a tension headache.

"And?" Bixie was all attention.

"And he's heading our way. Probably on Friday. Saturday at the latest. Evidently, his editor smells a story in the making. Paul left a couple of messages, too. He wants me to call him as soon as possible." I closed the phone and stuffed it into the back pocket of my jeans.

Bixie finished a text message before looking up. "Aren't you going to call Paul?"

"Later. You know what a drama queen he is. It's probably nothing." I opened the door and slid in behind the wheel. "Let's get over to City Park first and grab a picnic table." I started the engine and reminded myself yet again to stop at the Holiday Station and have someone check out the ominous rumble under the hood. "The evening cruise doesn't leave for an hour and a half, so the crowds shouldn't be too bad."

I inched my way out of the parking lot and waited while a family of five sporting Pictured Rocks hats and standing in the middle of the curb cut consulted their Chamber of Commerce map. Then I waited for a break in the traffic that surged along M-28. After two long minutes, I darted in behind a double-flatbed truck loaded with timber. We rolled down our windows and, within seconds, the car was filled with the intoxicating scent of freshly cut pine.

As usual, the intersection just north of the city dock was clogged with knots of jaywalkers, confused out-of-town drivers, and irate truckers trying to make their delivery schedule. Hard to believe that, in a typical season, Alger County's nine thousand residents will host more than one million visitors from every corner of the globe. Equally hard to believe that, not all that long ago, National Pictured Rocks Lakeshore was one of the Upper Peninsula's best-kept secrets. Which is how most of us preferred it.

After two close escapes from fender-benders, I gave up, headed back to M-28, and claimed the last remaining slot in the Dollar Store parking lot. Five minutes later, white bakery bags in hand, we were staking out a picnic table in the park. One minute more and we were pulling on our jackets to fend off the lake breeze and setting out paper napkins, catsup packets, and plastic dinnerware.

I was staring at my pasty, trying to decide whether to start with the crust or dive into the meat-and-potato center, when Bixie's phone let out a cascade of notes. From where I was sitting, I could see the name "Andrew" hovering at the top of her screen.

My heart stopped for a split second before going back to its dull, safe, normal rhythm. "Down, girl," I told myself sternly as I began pulling the crisp white paper away from my pasty.

After a few conflicted seconds, she put down her fork and threw me a quick glance. "Sorry, but I should probably get this." She tapped the screen, stood up, took a few steps away from the bench, and stared out at the lake. "Hey, Andrew. What's up?"

Chapter Eleven

Normally, I would have begun intensive eavesdropping immediately. However, making the first cut into a pasty is something of a sacred moment, so I tuned out the first part of the conversation. But after a minute or so, things got too interesting to ignore. There were long silences on Bixie's end, interrupted only by an occasional "What?" or "Why?" or "No!" There were two bursts of "Are you serious?" And finally, one "For how long?"

It was the second "Are you serious?" that hooked me completely. Fork down, I looked up from my half-finished pasty just in time to see Bixie's eyes widen and hear her blurt out, in a slightly desperate voice, "Andrew, I really don't think that's a good idea."

Evidently, Andrew disagreed because the next sound out of her mouth was a cross between a sigh and a growl. "Fine," she spat the word at her phone. "Have it your way. But you better be sure your friend is serious about that free cabin, because there isn't a vacancy within seventy miles of this place." After a brief pause, she muttered something that sounded like "I think you're making a mistake," then jabbed at the screen, put her head back, closed her eyes, and began taking breaths so deep I could hear them from my bench twelve feet away despite a rising wind and screeching gulls.

Suddenly, the nickel dropped, taking my appetite with it. I pushed away the remains of my pasty and looked up at Bixie. "Cabin? Did I hear the word cabin? Just where does this particular cabin happen to be?"

Free hand on her forehead, phone hand on her hip, Bixie closed her eyes for a few seconds before answering. She looked like a statue I saw in Paris once, something about suffering womanhood. When she spoke, the words came out in a slow, controlled cadence. "The cabin belongs to a friend of Andrew's in the department. Some guy whose family has a summer cottage up here."

"*Up here*," I repeated. "And *up here* is where, exactly? I mean, we are talking about more than twenty-six thousand square miles in this peninsula. "

The look she gave me wavered between anger and apology. "Up here is a place called Lost Lake. You know it?"

"Know it?" My stomach began doing gyrations that had nothing to do with dinner. "You could say that. My uncles built a cabin on Lost Lake years ago, and we used to spend our summer vacations there when I was a kid. And occasional weekends." Part of me refused to believe this conversation was happening. The other part plowed on. "It's not far, just outside of Wetmore. Maybe ten or eleven miles from where we are right now."

I gulped down some water. "So. Would you care to tell me why your brother has this sudden urge to drive over four hundred miles to the UP? And not just anywhere in the UP, but to this particular little patch of it?"

Everyone has her own tactics for evading questions she prefers not to answer. Bixie has more than most. The one she used now involved an elaborate shrug, a lot of head turning, and eyes that flitted around the park butterfly-style before finally landing on something just beyond my right shoulder. "He said he was stressed out, that he'd accumulated a ton of vacation time, and that a good friend of his had offered him the use of their family cottage."

"So…" I broke off a chunk of pastry crust. Delicious. Must be the lard. "So, what you're saying is, this spur-of-the-moment trip has nothing whatever to do with the fact that Ben Roberts died last night less than a mile from where his little sister and her pain-in-the-butt friend are staying."

"Well, not quite. Ben *was* one of the topics we discussed."

"One of them." I bit into another chunk of crust and gazed out at the lake. "What was the other? You seemed to be pretty worked up."

"It's not important. And it doesn't involve you."

I chewed in silence. What was she not telling me? I waited, knowing full well that no further explanation was coming. Note to self: In my next lifetime, my closest friend will not be the excessively private, sharing-averse, gossip-impaired offspring of a tediously well-mannered Midwestern mother and an upper-middle-class Brit father. Rather, she will be a bubbly, tell-all Diane Keaton type who shares everything with me, whether or not I want to hear it.

"Bixie, how long have we known each other?"

Her eyes swiveled away from the gazebo and locked on my face. "Just about forever."

"Right. So why is it that I'm usually the last to know what's going on in your personal life? Even though your personal life often tends to be entwined with my personal life?"

"Oh, Karin, stop exaggerating. If that's even possible for you." She pushed up from the table and began collecting the remains of our dinner.

Instinctively, I reached out a hand to shield her untouched pasty from the methodical clean-up. "Aren't you going to eat that?"

"I'm not hungry anymore." She began stuffing dinner debris into one of the white bakery bags. "And if we sit around, we're just going to argue about Andrew's decision to come up here. Even though there's absolutely nothing I can do about it."

I sighed, picked up the pasty and gently tucked it back into its aluminum foil jacket. "I'm going to put this in the cooler along with the rest of the cold stuff from the Marquette Co-op. In case you get hungry later tonight and need a snack."

Bixie glanced over at me with the tiniest of smiles. "Don't you mean, in case you get hungry tonight, the way you do every night?"

Choosing to ignore that last remark, I stood up, wrapped pasty in hand. "Okay. Just one simple question, which even you should have no problem answering. Did Andrew happen to mention when he's leaving for this little paradise of ours?"

I watched while Bixie used her napkin to brush crumbs off the picnic table. Only when the last stubborn crumb had finally been removed did she answer. "He's planning to leave on Saturday. His shift ends at three that day,

47

so he should be on the road by four, five at the latest."

Which, if he drove like most men and only stopped for gas and coffee, would put him in Munising around midnight. The good news just kept coming. First, Roger. Now, Andrew. I began to wonder when Paul would decide to join the exodus from Ann Arbor and become part of our happy little band up here in the True North. Then I banished that thought. Some things were just too bizarre to contemplate.

Before I could say a single sarcastic word, Bixie began walking toward the main drag, stopping at the trash bin along the way. "It's still early," she said. "Let's put that pasty in the cooler and then see who's playing tonight at Falling Rock. You can get a cup of coffee, and I'm going to try that new soy ice cream they've got."

At that moment, I desperately wanted to release the two-year-old self I keep locked away inside. I wanted to throw a tantrum to end all tantrums, toss myself on the ground, kick the air with primal fury. I wanted to scream, "No! No! This will not happen. I won't let Ben or Roger or Andrew or anyone else invade my vacation. I won't, I won't, I won't."

That's what I wanted to say. What I actually said was, "Good idea. We might as well enjoy our last days of freedom. Before Roger and Andrew arrive, and all hell breaks loose."

"Oh, stop it," Bixie tossed the words over her shoulder. "Nothing is going to break loose. We'll hardly even know they're here."

I closed my eyes briefly against the bright evening sun and consoled myself with the dark thought that a few days or weeks from now, I would have the perverse pleasure of reminding Bixie just how wrong she'd been.

Chapter Twelve

I'm convinced that good things tend to happen on Thursdays. Not earth-shatteringly good things, just quietly pleasant good things. My theory is supported by folk wisdom:

Monday's child is fair of face.
Tuesday's child is full of grace.
Wednesday's child is full of woe.
Thursday's child has far to go…

In merry olde England, where that nursery rhyme got its start, "far to go" meant a long and successful life. I rest my case. Except, of course, there's also Eartha Kitt's brilliantly understated rendition of *Thursday's Child* to consider:

Things look mighty black for Thursday's Child.
Trouble down the track for Thursday's Child.

Ominous. But note that the predicted trouble is down the track, not immediate. So I've continued to put my faith in Thursdays, and this particular Thursday did not disappoint.

In fact, despite the uncertainty surrounding Ben's death and the impending arrival of both Andrew and Roger, I woke up feeling, well, I won't say happy because those of us who haul around a lot of Finnish DNA rarely achieve that state. But strangely peaceful. Calm and settled.

It must have been the Grand Island Slam I'd had the night before at the café. Special of the day: one scoop each of Pictured Rocks Pecan, Lover's Leap Vanilla, and Chapel Rock Chocolate. Of course, it's possible that all the touristing around Marquette had worn me out. Whatever the reason, I collapsed into bed around ten, slept what Winston Churchill once described as the sleep of the saved and thankful, and woke early.

The morning news broadcast was more of the same, a retread of yesterday's stories with renewed assurances that police were continuing their investigations and that everything Ben had been eating and drinking—knowing him, probably more drinking than eating—had been sent to the Michigan State Police Pathology Lab in Marquette for thorough analysis. Stat priority.

I would have preferred hearing that all evidence pointed to death by natural causes. Case closed. End of story. But as my Aunt Ilsa is fond of saying, no news is good news. And except for Ben's knack of making enemies wherever he went, there was no reason to suspect that the path lab would turn up any alarming discoveries.

So, despite the uncertainty factor and the mild undercurrent of anxiety that came with it, the day passed in a blurry vacation haze. There was beach time. Novel reading time. Snack time. Agate searching time. Lake gazing time. Gift shop browsing time. And of course, moccasin buying time, because who can resist the lure of a new pair of Minnetonkas, never mind the price.

Late in the afternoon, there was also laptop time as I sat in the school library, one of the few free wifi spots in town, and slogged my way through forty or so emails, about a dozen of them from clients. Despite the fact that mine tends to be a crisis-prone profession, there were no stomach-churning messages. No emergencies. No nasty surprises.

There was also phone time, with me leaving voicemails for Evelyn and a cousin in nearby Chatham and a snotty receptionist at the Channel Six news desk because I couldn't reach Sandy at her office extension. Last on my list, I returned Paul's call, using his home landline number because it was, after all, Thursday, which meant that he was either at his workshop or swanning around his upscale furniture boutique in downtown Ann Arbor. So I could retreat into the safety of voicemail rather than risking a long, laboriously detailed and occasionally bitchy conversation.

Although Paul is one of my favorite human beings when he's behaving himself, and although it's true that he saved my life during our botched murder investigation, it's also true that he can be trying to even the most patient of souls. A group that does not include me. Besides, I knew that Albert the Magnificat was perfectly fine and had probably taken over the household by now. If anything had happened to my beloved feline, Paul would have found a way to let me know.

As I said, a sublimely sweet day. Exactly what a vacation day should be, and a respite from the tension surrounding Ben's death.

Friday was essentially a carbon copy, a sunny, beachy, errand-running, novel-reading day that almost lulled me into a false sense of security. Paul provided the day's entertainment in the form of three gossipy voicemails focused almost entirely on our new neighbor who according to rumor had— back in the day—carried on a relatively discreet but reputedly torrid love affair with Mick Jagger. On a less thrilling note, I checked in with my Aunt Ilsa and then accepted Evelyn's invitation to Sunday dinner, after she promised to make her mother's legendary meatloaf recipe.

For Bixie, the high point of the day was a phone call.

During breakfast, between sips of green tea, she had suggested that we pay a visit to the Ojibwe casino in Christmas. To show how little she cared about the topic, she kept her face turned toward the front window, pretending to be transfixed by the moving wall of fog that rolled across the glassy lake surface. Her exact words were, "Got any plans for the day? Because I thought it might be fun to check out the casino."

For a few seconds, I could only stare. Whoever was sitting across the battered kitchen table from me was not Bixie Murray. On a loose-ends day, the real Bixie might suggest trekking to a nearby lighthouse or a local artist's studio or a waterfall, or having a picnic lunch at Shelter Bay. Those were all very Bixie. But her wanting to visit a casino was the equivalent of the Pope break-dancing in Vatican Square.

"The casino?" I asked. "Really? Why?" Of course, I'd agree to go with her, eventually. But except for my Sunday School training, there was nothing to keep me from making her squirm a little first. "I mean, we're talking about slot machines and blackjack tables. And a sort of café run by a big burly guy with tattoos who would rather be doing something else." I put down my coffee cup. "That's pretty much it, except for some corporate spaces in back that are off limits. Although I suppose they wouldn't be if Charles were there."

A rosy flush bloomed on her cheeks, and she started fidgeting with that long blonde mane of hers. "Well, it was just a thought. And there are other things to do in Christmas. Didn't we pass a pottery shop? And…"

I relented. "Actually, the casino is a good idea." If she was that hot to see Charles again, why not? The man fascinated me as well, albeit for reasons that had nothing to do with lust. "Let's go." The words were barely out of my mouth when her phone went off.

She glanced at the screen, then up at me. "That's odd. It's a local call." After a wary "hello," her face went all soft and flustered-looking.

I can't tell you what she and Charles talked about because once the conversation started, she stepped onto the back porch. Better reception out there, as she later explained. The upshot was that she—and probably as an afterthought, I—were invited to lunch and a private tour of the casino tomorrow. Evidently, Saturday was a special promo day, and there were all sorts of exciting things going on. "Exciting" being a relative term.

I decided to do the right and good thing. "Thanks, Bix, but I don't think so. I've been to the casino and really don't need to see it again." Don't want to see it again. "Besides, you two will have a better time without me."

"Oh no, that's not true. He included you in the invitation." Jane Austen would have described my friend's response as dissembling, and I might have agreed, if it weren't for the slightly panicked look in her eyes and the slightly pleading tone of her voice. "You really should come. Please."

I sighed and thought, well, maybe this is just what happens to widows. Maybe this is one of our assigned roles. Chaperone. Maiden aunt. Comfortable presence. Fifth wheel or, in this case, third wheel.

"Okay," I said. "Might as well. I have nothing else to do tomorrow." Thereby proving yet again that clairvoyance is not one of my many gifts.

Chapter Thirteen

It was just a few minutes after noon when the news broke on Marquette's NPR station. Bixie and I were sitting in a long, tangled line of traffic at Munising's one lonely, overworked downtown stoplight. We'd been talking over the broadcast, chatting idly about what Charles might have in mind for our so-called casino tour, when an urgent female voice brought our conversation to a halt.

"Turning to local news, Alger County Police report a major breakthrough in their investigation into the death late Wednesday night of local entrepreneur and real estate developer Benjamin Roberts at his home in Munising. Tests conducted by the Michigan State Police Pathology Lab in Marquette have determined that Roberts' death was not accidental, as initially assumed, but was the result of deliberately induced anaphylactic shock. Based on new evidence, the Alger County Sheriff's Office has released a brief statement announcing that the department will be pursuing leads in cooperation with various law enforcement agencies in what is now presumed to be a homicide investigation. Roberts' home on Sand Point Road in Munising will remain an official crime scene for an indefinite period of time. Stay tuned for news updates throughout the day as more information becomes available."

Despite a hot breeze flowing into the car, I suddenly felt chilled down to my core, as if a Lake Superior tsunami had washed over me. It was only the pain of my hands gripping the wheel and the frantic honking of the Dodge Ram behind us that brought me back to the present. That, and my thumping heart and the sick feeling in my stomach. Bixie, who was staring fixedly at the radio, appeared to be in the same state.

Pulling away from the Ram driver who was now cursing me loudly and creatively through his open window, I raced through the light just as amber turned to red and then, on impulse, swerved into the parking lot next to a construction site. A small part of me stepped away from the thought tornado twisting through my brain long enough to wonder what the new place was going to be. A brewery? A bistro? A high-visibility home for the Chamber of Commerce?

"Ben. Murdered." Bixie shifted her stare from the radio to me. "Murdered," she repeated. Her voice was so monotone I couldn't tell if she was stating a fact or asking a question or making an accusation. She probably didn't know either.

A grief counselor once advised me, when in doubt...breathe. Deep breathing, she explained, not only calms the body and clears the mind but is incompatible with tears. You can't cry and take deep breaths at the same time. So I breathed. Not that I was in any danger of crying. What I most wanted, all I wanted at that dizzying moment, was to breathe my way into clarity and away from the incipient panic waiting patiently for me at the edge of thought.

"Okay." It was a brave start, meant to camouflage the fact that I had no idea what to say next. "Okay," I repeated. "There's no real surprise here. Remember what Charles said? That just about everyone in town had a reason for wanting to see Ben dead? And maybe even a reason for *making* him dead? The same thing is true for a lot of other people in a lot of other places. Ben cast a wide net. We don't even know the extent of his business dealings. He could have enemies all over the country, or beyond." At least we could hope so.

Bixie's face wore the look of a troubled four-year-old. "But murder. Again." A small wrinkle made its way across her forehead. "The people you know are supposed to die natural deaths. Normal deaths. From disease or accidents or old age. That's the way it works. But instead, here we are again. With someone we know being murdered."

"Well," I admitted, "the odds are definitely against something like this happening." I wanted to add that things were different this time, because this time we wouldn't be involved in a murder investigation. But of course that wasn't true.

"Tell you what," I turned the key in the ignition as I spoke. "Let's get ourselves to the casino and order a couple of glasses of wine. We're not going to sort this out here, and Charles is expecting us." I inched toward the parking lot entrance and turned right. "Besides, I'm sure he'll have something to say about this new development."

Neither of us uttered a single word during the five-minute drive. The silence, or maybe shock, continued as we walked through the door of the casino and into the lounge. When I ordered a Chablis for Bixie and a Riesling for myself, the bartender cocked an eyebrow, flicked an invisible speck of dirt from the counter and said matter-of-factly, "Better make that two Chablis. Unless you want to drive to Marquette for your Riesling."

From behind me, a man's voice said, "Two Chablis, Art. On the house."

Bixie and I both turned at the same time, but it was Bixie who spoke first. "Charles." For a split second, I had the distinct impression that they were both fighting an impulse to hug each other. But then maybe I was just projecting because I needed a hug so badly myself.

Charles measured out a warm, wry smile for each of us. "Ladies, it's good to see you both. Glad you could make it. Although from the look on your faces and the order you placed, I'd say you probably just heard the news about Ben Roberts."

I gave a nod, then followed it up with a long, deep swallow of wine, deeper than I intended, and nearly choked. Bixie attacked her glass at a steady but ladylike pace.

"I've got a suggestion," Charles put the coffee cup he was holding on a nearby table. "Why don't we postpone the tour for the time being and head back to my office? It's quiet there. And I can show you my collection of Indian artifacts, all local."

Grateful for the prospect of being in a safe, sequestered space for at least a little while, where police would never think to look for us, I tagged along behind Bixie. Charles led us around a corner and down a corridor lined with numerous doors and large photographs of local beauty spots. As we walked, I recognized one of the images as Face in the Rock, a huge sandstone sculpture made by a French explorer more than two hundred years ago. I stopped to take it in.

"Power of the Air," Charles said, moving to stand next to me as I gazed at the photo. "The only surviving Chippewa warrior of a devastating battle between Michigan and Minnesota tribes over two centuries ago. The Grand Island tribe had never fought anyone, ever, and never wanted to. They were forced into the fight by other tribes from the area."

"Yes." I couldn't seem to pull my eyes away from the faint outlines of that face in the stone. "If I remember right, Power of the Air was a fantastic runner. Very young at the time of the battle. And when everyone else was dead or dying, he raced away at what must have been a ferocious speed. I remember reading his recollections of the escape, the dying elder telling him to run, and all the arrows raining down just behind him as he raced along. Cutting through the air. Barely missing him. He was the sole survivor."

"That's right," Charles said in a dry voice. "I guess there are times in life when we can all relate to that. Moving as fast as our legs and our brains will carry us, dodging in every possible direction, hoping we'll out-run the arrows coming our way."

He walked on to the nearest door, opened it, and stepped back to allow Bixie and me to enter. "It looks as if we're all in for some interesting days ahead," he said as we walked past him through the open door. "But at least I can offer you a temporary escape."

Chapter Fourteen

One standard issue executive desk in chrome and black laminate. Two standard issue black vinyl chairs. Desktop computer and assorted office paraphernalia. Four tall filing cabinets, also black, also standard issue, with prominent locks on each drawer. Picture window featuring a view of the back parking lot and delivery area, fringed by evergreens.

It would have been just another office if it weren't for the glass exhibit cases that lined two of the walls. Every one of them was filled with artifacts. Bixie let out a little gasp as we both moved automatically toward the items on display. "Remarkable," she said in an Alice in Wonderland voice, to which I could only add, "Fantastic."

Together, we gazed at dark, unglazed clay bowls and plates of all sizes. Next to them were small fringed bags made from worn animal hide, decorated with the remains of beadwork created by women long dead. There were several pipes. Drums. Knives. Two hatchets. Something that looked like a set of utensils. Taking up most of one corner was a pair of men's leather leggings stained and weathered by time and, just above them, a magnificent headdress with most of the embroidery and feathers still intact. I stared at the headdress intently, as if by sheer will I could make it speak, share its memories, tell its stories.

Eyes shining, Bixie looked over at Charles. "This is amazing. It's like stepping into a private museum. Tell us about all this. How did you manage to collect so many pieces? Where did you find them? Where do they come from?"

I pointed to a tiny brown clay pipe with a broken stem, no more than three or four inches in length, lying next to what must have been a tobacco pouch but was now a dark, wrinkled, nondescript bag. "Start with this one," I said. "What is this? A child's toy?"

"A toy? Not at all." Charles stepped between us, inserted a key into a small lock, pulled open one of the sliding doors, tenderly picked up the tiny object, and placed it in the palm of his hand. "This was my grandmother's ceremonial pipe." He held it out to me and, after a few seconds, turned it toward Bixie on his other side.

Strange, how comforting it was to stand so close to a man again, a big man, to feel the warmth radiating from his body and smell the faint aroma of, I took a quick breath, yes, it was Old Spice. My father's favorite, and something that occasionally appeared on Terry's side of the bathroom cabinet as well.

With more discretion than I'm usually capable of, I moved away from Charles and Bixie, who were in deep and, from where I stood, close conversation about some piece in the collection. The exhibit cases on the other side of the room held larger items. My eyes came to a full stop on the remnants of a small headdress and the tattered remains of two beaded, fringed deerskin shirts.

"Those large fabric pieces are hard to come by." Charles aimed his voice at me from across the room. "The ones you're looking at were handed down through my father's family. Heirlooms, I guess you'd call them. In this part of the country, it's unusual to find any Indian relics that are intact. The climate here is so harsh that most of the clay utensils have been destroyed. And with all the dislocation our people went through, moving to the mainland in order to survive and living out on the edges of the city in shacks and tents, a lot of the leather work and ceremonial clothing disappeared."

"So then," I turned again to stare at the beaded scrap of shirt, "are all of these things from your family?"

"No." He walked over to stand beside me. "Some of them are from archaeological digs on Grand Island. The University of Pennsylvania led a major expedition here a few years back. I'm what you might call a temporary curator for the tribe. But a lot of these pieces were salvaged by men, mainly Ojibwes, who worked on construction projects along Sand Point. All kinds of artifacts turned up, literally turned up, when roads and houses were being built out there years ago. And that continues to the present day."

"There must be laws about that now," Bixie piped up. "About all Indian artifacts being the rightful property of the tribe or, maybe, since it's part of a national park, belonging to the federal government." Having grown up in one of the state's liberal strongholds, Bixie is an unapologetic Progressive. She's also just naïve enough, sometimes, to believe that most people share her views on social justice. So naturally, in her world, there would be laws to protect all historic Indian relics.

Charles' eyes took on a flinty look. He shook his head and let out a short laugh that wasn't a laugh at all. "Laws? Not until nineteen ninety. For years, any relics were ignored or stolen. Things are supposed to be different now. The rule is that every artifact belongs to the tribe. And when bones are churned up…"

"Bones?" I jumped in. It's one of my many rude habits, interrupting people in mid-sentence. Irritating, I know, but I can't seem to stop. "Human bones are turning up on Sand Point?"

"Sure. Around the lakeshore mainly. During my grandparents' time, the tribe had to leave Grand Island for the mainland, since they couldn't support themselves anymore in traditional ways. They settled in encampments on the outskirts of Munising, including Sand Point. They lived there, and they died there. So their bones are there, in tribal burial sites. And they're still turning up, especially with so many people buying prime lakeshore property and building on it. Whenever human remains are discovered, all work is supposed to stop. Local officials are supposed to be notified. Then they're supposed to contact tribal leaders, who arrange for reburial ceremonies in a sacred site."

"So that's what happens now?" Bixie had no intention of giving up her hopes for humanity. "I mean, it would be indecent to disturb a grave and not make it right."

"Sometimes. Not always." Charles put the tobacco pouch he was holding back in the case behind him. Then he closed the sliding door, inserted the key in the lock, walked back to his desk, picked up the receiver from his complicated phone console, and pushed a button. "Anna? Hey, do me a big favor, would you? Have someone bring three coffees down to my office. Cream, sugar, and, if they can find it, some honey." Brief silence. "Perfect. Thanks."

As Bixie and I settled ourselves in the standard issue chairs, which were surprisingly comfortable, Charles picked up a pen and studied it for a few moments. Still holding the pen, he looked up at me, then at Bixie.

"You ask what happens now to the artifacts?" His fingers tightened into a fist around the pen. "What happens now is that, when developers like Ben Roberts build their big, expensive condo projects, they usually make sure that nothing stops the work. Time is money, right? So, in some cases, not all but some, when bones are churned up by heavy equipment, they're treated like debris and churned right back into the soil or dumped into piles of slag. And woe be to any worker who reports it to the authorities."

"And you know this how?" Given the look on our host's face, I was almost afraid to ask.

"I know this because two of my cousins were part of the construction crews that built Ben's house and also did the site prep work for his luxury condos. They saw bones being dug up, nothing done about it, no phone calls, no work stoppages. When the bones surfaced, they became part of the building site. It was Ben's policy. Of course it was. Why not? They were just the remains of dead Indians, so why should they matter? And when other things were disturbed, the kind of stuff you see in these cases, it was set aside. Supposedly to be picked up by tribal officers. There was a space, a small shed, where they were kept. But my cousins never saw any members of the tribe at the site. Never. As far as they could tell, nothing was ever picked up. But somehow the artifacts always disappeared."

He unclenched his fingers. "I figured they all ended up in one of those artsy galleries operated by Ben's lady friend, or people like her." There was a knock at the door that made me jump in my seat. Charles stood up. "But that's just my guess."

He walked over to the door, opened it, and took a large serving tray from a young man dressed in the white shirt and black pants of a professional dealer. "Thanks, Bob. Much appreciated. Tell Henry I'll be out on the floor in a while, showing my guests around, in case he needs me for anything."

Carefully setting the tray on a side table, he looked over at us with a smile. "How do you take your coffee, ladies?"

Chapter Fifteen

I like anomalies, and Falling Rock Café is one of my favorites. But like all anomalies, it's hard to describe.

The café is an oasis for townies, a mecca for tourists, and a five-star favorite with online reviewers and guidebook writers. Think small-town urbanism. Rustic cool. Woodsy chic.

It's the kind of place you'd never expect to find in the far reaches of the UP. And yet there it is, taking up two funky storefronts on Superior Avenue, better known as M-28.

Falling Rock was the brain child—or love child—of a downstate couple who came to Munising as tourists and decided not only to stay but to give their new home the one thing it was missing: a destination café/bookstore/deli/art gallery/performance venue/meeting place/co-work space/community center/ice cream parlor/reading nook/winter sanctuary/home-away-from-home. It's also an ideal escape pod for those times when life is overwhelming and scary around the edges.

Needless to say, in the summer months, the place tends to be crowded. Impossibly crowded. Too often, the queue snakes out the door, around the corner, and halfway up the block to the local dive bar. But tonight was different. Maybe it was the lure of the whispering lake breeze or the high, strong sun that substitutes for twilight during northern summers. Whatever the reason, and despite it being a Saturday night, the line was mercifully short.

In less than five minutes, I was holding a large steaming latte. Large. Not grande. Falling Rock doesn't do grande. Falling Rock does small, medium, and large, as God intended. Bixie stood next to me in the shoulder-to-shoulder throng licking a double-scoop, French vanilla, non-dairy, gluten-free, something-like-an-ice-cream cone.

I led the way across the uneven pine floor boards, past shelves and freestanding displays crowded with books and birch bark postcards and Lake Superior agate jewelry and locally made whatnots, down a worn step and into the adjoining space. There, a dozen mix-and-match wooden tables had been pushed back to make room for a small stage and rows of metal folding chairs, half of which were already occupied.

We nabbed two chairs on the aisle and settled into them. With just five minutes to show time, people were starting to crowd in, and folks who had been standing around in chatty groups began sorting themselves out, claiming tables in the back or looking for empty seats among the folding chairs. Swiveling her head to take in the crowd, Bixie applied a paper napkin to some stray drops of soy ice cream on her chin. "Who's playing tonight?"

I picked up the flyer on the seat next to me. "A group based in Nashville. The New Nevilles. Looks like they play a little of everything. Folk. Cajun. Classic rock. R and B."

Bixie downed the last soggy bite of her ice cream cone and used what was left of the napkin to wipe her fingers and mouth. "The New Nevilles? Talk about setting the bar high."

Musicians who pass through the UP tend to be a mixed bag, but the New Nevilles lived up to their name. After the usual banter and lame jokes, they dove into the music. Within a few minutes, everybody was swaying in their seats. Two songs later, when they launched into *Yellow Moon*, the dancing started. Of course, it never takes much to get people dancing in the narrow aisles at Falling Rock. The instigator is usually Anna, a large-boned blonde with a perpetual smile who manages the deli counter.

In less than half a minute, the room was filled with good-natured chaos. Kids. Teens. Twenty- and thirty- and forty- and fifty- and sixty-somethings. Couples. Singles. Girlfriends. They were all on their feet, dancing. I was doing some serious swaying in the comfort of my chair when Anna appeared, grabbed my wrist, and began pulling me up. I resisted. Anna kept tugging.

Bixie gave me a gentle nudge, then got up herself. And suddenly we were dancing, a female tribe of three.

It felt good to be moving. So good that, when the sax player and the guitarist revved it up, I got carried away and attempted a spin. That would have been fine, except for the fact that I failed to remember just how tight and crowded the space was, and plummeted backwards into a large, solid body behind me. As I started babbling out an apology, two strong arms turned me around, and I found myself finishing up with "I didn't hurt you, did I?" while looking into the face of none other than…no…it couldn't be…

"Roger," I gasped and found myself thinking, not for the first time, that my so-called guardian angels have a truly warped sense of humor.

Without releasing his hold on me, Roger gave a cocky grin. "Hurt me, darlin? Hurt me? It's what you do best. But don't stop, ever. I love it." He waited until I was steady on my feet before letting go of my shoulders. "Care to try that move again? It was quite thrilling. Very Michael Jackson."

"Roger," it was a hiss this time, barely audible over the music. "What are you doing here? Why aren't you having dinner somewhere? Or checking into a motel?" I pushed damp strands of hair away from my face.

"I got in an hour ago. Then I found myself feeling irresistibly drawn to this place," he half-shouted above the din. "Must have been your presence, pulling me in." He staggered slightly when a grey-haired couple did a hit-and-run with their dance moves. "What do you say we go outside where we can talk?"

He put his hand on my left shoulder as he spoke. I tried to shake it off, but it didn't budge. "What do you say we don't?" I answered. Reaching over with my free hand, I put it on top of his and pushed, then pushed again, harder. His hand stayed where it was. My anger meter clicked on and began inching upward. "Look. It's been a long day, and I'm too tired for chit-chat, so let's talk tomorrow. We can meet somewhere for coffee. Here, if you like."

Before Roger could respond, another voice, slightly familiar, also male, broke into our little tête-à-tête. "Is this man bothering you, Karin?"

I hate it when things go from bad to worse. Rob was wearing civvies now rather than his neatly pressed Alger County police uniform, which is why it took me a few seconds to recognize him. But the one thing he hadn't changed was the suspicious look on his face. I wondered briefly if that reptilian squint always made people feel guilty, even if they had no reason to. If so, it probably came in handy during interrogations.

Rob stared hard at my tormenter, whose smile had by now turned to a rictus. "Why don't you put your hand back where it belongs?" It wasn't a question so much as an order.

"And why should I do that?" Roger's voice was civil, but just barely. "Karin and I go way back. We're friends. And I'm just being friendly."

"Why? Because I told you to." Rob was doing his best to channel a young Clint Eastwood. Actually, there was a vague physical resemblance, but his voice lacked Clint's quiet menace, and he came across more as an overgrown schoolyard bully. "And because," he opened the front of his jacket enough to reveal a bright shiny badge, "because if you don't, I'll haul you in for assault. Along with any other charges I can think of."

It was the first time I'd ever seen Roger when he wasn't in control of a situation. And if I hadn't been enjoying it so much, I might have felt a little sorry for him. After a few stunned seconds, he released his grip on my now-throbbing shoulder. I resisted an impulse to rub the spot.

"Well, Karin, my love, it appears you've been rescued, whether or not you want to be." Roger brushed back a few strands of clay-colored hair with the hand that had been squeezing my shoulder and looked hard at Rob. "Glad to oblige, officer. I've always believed it's important for the press and the police to be on good terms."

Rob cocked an eyebrow at that. Roger turned his bloodshot blue eyes back on me. "Call me tomorrow, darlin'. One way or another, I'm sure we'll be in touch." He gave a chilly smile. "And now I'll be saying good night."

"That's some friend you've got there." Rob kept his eyes riveted on Roger's retreating back as he spoke. "And a reporter, no less. From downstate. Just what this investigation needs."

"Yeah, Roger's quite a character," I agreed. "He can be a real pain sometimes, but he's generally harmless. And he's a very good reporter." I glanced over at

Rob's profile to see if I'd piqued his interest. "It's because he's so persistent. Once he gets a lead, he doesn't let go."

Rob slid his eyes my way. "I'll keep that in mind. In fact, I'll be sure to keep an eye out for him. When you talk to him tomorrow, you might want to tell him that." He nodded, half-turned to leave, then looked back at me. "Also, don't be surprised if you get a call from Lieutenant Harris. He's heading up the murder investigation. I think he'd like to have a little chat with you and your girlfriend."

And with a farewell tug at his baseball cap, my hero disappeared into the dancing crowd.

Chapter Sixteen

"Looks like you've got yourself a bodyguard. Just what you've always needed." Bixie was still breathing hard from her exertions, and two rosy patches hovered like clouds on her cheekbones.

If my cheeks were rosy at the moment, it was from a combination of rage and embarrassment. I used both hands to push the hair back from my forehead, and a burst of anger spilled out. "Where were you? I could have used some help with both of them. That whole thing with Roger was very weird. I mean, he's never so much as touched me before, and suddenly he was getting all physical. If you'd been there, both he and Rob might have backed off." I rested a hand, feather-lightly, on my shoulder and hoped that Bixie had brought her usual arsenal of homeopathic remedies.

"Sorry. I was about twenty bodies away, dancing with some older guy. I'm not even sure how that happened." She tried combing her hair with her fingers, then gave up, reached over, and touched the spot where Roger had done his damage. I winced. "He really did get physical, didn't he? I've got a bottle of arnica in my purse. You should take some now. And there's ruta graveolens back at the cottage."

With me still fuming, we worked our way through the small forest of bodies and settled into our seats just as the group launched into *Bird on a Wire*. Shoulder pain forgotten, Bixie and I leaned back in our folding chairs and let the music wash over us. When the last chord had faded and we'd both taken a quick swipe at the wet patches under our eyes, the lead singer announced a fifteen-minute break.

We stayed where we were, watching the bodies around us stand, shift, stretch, and inch their way toward the café counter in the next room. "One thing you should probably know," I hated breaking the restful silence. "Just before he took off, Rob told me that the lieutenant in charge of the investigation wants to talk to us both."

Bixie's face went from drowsy contentment to high alert. "Talk to us? Why? Are they planning to interview everyone in town who had any dealings with Ben? Or is it just us? What could we possibly tell them?"

I took a breath and reminded myself that, although patience was not one of my more notable virtues, it could be cultivated. At least according to my Aunt Ilsa.

"Think about it." I kept my voice low. "We both know that Ben was allergic to penicillin. In fact, everyone in the agency knew it because he was always bragging about how hale and hearty he was despite his endless vices and how, as long as he avoided penicillin, he'd outlive us all. We knew that, even though we were just employees. Considering how much Ben liked talking about himself, it stands to reason that other people, probably a lot of other people, knew about his allergy too. So my guess is the police are casting a wide net and looking for a motive among a whole lot of suspects. Including us." I raised an eyebrow, waiting for Bixie to let in all the possibilities.

Her eyes flared, never a good sign. "A motive," she repeated. "A motive for murdering Ben." Pause. "It sounds so far-fetched. I mean, granted, Ben got under everyone's skin. He had a gift for finding your weak spot and then pressing hard. Hard enough, I suppose, that some people might have thought about how much better the world would be without him." I nodded. "But nobody we know would think seriously about killing him." I raised my eyebrows. "Well, maybe in the heat of the moment, someone might consider it. Briefly. But no one would actually do it. And in any case, how many bona fide Ben-haters would have access to penicillin?" She gave her head a few furious shakes.

"If your brother were here," I reminded her, "he would tell you that under the right circumstances, pushed far enough and hard enough, anyone is capable of murder." Time to lighten the atmosphere, if possible. "Also, it could be that we're on the list because the police want a little more background on Ben from a couple of people who worked for him. And let's face it, the fact that we just happened to be staying in the same town, on the same road where Ben died, on the night he died, would make anyone suspicious. Anyone. And the police are naturally suspicious. It's their job."

I leaned over and picked up my purse off the floor. "Well, as my mother used to say, 'Sufficient unto the day are the troubles thereof.'"

I pulled on my denim jacket and slung the purse over my good shoulder. "There's a bottle of scotch calling my name, and I could do with some quiet time in one of those rickety beach chairs." Without waiting for an answer, I started moving.

I'd expected some push-back from Bixie, who was still relatively calm, having dodged any direct contact with either Rob or Roger, and was clearly enjoying the music. But without so much as a murmur, she got up from her chair, reached down to pick up her purse, and settled the strap on her shoulder with a "Let's go."

Walking back to the parking lot, I scanned every vehicle for bumper stickers. It's a habit, something between a hobby and a compulsion. I collect bumper sticker messages the way other people collect seashells or baseball cards or prize wines.

Tonight, I was rewarded with some winners. The first one was pasted on the rusty bumper of a tired-looking Ford 150: *I'd tell you to go to hell, but I work there and don't want to see you every day.*

Next to it, on an aging Accord, was a black-and-white message: *Jesus Loves You. But I'm his favorite.* The owner of the Forester parked next to Amelia had a sticker that was pure Ann Arbor: *I'll believe corporations are people when Texas executes one.*

Strange how people are willing to advertise little bits of their identity in such a public way. Feeling ever so slightly cheered, I drove back through the M-28 intersection, along the highway next to the paper mill, then slowed to a crawl as I turned off on Sand Point Road guided only by my headlights. Tainted by light pollution, we city slickers forget what true night-time darkness is really like. I confess, even having grown up in small northern towns, it spooks me a little.

Not bothering with conversation, Bixie and I unloaded the car and dropped our incidentals on various pieces of furniture. Then, while Bixie washed off the day in the rust-stained confines of our shower stall, I went over to one of the Formica cabinets, pulled out an almost virgin bottle of Chivas Regal, grabbed one of the few chip-free drinking glasses in the cupboard, and poured out a finger's worth. After considering what was likely waiting for me tomorrow, and who, I measured out another finger, added two ice cubes, and headed over to the door leading to the back porch.

Using the dim light that seeped out of the kitchen windows to guide me across undulating patches of grass and sand, I made my way toward the lake and eased myself into one of the creaking Adirondack chairs that waited there with infinite patience. Moving carefully to lessen any chance encounters with nails and wood splinters, I settled in.

Finally, holding the cold glass in both hands, head braced against the wide chair boards behind me, I closed my eyes and breathed in the smells of lake and sand and driftwood and forest all melded together in air that was so sweet and clean, it almost made my lungs ache. I tuned into the night sounds, the soft swish of waves, the mating calls of frogs, the chirruping and rustling, the occasional plaintive cry of an owl, the distant wail of a coyote. Or was it a wolf? Then, and only then, did I lift the glass and savor the hot-cold sensation of ten-year-old scotch slipping across my tongue and down my throat.

Turning my eyes upward to the tangle of stars, I located what seemed to be the brightest and tried to think of a wish. Nothing. I concentrated and tried again. Nothing. Only after the third attempt did I accept the fact that I was wish-less. There was nothing I dared hope for because everything I truly wanted was impossible, even for a star. And I knew very well there were places in our lives, pains and losses, and sores in our souls that even magical thinking couldn't reach.

I'll never know whether or not, given a high enough dose of lake air and scotch and night sounds, I could have fumbled my way to a wish. My cell phone cut through the solitude with its usual imperious ring and, against my better judgment, I yanked the bloody thing out of my jacket pocket.

I stared at the lit-up screen in my hand, which seemed to float in the surrounding darkness.

Andrew Murray.

Calling me? At ten-thirty on a Saturday night? When he could have left a voicemail for his sister? Suffering as I do from terminal curiosity, I did the only possible thing under the circumstances and pressed the talk button.

"Andrew. What's up?"

Chapter Seventeen

"Karin."

I'd like to be able to tell you, without relying on one of my trusty white lies, that I had no reaction whatever to the sound of Andrew's voice speaking my name. I'd like to be able to say that, except for a mild mix of irritation and curiosity, it moved me not at all. That he might as well have been a robo-caller. That a little shudder didn't sweep over me. That my heart didn't sound like a snare drum. That my stomach wasn't churning in an adolescent way.

But the truth is, before daring to say a word, I had to pull in a quick, deep breath to steady my voice.

"Yup, it's me," I aimed for a cocky-casual tone and just missed. "You sound surprised. Did you misdial?"

"No. I mean, not exactly." I smiled into the darkness. Andrew was always supremely self-assured, in control of every situation, from a crime scene to a simple conversation. But tonight he sounded tired and human. "Thing is, I've been trying to reach Bix, to let her know where I am. But she isn't picking up."

"That's because she's enjoying our luxurious shower right now. And your sister tends to take marathon showers." I thought about the tiny water heater that lived in one of the cottage closets and wished I'd claimed the bathroom first.

"When she gets out, would you tell her I'm in Saint Ignace right now? I figure it's another couple of hours to Munising."

"More like two and a half," I corrected him. "If you don't break the speed limit. But of course, you can probably drive as fast as you want. Do cops ever ticket other cops for speeding?"

He ignored the bait. "Just tell Bixie I'm okay, would you? And that I'll call her tomorrow. We can have breakfast somewhere, and then she can show me where to get some groceries. From what Tim said, that cottage of his is way out in the boondocks, so I'll need to stock up."

"Oh, right. Bixie mentioned Lost Lake." I dropped the banter and got serious. "I hope you've got a good GPS. And a map. You're going to need them. Plus a searchlight. It's hard to find cottages on Lost Lake even in broad daylight, when you know where you're going. Most of the roads are just bulldozer ruts, and they wind all over the place. Seriously, Andrew. I am not exaggerating." For once. "Your friend did make you a map, didn't he?"

"Yeah, he did. It's somewhere. I'll be fine." He spoke with that sometimes irritating, sometimes irresistible male confidence that came so naturally to him. Staring into the moonlit air, I pictured Andrew in the absolute darkness of dense northern woods, trying to navigate the roller-coaster ruts, the tree roots that reached out for tires, the dizzying twists and turns.

Typical downstater, I thought. Nothing up here in the boondocks that he can't handle. After all, he's lived in metro Detroit all his life. Big city, bright lights. Done it all, seen it all. To him, roughing it means having to put up with two-lane roads, two-star motels and two-bit bars. Part of me wanted to abandon him to his hubris. The other part knew that he needed saving. After all, pain in the butt though he might be, he was also Bixie's brother. And my friend. Sort of. In an uneasy kind of way, my friend.

There are good impulses. And then there are impulses which, if you follow them, will have you kicking yourself for a long, long time. Before I could stop myself, and before common sense prevailed, I gave in to what was probably the second kind.

"Maybe you should crash here, at our cottage, just for tonight." The words rushed out faster than I could think. "Honestly, Andrew, Lost Lake is a nightmare to drive. It doesn't have roads. It has trails."

The silence on the other end of the line made me squirm. I took a sip of watery scotch.

"Thanks, Karin, but no need. I'll be fine. See you tomorrow. Bye."

Cheeks burning, thoughts racing, I slapped my forehead hard three or four times while repeating the most appropriate word I could think of: idiot. After wallowing in self-loathing for a minute or two more, I dragged my sorry self back to the cottage and walked past Bixie who, totally oblivious, was snuggled up on the couch with a blanket watching the news and probably hoping for an update on Ben. Two minutes later, pajamas in hand, I trudged into the bathroom, set a new Guinness World Record for hottest, shortest shower by anyone, brushed my teeth, ran a comb through my wet hair, made my way across the living room, closed the bedroom door, collapsed onto the mushy mattress, and pulled the blankets over my head.

The last thing I remember was the fluorescent hands of the bedside clock telling me it was ten-thirty.

Normally I sleep like a cat, alert to the smallest noise and likely to be woken by the slightest sound. It was one of the few things that infuriated Terry, the fact that every time the poor man rolled over, my eyes would snap open and my head would rise from the pillow.

That hasn't changed. In fact, since the day Terry left this world, sleep— when it finally comes—is even lighter and thinner and closer to waking consciousness. But for the next three hours, I slept the sleep of the dead. Or, more accurately, the sleep of the horribly humiliated in need of escape.

In my dream, I was lying in bed and someone in the far, far distance was pounding on a door. Gradually, the pounding grew louder and more demanding. I didn't want to answer it. Instead, I kept repeating the words "Go away" over and over, as if they were a magical incantation. But it was weak magic, because the knocking got louder and more insistent.

That's when I woke up. To a real knocking sound. At a real door.

By then, the alarm clock read one-thirty. Instinctively, heart banging against my ribs, I froze. Is there any human being, anywhere, who doesn't feel a primal fear at the sound of some nameless, faceless other trying to enter their space in the deep, dark, early hours of the morning? It's no wonder, when you consider how the night seems to invite raiders and marauders into the safe little worlds we try to make for ourselves.

Knowing that nothing short of the Second Coming was likely to rouse Bixie, I grabbed the police issue flashlight my brother Joseph had given me for Christmas. It was a heavy, club-like thing with a surprisingly comfortable grip and, supposedly, a five-mile beam. Adrenalin pumping, I made my way to the door, fully prepared to scream my lungs out if need be.

With my free hand, I pulled back the oversized deadbolt, which, given the flimsiness of the door, seemed slightly ridiculous. Holding my breath, I clicked on the flashlight. Yanked the door knob. And aimed the beam outside, at face height.

"Jesus!" Instinctively, Andrew's hands flew up to shield his eyes. "Are you trying to blind me with that damn thing?"

Too shocked to lower the beam, I stood there, motionless and mute in pajamas and bare feet, until Andrew reached out and pushed the flashlight away.

"Andrew." It was a start anyway, and the best I could manage at the moment. "What are you doing here? It's one-thirty, for God's sake."

Even in the reflected glow of the flashlight beam, which now focused on the cracked floorboards of the front porch, Andrew's face was haggard. Leaning one hand against the door jam, he squinted at me in the semi-dark. "You win."

"I what?"

"You win. I give up. Much as I hate to admit it, you were right." He lowered his head and closed his eyes. Exhausted as he was, he still looked better than any man had a right to.

After a few seconds, he forced his eyes open and rubbed the back of his neck. "When I got off the county road, it was like trying to follow a deer trail through the woods. I'm pretty sure I left my muffler along one of those tracks somewhere." He sighed. I stared. "It was crazy. The GPS was useless. And in the dark, Tim's map was no help." His pale grey eyes latched onto mine. "Why the hell do the people who live out there put up with those...I don't even know what to call them. They're not roads."

My answer came automatically. "Because it would cost money to make real roads. A lot of money. And besides, why do you think they call it Lost Lake? Everyone with a cottage out there likes things just the way they are. Lost. Hard to get to. Hard to find. Hard to break into. Except in broad daylight."

I reached over, switched on the kitchen light, and held the door open. "Come on in." I took a few steps back. "There's an extra room with a cot in it. It won't be very comfortable, but at least you'll be horizontal and away from most of the mosquitoes. I'll help you bring your stuff in."

Andrew lowered his head, and those icy grey eyes of his found mine. Falcon eyes. For once, they didn't seem guarded or mocking, though. Just tired and honest. Walking past me into the living room, he did his best to grin. "I owe you, Karin."

I led the way to the small third bedroom. "Bathroom is over there," I pointed at the door next to Bixie's.

He nodded. "Thanks. Don't worry about my stuff, I'll take care of it myself. And I'll lock up. You get yourself some sleep."

I nodded, turned, and, flashlight in hand, scuffed my bare feet across the living room. Sleep, he said. Get yourself some sleep.

I reached for the doorknob, stepped into the moonlit room, and stared at my rumpled bed.

Sleep. As if.

Chapter Eighteen

When the alarm went off, I rolled over instantly and jammed my hand down on the stop. Seven a.m. More than enough time to linger over coffee, devour a few of Aunt Ilsa's cardamom rolls, enjoy the lake view, and still get to the ten o'clock service at Eden Lutheran. Or as they called it these days, Eden on the Bay.

Tossing off the covers, I stretched, sat up on the edge of the bed, and wiggled my feet into the beaded moccasins my mother had bought me years ago. They were her last gift to me before the accident. Staring at the tattered moose hide fringe, I thought how strange it was, the way simple, humble objects can become time machines. The years dissolved. I watched a younger version of myself pick up a telephone. I listened again to the heart-stopping news that my parents were dead. Head-on crash with a drunk driver.

A well-worn sadness settled around me like an old sweater, but just for a moment. Without warning, my brain synapsed or whatever it is brains do when they suddenly change direction, and a far more recent memory jolted me into the now. I sat up ramrod straight.

Andrew.

Omigod. Andrew Murray was here. In this cottage. At this moment. Hopefully still asleep after his wilderness exploits. But maybe not. Glancing at the dim, fly-specked mirror above the bureau, I took stock of my present state: hopelessly tousled hair, sleep-smudged eyes, mouth desperately in need of a toothbrush. And the bathroom was clear across the living room. I envisioned myself scuttling out and being intercepted by those searchlight eyes of his.

Then, summoning my inner feminist, I straightened my shoulders and gave myself a pep talk. It didn't matter. Why should I care? He's probably no prize himself at dawn's first light. Besides which, the guy has been married for nearly twenty years. He knows what women look like in the morning. Of course, Helen isn't just any woman. She's of the Stepford Wives variety. Blonde right down to the roots. Blue-eyed. Porcelain-skinned. Bountiful in all the right places. Probably wakes up looking as if she just stepped out of a Victoria's Secret catalog.

Channeling Gloria Steinem, I walked to the door, opened it just enough to stick my head out, and did a quick survey of the living room and the kitchen beyond it. Empty. Thank you, God.

Half-walking, half-tiptoeing, grateful for the soft soles of my moccasins, I made it to the bathroom and attempted to carry out my morning ablutions with minimal noise. Of course, my efforts were defeated by the ancient plumbing, banging pipes, squealing taps, and a vintage toilet that used water with glorious abandon and always let out a resounding flush that let the world know exactly what its job was.

I inched open the door. Still no sign of Andrew. Things were looking up. He might sleep away the morning, or at least enough of it for me to escape.

I had just poured myself the day's first cup of coffee when the door next to Bixie's opened. Wearing a V-neck undershirt, pajama bottoms, and a sun-dazzled squint, Andrew stood in the doorway, looking around, getting his bearings, remembering what happened and where he'd landed the night before. It took him a few seconds to notice me back by the stove.

By then, I had pulled out a supersized mug, filled it with coffee, added a teaspoon of sugar from my secret stash under the sink—anything to avoid triggering Bixie's white-sugar-is-death tirade—and started walking toward him.

"Here," I held out the mug. "You look as if you could use this. Black, one sugar, right?"

Rubbing his forehead, eyes half-closed, Andrew nodded, reached out, grasped the mug with one hand, breathed in the coffee aroma, took a long sip, sighed, and, with the other hand, lifted my fingers to his mouth. I watched, speechless, as he bowed his head, kissed the top of my hand lightly, touched it to his forehead, and said, "My lady, I am your vassal."

Glancing up at me, he dropped my hand and let out a quiet laugh. "Don't look so shocked. Even cops can be gallant occasionally." He took a long swallow of coffee. "Especially if they were brought up by a Classics scholar fixated on Medieval manners. Otherwise known as *courtoisie*." Another swallow. "Did you know that my father is a world-renowned expert in Medieval and Renaissance love tales?"

Still at a loss for words, I reclaimed my hand and shook my head. He grinned and walked over to the plaid armchair. Without thinking, I moved closer to the chair. Maybe a little too close for propriety's sake.

"Well, he is." He leaned back against the faded headrest. "Dinners at our house were usually run like graduate seminars. At least they were when Dad wasn't at a faculty meeting or some international conference. I can quote passages from *Troilus and Cressida* as easily as I can load a gun. It's second nature. I can even do a little Dante, and toss in a few choice quotes from *The Wife of Bath*."

Determined to reclaim at least a little composure, I looked at my guest with what I hoped was a cool and appraising gaze. "Lieutenant Murray, you are clearly a man of many parts."

It was at that moment, with both of us in pajamas, talking in low voices and drinking coffee at close quarters, that a familiar voice from the far end of the living room cut through the sun-drenched air. "Would someone please tell me what's going on? Andrew, what are you doing here? In your pajamas?"

As if cued by a prompter, Andrew and I turned our heads at the same exact moment. By then, Bixie was just a few feet away from us, looking by turns surprised, suspicious, and disapproving.

I glanced at the kitchen clock. It was a cheap Shopko model with a bad habit of slipping off its wall mount and tilting to the left, so that the number "12" was generally in the "10" position. "Oh my gosh, look at the time. I've got to get ready for church. And I promised to meet Evelyn for breakfast before the ten o'clock service."

That wasn't entirely a lie, since Evelyn and I had talked about meeting before church on Sunday. I simply neglected to mention the fact that she'd changed our date from breakfast to dinner. "So, I'll just grab another cup of coffee and get dressed. Andrew can tell you what happened last night." Unfortunate choice of words. "I mean, why he ended up here instead of at his friend's cabin."

Moving as quickly as my full coffee cup would permit, I walked from the kitchen to the safety of my bedroom door and called out over my shoulder, "There's hot water for tea if you want it. And cardamom rolls on the counter." Just for good measure, I put on an innocent voice and added, "Oh, and if either of you want to come to church with me, you're more than welcome."

Of course, the invitation was totally disingenuous. I knew full well that, except for weddings and funerals, neither of them had set foot in a church for years or had any intention of doing so. As the Psalmist said, God is our refuge and strength, an ever-present help in trouble. Although, I'm not sure that my situation was quite what he had in mind.

It didn't take me long to slip into a pair of white jeans, a boat neck top, and, in case the morning lake breeze was gusting up cool, my trusty Land's End blazer. Finally, as an afterthought, I dug out my boarding bag from the closet, found the battered jewelry case I keep meaning to replace, and pulled out the Celtic lover's knot pendant Terry had given me on our third anniversary. Such a long time ago. Such a short time ago. From the moment I slipped it on, the necklace had become a kind of talisman, an amulet to ward off negative energies and evil forces.

I spent longer than usual on my make-up, partly because I like putting on make-up and partly because I wanted to give Andrew and Bixie as much time as possible for their confab. Finally, just after nine, purse in one hand and car keys in the other, I was ready to make my escape and head to the Navigator Café for some scrambled eggs.

When I opened the door, two sets of eyes swung over to me.

"So," I asked brightly, "what's the plan?"

Bixie's face was still flushed, and her eyes seemed to spark, but at least her voice was calm. "After breakfast, Andrew and I will pick up some groceries and head out to find the elusive cabin, assuming it actually exists."

The Yooper in me couldn't resist offering some native wisdom. "When you get there, you may find that things are in pretty rough shape. Unless it's been used on a regular basis, there could be some, uh, surprises waiting for you."

"Surprises?" Andrew didn't seem to care much for the word.

I shrugged. "Well, nothing too terrible. Moldy, musty smells. Some rodents, dead or alive." Bixie's shoulders tightened as if to ward off invisible vermin. "Mouse and rat droppings. Spiders. Lots of those. But the Black Widows prefer outdoor settings, so you'll be okay."

I was beginning to enjoy this.

"You'll want to wash the bed linens and clean things up a bit. Vacuum. Sweep. Dust. Check the mousetraps. Oh, and be sure to wash the dishes and cooking utensils before you use them. Otherwise, with all the mold and animal whatnots, you could get sick." I noticed that Andrew was looking a little peaked. "But I'm sure everything will be fine. The family has probably been out there, using the place and keeping it in good working order." By now, I was within three feet of the front door. "I'll keep my phone on. So call me later, and let me know how things are going."

Turning to face them both, I backed up the last few steps as I grabbed the knob and pulled the door open. Then, seeing their stunned, wide-eyed looks, I whipped my head around.

There, taking up most of the doorway, stood a man. At least I assumed it was a man. It was hard to be certain since the upper half of his body was completely hidden by masses of grocery store flowers—there must have been twenty cellophaned bouquets at least—that were gradually and inevitably slipping out of his bear hug grasp.

I was just about to break the silence when suddenly, from somewhere behind the flowery mass, an all-too familiar voice boomed out.

"Karin, darlin' girl. I was a complete beast last night. A thousand apologies. What can I say to make you forgive me?"

Chapter Nineteen

"What the hell?"

At the sound of Andrew's voice, Roger dropped most of his flowery cargo. Holding a salvaged bouquet in each hand, he took in the scene. Then, grinning like a demon, he clucked his tongue. "Well, well. So you weren't putting me on about the new man in your life after all." The grin stretched into a leer. "Darlin', you are full of surprises." A surge of heat flashed across my face.

He nodded at Andrew. "Good morning, Lieutenant Murray. I must say I didn't expect to find you here. At this time of day. Out of uniform."

By now, Andrew was on his feet. I positioned myself between the two of them and shot nervous glances back and forth, like a spectator at a high-stakes tennis match.

"Roger Sullivan." Coming out of Andrew's mouth, the words sounded like an accusation. He swung his eyes over to me while he spoke, as if to make sure I felt included, as if I'd arranged this bizarre encounter. "This is a little off your usual beat, isn't it? By about four hundred miles or so? What brings you here?"

For someone who was standing ankle-deep in grocery store flowers and facing down three unhappy people on a Sunday morning, Roger showed admirable sang froid. "The same thing that brought you here, Lieutenant. Looking into the Ben Roberts matter."

His eyes swerved over to Bixie and then me. "Only I suspect you're more interested in doing what you can to keep your sister and Karin here from falling into the hands of the local constabulary. Who are likely to be very curious as to why two of Ben's former employees just happened to be staying in the same town and in the same general vicinity where the poor man met his maker, helped along by some earthly agent. Why just last night, Karin was keeping company with a good-looking but very intense local cop."

The thing about Roger is, sooner or later, whatever the circumstances, he manages to push every button on my console. Right now, they were all blinking bright red. Of course, he hadn't noticed the warning signals, so my explosion probably surprised him.

"Enough!" I practically shouted the word, turning the full force of my fury on him. "Not one more word from you, Roger. Not one." He opened his mouth, and I held up a warning finger. "Not. One. Single. Word."

I took a deep breath, squared my shoulders, straightened my purse, and pushed back my hair, being careful not to let my glance settle on Andrew or Bixie. "Alright," I continued. "You want my forgiveness? You can start earning it right now. Pick up those flowers. Every bloody bouquet. We are going to load them into my car, and you are going to follow me in your car to the nursing home near the docks. We are then going to take all the flowers into the nursing home, and you will help me deliver them, room by room, until we run out of bouquets. Is that perfectly clear? Nod if it is."

I riveted my gaze on Roger's pale blue eyes. He nodded. "Good. Let's go. I'm not going to miss the ten o'clock service because of your…because of all this. You can come back later and apologize to Bixie and her brother."

Roger was clearly aching to say something, but managed to swallow the words that were waiting to jump off his tongue on a suicide mission.

Turning to Bixie and Andrew, I offered a quick "Sorry about this."

Andrew was wearing his stony cop face, and I couldn't begin to decipher whatever his eyes might be saying. "We'll talk later today, Karin. I have a lot of questions." He looked at his sister. "For both of you."

It took us about five minutes to pick up all the flowers, tap the dust off, and load them in the trunk of my Malibu. Traffic was light and tourist-free, a pleasant drive really, except for my righteous rage.

To his credit and my relief, Roger was amazingly docile. We divided up the bouquets between us and carried them into the building. The woman at the front desk said she remembered me from the days when I used to visit my Uncle Arnie. When I explained what Roger and I were planning to do, a smile lit up her broad face. She pointed to one of two hallways, told us to start there and circle around, and asked a passing nurse's aide to round up as many vases as she could find.

I like to think that the next fifteen minutes did Roger's soul—and mine— some genuine good. His especially. Assuming he has one.

Handing out bouquets to the residents, navigating their cramped rooms, watching them straighten up in their wheelchairs or their beds, seeing surprise and gratitude light up their faces, the way they reached out to thank us with a touch, the "God bless you's" bestowed on us, all of it seemed to reach down into some seldom-visited place in Roger. A place I didn't think existed.

By the time I was tapping the code numbers on the pass box to unlock the front door, Roger's eyes were suspiciously shiny. Noticing that I noticed, he turned his head and, with a quick gesture, brushed away the wetness with the back of one hand.

That momentary glimpse of humanity did almost nothing to soothe my outrage or, let's be honest, the shimmer of fear I now felt in his presence. Except for occasional shoving matches with my brother during our pre-teen years, no male had ever manhandled me the way he had. No man had ever hurt me, at least not physically and deliberately. That made me exceedingly lucky, I know, one of those statistical blips at the far end of the bell curve. But it also made me more unprepared and vulnerable in some ways. The net result was that Roger's physical bullying wasn't something I was inclined to forget, or capable of fully forgiving.

Of course, he had no way of knowing that. And, being Roger, he was prepared to pick up where we'd left off. As we approached my car, he opened the driver's door for me. "That was quite an experience, and I thank you for it. I'm feeling a bit chastened."

"Chastened would be good," I said, pushing past him and settling behind the wheel. "Especially if it's permanent."

"So, can we call a truce then? I'll buy you lunch to earn a bit more of your forgiveness, and then you can watch me apologize to Andrew and Bixie. How about it?"

I turned the key in the ignition and did some fast thinking. As noxious as the prospect of lunch with Roger was, maybe there was some way I could use it, leverage it, pick his reporter brain, find out what he knew. I couldn't stop thinking about his earlier comment that Andrew was here to help fend off possible legal dangers to Bixie and me. And with all of his contacts, I might at least get some idea of where the case was heading, who was under suspicion. Heck, Roger would be the first to know whether any of Ben's kids were in town, which of his past wives might be prime suspects, and what kind of shady business dealings might have resulted in his midnight murder. If it was murder.

As if he'd read my mind, Roger piped up. "Think of all the things I probably know about this case already. Things that you don't. Even if my good looks and charm won't tip the scales, surely all that juicy information will tempt you. Besides, we might as well kiss and make up."

If he noticed my wince, he chose to ignore it. "I'll probably be around for some time, and I'll just keep pestering you. I have no intention of leaving this burg until I find out who killed Ben Roberts."

"Lunch is remotely possible." I slipped on my sunglasses. "But only if you're willing to share some of that juicy information you referred to. Otherwise, forget it."

He grinned, "There's only one way to find out, isn't there?"

I let my hand rest on the gear shift while I wrestled with my self-respect. "Okay. If you promise not to be overly annoying. Quarter to twelve. Foggy's Restaurant. It's always crowded at dinner, but a lot of tourists don't know it's open for lunch."

He nodded, looking far too pleased with himself. "And where do I find this Foggy place?"

I put Amelia in drive, and she gave a satisfying jolt that dislodged Roger's hand from the rim of my open window. "Do a little research. After all, you're the star reporter. If you're so certain you can find a murderer, you shouldn't have any problem finding a restaurant."

Chapter Twenty

I was still basking in the afterglow of church when a server who was doubling as a receptionist put on an absent-minded smile and led me through the dim comfort of Foggy's bar area, into the dining room, past the open grill and salad bar, and finally dropped two menus on a table in the far corner.

Always sit with your back to the wall.

Someone once told me Wild Bill Hickok said that. It's unlikely, though, since he himself was shot from behind. Whatever the source, I take the advice to heart. At the moment, that meant wedging myself into the corner chair and pushing the table out far enough to allow for a speedy escape if the situation called for it. If Roger got out of line even slightly, if his elbow so much as brushed against me when he reached for the saltshaker, he'd find himself talking to an empty chair.

I was weighing the merits of the Whitefish Salad versus the Superior Burger when a shadow fell over my menu. Unfortunately, it wasn't the server.

"As you can see, my investigative skills are still intact." Roger pulled out the chair on my right, and I cursed myself for loading up the seat on my left with purse and jacket but failing to create a buffer on my other side. "I found the place, no problem, thanks to an obliging gas station attendant. He seemed like a nice enough gent, despite the fact that he's probably answered the same question a thousand times."

"He was nice because he doesn't know you," I rasped. "Give him time." Ten seconds and already the man was grating on my nerves. I turned back to the menu and located the priciest entrée. "Besides, people who live in the UP tend to be nice in general, until someone gives them reason not to be."

Like most first-timers, Roger was fascinated by the do-it-yourself open fire grill in the middle of the room, which gave me the small satisfaction of informing him that the grilling option was only available at dinner. He settled on a hand-crafted beer made in Marquette and the Superior Burger with fries. I ordered an iced coffee and the full-course salmon dinner, with extra butter and sour cream for the baked potato. Roger handed our menus to the server and then turned to me with a sly, knowing smile. "Thank God for expense accounts."

I planted my elbows on the table. "Okay. You're here. And to my surprise, I'm here. Now start keeping your end of the bargain." I leaned in a couple of inches and lowered my voice. "Tell me what you know about Ben's death. Who have you talked to? What are the police thinking?"

As if the universe had decided to answer that last question for me, my cell phone rang. Intending to cut off the call and mute the damn thing, I pulled it out and got a stomach-wrenching jolt when I saw the caller ID. Alger County Police. It rang twice more before I had the presence of mind to push the off button.

"Something wrong?"

Ignoring the apparent concern in Roger's voice, which was probably just a cover for his incessant curiosity, I shook my head, reached for the water glass, and wished to high heaven I'd ordered a scotch.

"No, it's nothing. Just Bixie. I'll call her back later." I clasped my hands, which were trembling slightly, and willed myself to sound calm. "Now answer my questions."

Roger had just opened his mouth to speak when the server arrived with his beer and my coffee. When she asked if there was anything else, I piped up instantly. "Yes, you can bring me a glass of Chardonnay. In fact, save yourself an extra trip and bring me two."

"At the same time?" she wanted to know.

"Yes," I said. "Two glasses. Please." She walked toward the bar accompanied by the soundtrack of Roger's raucous laughter.

"Are you still going to insist that phone call was nothing at all?" He picked up his schooner. "Never mind. I know I won't get a straight answer." He sampled the beer once, twice, then held the glass up to the light. "Now that is as good as any pilsner I've ever had. These local brewmeisters really know what they're doing. Who would have thought?"

After another couple of swallows, he was ready to talk. "So, what do I know? In terms of hard facts, not a lot. Not yet. But in terms of hearsay and second-hand reports and what you might call local knowledge, some interesting stuff has emerged. And of course, based on what we know about Ben's history, there are all kinds of possibilities."

"Such as?" I stirred more cream into my coffee and wondered what could be delaying the Chardonnay.

"Such as his first wife, Dorothea, who has never made a secret of the fact that she got screwed in the divorce settlement. Did you ever meet her?" I shook my head. "Well, you didn't miss much. Beautiful but boring. Evidently, when they split ten or twelve years ago, Ben got himself a barracuda of a lawyer who managed to help him hide a boatload of assets. There's a rumor that some documents transferring properties and business interests to his son and daughter were backdated." Roger finished the last two inches of his beer, looked around, spotted our server, lifted his empty glass, and raised his index finger. She nodded and began walking toward the bar.

He put down his glass. "Where was I? Oh yes. Ben's marital misdeeds and divorce shenanigans. The problem is that, after ceding a considerable amount of his holdings over to his two brats..."

"The son's name is Devon," I interrupted, not willing to be sidelined during Roger's gossip fest and, oddly, perversely, needing to prove that I'd known Ben as well as he had. "He used to come by the office, doing his best to look bohemian and counter-culture. Long, wild hair. Torn designer T-shirts. Salvation Army jackets. For a while, he was dating one of the junior graphic designers, so he'd come by to see her."

Memories were coming fast now, one after the other, like a line of falling dominoes. "And I remember his daughter, too. Audrey. She'd show up from time to time, looking preppy and perfect. People always commented on how much she resembled her father—same hair, same fair skin, same eyes. Same attitude, too. Completely self-absorbed."

Roger nodded his thanks as the server deposited a fresh beer in front of him. He inhaled about a third of his drink before setting down the glass. "Right. To continue. After ceding a considerable amount of his worldly goods to the two kids, and getting off with a painless divorce settlement, he immediately set his legal minions into motion again to claw back all the giveaways, revoke the gifts, and get the major holdings back in his own name."

That was news to me, good news. Hearing Roger expand the list of suspects beyond Bixie and myself, I could feel the tension begin to flow out of my shoulders. "So what happened?" I asked. "Did he succeed? Knowing Ben, it's hard to imagine he wouldn't. How did the kids react?"

Roger wiped a foam moustache off his upper lip. "He did indeed succeed in revoking the bequests, for the most part anyway. According to my sources, he also succeeded in alienating and enraging both of his progeny. Even now, he and his kids barely speak. Or, rather, spoke. He did bestow a monthly allowance on both of them. And they'd show up for holidays and birthdays. His birthdays, not theirs. Largely out of fear, I suppose, that he'd leave his money to his current wife, even though they were separated. Or worse, that most of his estate would go to Meredith Wood. As you know, those two have been close for years. On a business and personal level."

I was about to speak when I noticed our server approaching with a loaded tray raised high and balanced on one backwards-bent wrist. How did they do that? And why not use trolleys like they do in Europe? Some things are beyond our knowing.

There were a dozen questions I was aching to ask, but I managed to rein them in until our meals were in front of us. After two blissful bites of salmon, I returned to the subject at hand. "How do you know all this?"

Instead of responding, my tablemate took a huge bite out of his Superior Burger, chewed slowly, and chased it down with a long swig of beer. Then he pulled a napkin across his mouth and locked his eyes on mine.

"Because Ben is, was, a fascinating human being. What you might call a worthy subject. Larger than life. Impossible to ignore. He was also a mover and shaker. I was assigned to the business beat for years, so he was on my radar. We were always crossing paths. I can't tell you the number of times I ran him down for a story or a comment. We were invited to the same parties, attended the same events." Roger paused and took a pull at his beer. "He never liked me, and I never liked him, but in a way, we needed each other. He thrived on attention, and I held the spotlight, at least in terms of the local press. The more I learned about Ben, the more fascinated I became and the more I wanted to know. So I dug and dug and dug."

Roger went back to his burger. "You made him your project," I said, trying to suppress a shudder as I spoke. "As if you were some kind of professional stalker. Thank God you never found me fascinating."

He grinned. "Oh, but I did. I do. You'd be surprised at all the things I know about you. And from what I saw this morning, I've added yet another fact to the inventory. Tell me, what does Bixie think about you and her brother getting it on?"

Chapter Twenty-One

Roger's comment was loud enough to draw mildly interested looks from surrounding tables. I lowered my voice to an angry whisper. "Andrew bunked in with Bixie and me, in one of the extra bedrooms, because he got to Munising late last night and couldn't find his way to the remote cottage he's renting or borrowing or whatever from a downstate friend of his. That's it. The truth. End of story. Besides," I fortified myself with a long sip of Chardonnay, "he's not just the brother of my best friend, which by itself would make a romantic relationship slightly creepy. He also happens to be married." Helen's calm, controlling Gwyneth Paltrow face floated across my mental screen. "Very married."

Having devoured his burger, Roger turned his attention to the French fries mounded on his plate, dipped one of them in catsup, and fixed his eyes on mine. "I don't for a moment think that you really believe what you just said. That Andrew is very married, as you put it. Still," he nibbled at the fry, "you do have a naïve streak, and you're sometimes woefully uninformed about Ann Arbor gossip. So if by some remote chance you're not aware of the fact, let me be the first to inform you that Andrew is not very married. At least not for much longer."

I stared at Roger, gobsmacked. Words deserted me. For a few seconds, I forgot to breathe.

Roger sipped his beer and gazed at me in silence, like a research tech studying a lab rat. Finally, he dabbed at his mouth with a napkin and put on a supercilious look that, under normal circumstances, would have been seriously annoying. As it was, the only thing I felt was confusion. Roiling confusion.

"So then you weren't lying after all," he mused. "For a change." Leaving his smug grin in place, he put down the beer, leaned back in his chair, and crossed his arms. "You really do need to work on camouflaging your emotions, darlin'. Right now, your thoughts are utterly transparent. You'd make a terrible reporter."

I swallowed hard and somehow managed to reconnect with my voice. "How do...? What...?" Deep breath. "If *you* were the reporter you think you are, you wouldn't be spreading rumors. Which this has to be."

Roger caught the attention of our server as she brushed by the table, flashed a momentary smile, and ordered coffee. Then, the smile switched off, he turned to me, and shook his head. "Oh no, I assure you, it's a cold, hard, ugly fact. And it's been vetted by numerous sources, including the manager of All Around Fitness, who's a longtime friend of mine. He also happens to be the employer and close friend of Helen Murray's personal trainer. The new love of her life."

"Helen? And her trainer?" My brain slipped back into free fall, reeling at the impossibility of it all. When I spoke again, it was more to myself than Roger, a case of me trying to think my way through the absurdity. "But she's so chilly and distant and elegant. So above it all. So totally in control of herself. I can't imagine Helen doing anything as sleazy as having an affair. And if she did, it would be with a dean or a celebrity professor or the CEO of something or other."

Roger ripped open the Velcro closure on one of his vest pockets and pulled out a credit card case. "Sleazy or not, it's been going on for some time. Love at the gym. Sex on the StairMaster. A classic tale of a beautiful, bored, neglected policeman's wife and her muscle-bound coach." He picked out a card and put it on the table near his coffee cup. "I'm surprised you weren't among the first to know. Bixie had to be aware of all this."

Bixie. Of course. The theatrical phone call with Andrew during our picnic dinner. The fuming silences. The disapproving tones. The faraway gaze.

I felt a pang. The kind of pang that comes when you realize, yet again, that the person you've chosen to be your best friend isn't quite as best as you'd always hoped, that other people matter more to her than you do or ever will, that she keeps large chunks of her life sequestered and secret, inaccessible, unshared. Fortunately, at that moment, my Aunt Ilsa's firm, Finnish-accented voice—which lives deep inside my brain—ordered me to stop feeling sorry for myself.

I re-entered the present moment just in time to watch Roger sign the credit card slip and reach for his fedora. "Well, darlin', it's been fun, but duty calls." He arranged the hat at a rakish angle on his thatch of red hair. In spite of myself, I had to admit it was a good look for him. "That apology to Bixie and Andrew will have to wait. I plan to stake out the Holiday Inn lobby this afternoon. Rumor has it that Meredith has settled herself in one of the luxury suites, and she's got to come out of her hidey hole sometime. When she does, I'll be there." He picked up his canvas bag, which, I knew, contained not only notebooks, pens, and digital recorders but also some devious surveillance equipment.

He leaned over and, before I could duck out of reach, landed a kiss on my left cheek. "Try not to miss me too much. But that probably won't be an issue, given all you have to think about right now."

He took a few strides, then turned around suddenly and said, in an unabashedly loud voice, "But don't think for a second that just because Andrew is now officially free, I won't keep trying to tip him out of first place. As you know very well, darlin', I don't quit easily. And when I want something, I generally get it."

Cursing the man inwardly, I tried to muster my composure as I gathered up my purse, keys, and sunglasses. Not easy when you've suddenly become the day's entertainment for a dozen strangers whose tables gave them a ringside view of Roger's soap opera exit.

Reaching the front of the restaurant was like running a friendly gauntlet. Once the door had closed behind me, I made a beeline for Amelia, turned on the air conditioning, pushed the lock button, and stared out past the parking lot, over the dunes, and into the white-capped waves of the Big Lake. When the heat in my cheeks had subsided and I could think again, I began mapping out the rest of my afternoon.

Options abounded.

I could do the good, right, and sensible thing and return the phone call from the Alger County Sheriff's Office.

I could call Evelyn and spend the afternoon telling her about my morning's adventures and listening to her gossip about the local goings-on since our last conversation.

I could be very drama queen, phone Bixie and confront her with what Roger had just told me.

I could find myself a bar stool at the Roam Inn, where a four-star menu and pricey drinks kept the locals at bay, and ponder the situation with Andrew over a third glass of Chardonnay.

Or I could head back to the cottage for some R&R, to reconnoiter and hide away from everyone and everything, and sink into the broken-down beach chair with my Nero Wolfe novel.

Once again, my cell phone made the decision for me. When I pulled it out for a quick check, there was a voicemail waiting. The caller was male. The time-date was five minutes ago. The message was terse, official, and unmistakably clear.

> *Hello, Ms. Niemi. This is Lieutenant Bill Harris from the Alger County Sheriff's Office. We, uh, require your assistance with our inquiry into the death of Ben Roberts. This is our third phone call to you. I'm at your rental cottage now and will be for the next twenty minutes or so, in case you prefer to answer questions here. Otherwise, we'll expect to see you at the police station no later than three p.m. today. If you need to reach me, you have my number on your caller ID.*

Chapter Twenty-Two

By the time I arrived back at the cottage, the small gravel parking lot was so crowded I had to improvise. Maneuvering carefully around the police cruiser and puzzling over the fact that Andrew and Bixie were back so soon, I put Amelia on a sandy patch in front of the picture window. Which, of course, ruined the element of surprise.

Making matters worse, Bixie opened the door just as I started to push on the knob, causing me to stumble past her and into the burly arms of a police officer who, despite his size, moved with the speed and agility of a professional dancer. He held me at arm's length until I regained my balance. "You alright?" Why do people ask that question even when it's obvious that you're absolutely fine except for some serious and possibly permanent damage to your self-esteem?

"Oh sure. This sort of thing is a habit with me. I like to make a dramatic entrance." Ignoring Andrew's grim look, I made my way to the far end of the couch, then wished I'd chosen one of the straight-back dining room chairs instead. The cushion felt like quicksand.

"Lieutenant Bill Harris," my rescuer said by way of introduction. "I'm heading up the investigation into Ben Roberts' death. Ms. Murray and I just finished up our conversation. Glad you could finally join us, Ms. Niemi."

He pointed to a digital recorder on the scarred coffee table, next to my stack of mystery novels. Looking at the tiny, traitorous machine, my shoulders tensed. "As you can see, I'll be recording this." I nodded. "I understand from Ms. Murray that you also worked for Mr. Roberts' ad agency in Ann Arbor. In what capacity?"

"Copywriter." I knew from experience that the safest answers were the shortest answers. "I was with Ben's agency for about five years and left ten years ago to start my own freelance business."

"And how would you characterize your relationship with Mr. Roberts?"

I resisted the impulse to look at either Bixie or Andrew. "Businesslike. He was my employer. I was one of three copywriters. Actually, I answered to the creative director, not to Mr. Roberts." As if Ben didn't micro-manage every bloody project.

"Ah, yes. The creative director." Officer Harris flipped through his spiral notepad and found the entry he was looking for. "That would be William Hardcroft. Retired and moved to Seattle two years ago. Hasn't returned to Michigan since." Officer Harris looked up from his notes and sent a cool, official gaze my way. "According to Mr. Hardcroft, you were a first-rate writer, which was the only reason Ben put up with you. He said that you two had a stormy relationship. Those were his exact words."

Good old Bill. He never did like me much, and he never could resist an opportunity to be a jerk.

I darted a quick look at Bixie, who was registering barely restrained panic, and Andrew, who was staring at me so intensely I had the feeling he was trying to put words into my head. Unfortunately, they weren't coming through.

I turned back to my interrogator. "As you probably know from your past interviews—assuming that people have been honest with you—stormy relationships were the only kind Ben was capable of. He thrived on drama. He loved a good argument, and he got a real kick out of insulting people. In fact, he was very creative about it. That's just the way he was, with almost everyone. Certainly with everyone who worked for him. Including Mr. Hardcroft." I was proud of the fact that I managed to keep my voice flat and matter-of-fact.

"The difference being that Mr. Hardcroft—and a lot of other people in Mr. Roberts' life—haven't seen him for quite some time." The lieutenant paused for effect. "You, on the other hand, attended his open house last summer. That's according to eyewitnesses."

"Yes," I agreed. "And the fact I was on that list should tell you that Ben and I were on good terms. Generally, even when he was showing off with a big, lavish social event, which is what the open house was all about, he wouldn't invite people who worked for him. He'd invite trophy guests. People who could be useful to him. That's partly because he was a snob and partly because big parties are expensive, and he was notoriously cheap." Bixie gave a small, almost inaudible gasp, not enough to stop me now that I was on a roll.

"So he never fraternized with employees?"

"Oh, late every Friday afternoon, the receptionist would break out the booze, and there would be a mandatory staff cocktail party. Clients and freelance help also had a standing invitation." I glanced at Bixie, whose face was so pale she looked like a Kabuki player.

"Cocktail party?" Officer Harris seemed both stunned and amused at the idea.

I shrugged. "Ben convinced himself it was all about building camaraderie. But that was a lie. He did find some of us amusing. Mainly, though, he just liked to remind himself how much power he had over us. Those Friday parties were an opportunity for him to torment his wage slaves." Andrew winched up one eyebrow and, unless I was mistaken, Lieutenant Harris struggled to keep his mouth from slipping into a grin.

"Were you one of the tormentees?" he asked.

"Not too often. Being Ben, he'd try every once in a while. But I always fought back, insult for insult. The odd thing is, he seemed to like it." Andrew, who was sitting in the chair next to the lieutenant, raised his eyes heavenward.

Harris glanced up from his notebook with the look of a cat about to spring on an unsuspecting mouse. "But evidently, there were other sides to your relationship as well. According to several guests at the open house, you and he appeared to be quite close. And in fact, there was an encounter at the door that included a passionate kiss."

As Andrew and Bixie shared astonished looks with each other, I let out a gasp of protest. "Passionate?" I half-shouted. "That wasn't passion. That was an assault. And it was typical Ben."

My interrogator looked at me with a mild expression. "And now you're here, less than a mile from where he died."

"That's right," I said. "But my being here has nothing to do with Ben, and everything to do with the fact that this is my hometown. I've got family up here. And friends. I love the UP. I visit as often as I can. Anyone who knows me will tell you that." What the heck, I thought, why not take the offensive? I gave him a wide-eyed look. "Lieutenant Harris, is there some reason you're asking me all these questions? Because I'm getting the distinct impression that I'm a suspect."

He met my gaze full-on, and I was surprised by the force of his hazel eyes. "Just trying to get a complete picture of the victim, Ms. Niemi. And that means getting as much information as possible from as many people as possible."

He paused. I braced myself.

"Also, one of your neighbors here reported seeing a woman of your height and build walking north along Sand Point Road on the night Ben Roberts died. I find that very intriguing."

Damn. That information would have reached the local police compliments of the ever-nosy, perpetually paranoid Eileen Savola. Her cottage, just next door, was notable for its high-intensity floodlights and high-power binoculars on every windowsill.

"Yes, that was me." Seeing the unanswered questions in the lieutenant's face, I went on. "My late husband and I used to walk Sand Point Road in the evening. I was having a grief attack that night. I needed to be alone, and I wanted to feel close to Terry, so I started walking." Somehow, I kept my voice steady and managed not to glance at Andrew or Bixie.

"And you were gone for how long?" Harris wanted to know.

"I'm not sure exactly. Sand Point used to be a fairly safe road. But now, with all the tourist traffic, it's downright dangerous. I'd only been walking five or ten minutes when a car nearly sideswiped me. So I turned around and went back to the cottage, but couldn't make myself go inside. I sat on the beach for another forty minutes or so. Thinking."

He nodded. "So you were gone for about an hour. That concurs with Ms. Murray's account." Of course. Bixie would feel compelled to tell the truth, but I could imagine how she'd embroidered and explained and excused my seemingly odd behavior. Which probably had the reverse effect, increasing rather than lessening any likely suspicion.

"This is all just standard questioning," the lieutenant assured me. "We're talking to a lot of people. The more we know about Mr. Roberts, his habits, his comings and goings, his personal life, his business dealings, the faster we'll find his killer."

Bixie and I both jerked upright at the word "killer." I knew very well that my best strategy was to keep quiet and wait for questions, not ask them. But I was doing a slow burn, so, despite a warning look from Andrew, I spoke again.

"Ben died from anaphylactic shock. That means whatever killed him was in something he ate or drank, right? I haven't seen Ben for nearly a year. Bixie hasn't seen him for longer than that. There was no way we could have tampered with anything in his house recently."

Lieutenant Harris closed his notebook slowly without taking his eyes off my face. "No way that we know of." He stood up, all six feet and assorted inches of him. "I think that does it. For now."

Chapter Twenty-Three

Reaching down to retrieve the digital recorder, our guest let his hand stray to the stack of books next to it. He picked up my half-read copy of *Death of a Demon*.

"I see you're a mystery buff, Ms. Niemi." He riffled through the pages. "I'm a fan of Rex Stout myself, but I'm not familiar with this one. What's it about?"

Honesty, they say, is always the best policy. Why then does it almost never feel that way?

"It's about the death, the murder, of the owner of an advertising agency," I said.

"Hmmm. Lots of suspects?"

"Yes. Typical Nero Wolfe case. Lots of motives. Lots of suspects."

He returned the book to the pile and picked up his digital recorder. "Interesting coincidence."

At the door, he pulled on his Alger County Sheriff's Office baseball cap and turned to face our little group. "Lieutenant Murray," he sent a sharp nod in Andrew's direction, "good to meet you." Another nod for Bixie and me. "Ms. Murray, Ms. Niemi, thanks for your time. You've been very helpful." Why did that make me feel uneasy? "I assume you all plan to stay in town for a while." Registering our surprise, he added, "Since your vacation has just started."

Door half open, hand on the knob, he stopped and turned back to us. "If, for some reason, you do decide to head out, we'd appreciate it if you let us know. I'm sure we'll have more questions. But in any case, we know how to get in touch with you. Wherever you are."

Andrew stood at the door, watching in silence until the cruiser had pulled out of the parking area. Then he lowered the boom.

"That went well." He shut the door with so much force the floorboards shivered under my feet. "Jesus, Karin. What is it with you and police? Do you get some kind of thrill out of provoking them?"

I managed to hold my ground, despite a natural urge to back up a few steps. "He wanted to know about Ben," I said. "So I told him. Maybe I was more honest than I should have been, but eventually, he's going to get the same story from everyone, in bits and pieces. I decided to save him the time and effort of asking a lot of devious questions."

I walked over to the armchair and tossed my purse on the seat cushion, which released a puff of dust particles. "Besides, Lieutenant Murray, how likely is it that a murderer is going to badmouth her victim during an interrogation?"

Andrew let out an exasperated growl. "More likely than you'd expect. Especially when the interrogator is good at his job. And in case you hadn't noticed, Harris is very good."

"Enough! Stop it, both of you." I'd forgotten that Bixie was still in the room and taking in our little scene from the couch. Head flung back on one of the cushions, eyes fixed on the ceiling, she looked like the long-suffering heroine of an afternoon soap opera.

With a dramatic sigh, she sat upright. "Andrew, give it up. You know Karin can't help being...herself." She made it sound like a disability. "And besides, if she was messing up so badly, and if you were so bothered about the way the interview was going, why didn't you step in?"

"Why?" Andrew shifted all his angry attention to his sister. "Because, as you should know, I couldn't. I'm out of my jurisdiction, and the law is absolutely clear. This investigation is off limits to me."

As he moved closer to the couch, I tiptoed into the kitchen. This conversation was definitely safer at a distance. Also, I was in dire need of a cookie fix and a reviving cup of coffee. Fortunately, Andrew was still flaming, in the full throe of making his point. "And it's not just that I'm an outlier here," he went on. "I'm contaminated by the fact that the suspect list includes not only my sister but also a friend."

By now, Bixie was on her feet, and the two siblings were facing off, almost nose to nose. Given their height and the fact that both of them were incredibly good-looking, it was a sight worth seeing. Kind of like watching two minor Greek gods having a family squabble. I half expected to see lightning bolts flash around the shabby living room.

Still, things were escalating, and an artful interruption seemed in order. In my experience, a non-sequitur often works best. Half-eaten oatmeal cookie in one hand, cup of warmed-over coffee in the other, I spoke up. "Why are you both back so early from Lost Lake? Don't tell me you managed to clean up the cottage already. I didn't expect to see you for hours yet."

Two startled faces turned toward me. In the lengthening silence, brother and sister froze in place, only moving their eyes to cast sidelong glances at each other. The same way they must have done as children, back in the long ago, when one of their parents discovered them in the midst of some serious mischief.

I tried again. "Well, isn't someone going to tell me what happened? It can't be that bad."

Andrew let out a noise that was part groan and part sigh. "Yes, it can be that bad."

Sensing that her brother had temporarily run out of words, Bixie took over. "The place was a disaster. When we drove up, it looked like part of the roof had caved in. We couldn't believe what we were seeing. And when we got inside, there was water everywhere on the floor. Most of the ceiling in the living room had given way. There were chunks of wet wood and shingles and ceiling tiles and all kinds of debris scattered around." Her purple-blue eyes were wide with the memory. "The stench was awful. Moldy and rancid. Like a swamp. When I went into the kitchen to check out the damage, a raccoon ran out from one of the lower cupboards." She gave a shiver of disgust. "I don't even want to think about what else is living in there."

I could picture the wreckage as clearly as if I'd walked through it myself. "Well, it's not all that unusual for things like this to happen, especially after hard weather." Over the years, I'd heard worse stories about the toll of heavy snows and torrential spring rains on unoccupied cabins. Worse, but not much worse. "Any idea how long it's been like this? When was the last time someone from the family checked up on the place?"

"I called Tim as soon as we could get a signal," Andrew explained. "He said one of his uncles had gone out there in mid-April to check on things. At the time, everything seemed okay. But apparently, along with record snowfall last winter, they got hit with non-stop rain all spring, right into June."

I nodded. "Same as we did downstate."

"Tim told me the roof was overdue for replacement. That was going to be his big project this summer. Obviously, it couldn't stand up to the combination of all that snow followed by heavy rains. He said the total snowfall was over three hundred inches, nearly a record. And no one could make their way through those back roads to clear off the roof. So the result was…"

"Disaster," Bixie finished the sentence for him.

"Anyway," Andrew went on, "one of Tim's cousins volunteered to get a crew out there to tarp the roof for the time being. Tim's calling the insurance company, and he or one of his brothers will be driving up in the next day or two to meet with a claims adjuster and get the repairs underway."

Someone had to ask the unspoken, uncomfortable question floating in the air. As usual, that role fell to me.

"Last I heard, every motel room, campsite, B&B, and quonset hut between here and the bridge has been rented out for the rest of the summer and into early fall. So, where are you planning to stay? Or *are* you planning to stay?" The coward in me gave a hopeful little surge at the thought that this might be the shortest UP vacation on record.

Andrew locked his eyes on mine. To keep from squirming, I channeled my Aunt Helmi, who had been gifted with the face of a professional poker player.

"With everything that's going on here right now, I need to stay." He paused as if deciding how much of his usual in-charge, alpha-male attitude he was willing to set aside. Still holding his eyes on mine, he took a deep breath. "I want to stay."

"So," Bixie chimed in, "I thought, since we've got an extra room, Andrew could bunk in here for a few days. Until he finds another place. I mean, something is bound to open up, maybe one of those mom-and-pop hotels in town." She put on an uncharacteristically sweet smile. "Is that okay with you?"

The human brain is capable of processing eleven million bits of information every minute. Which means that, in the five or six seconds that elapsed between Bixie's question and my answer, my brain sorted through approximately one hundred ninety thousand permutations, possibilities, pros and cons.

I flashed back to Psych 101. Approach-avoidance conflict. A classic conundrum. A situation that is simultaneously attractive and appalling. An event that holds both positive and negative possibilities. A decision certain to result in both positive and negative outcomes.

Finally, it all comes down to doing and saying the right thing. And of course, there was only one thing I could possibly say to my best friend and her brother. Her bossy, contrary, infuriating, secretive, always-knows-best brother. Her smart, tough, witty, well-intentioned, disturbingly attractive brother.

I took a breath, hoped that I wasn't making a hugely regrettable mistake, suspected that I was, and said, "Well, you probably won't be very comfortable on that cot, but if you really want to, then yes. Of course. You're welcome to stay here."

Chapter Twenty-Four

"**B**iindigen! Hello and welcome!"

Evelyn pulled me into the house with one hand and beckoned to Bixie and Andrew with the other. "Come in, come in. So glad you could all be here." She transferred the grocery bag I was holding to Charles, who headed off in the direction of the kitchen.

I'd called Evelyn right after Lieutenant Harris left to let her know all that had happened. When she heard about the grilling by Munising's finest, the cottage catastrophe, and the change in our housekeeping arrangements, she did a typical Evelyn thing. Instead of rescheduling dinner, as I suggested, as I would have done, she extended the invitation to Bixie and Andrew.

When I worried out loud that we'd be imposing, she brushed it off. "Don't be ridiculous. You know I always cook enough to feed an entire clan. Besides, I've already invited Charles, so two more people won't be any problem. I'll expect you all at six."

So it was that, promptly at six, we appeared on Evelyn's doorstep. Since her flower garden qualified as one of the wonders of the world, we didn't bother with a hostess bouquet. Instead, I'd picked up half a dozen bottles of Pellegrino, her favorite.

Once introductions were made, I retreated to the kitchen—knowing that soon everyone would be chatting away as if they'd known each other for years. It's the Evelyn Effect, a magical spell she weaves. I've seen her walk into a room full of chilly strangers and, within fifteen minutes, it's auld lang syne time.

That night, the magic was as strong as ever. As I arranged cheese slices and crackers on a platter, grateful for a few minutes of solitude, I could hear Bixie talking, could hear Charles, and then Evelyn responding. And unless I was mistaken, that laugh belonged to… Andrew? If so, it was the first time I'd heard it since he arrived.

When I walked the platter into the living room, everyone was still nattering away. Charles was sitting next to Bixie on the small settee, the very small settee, and he and Andrew had struck up a conversation about the cottage disaster. Bixie and Evelyn were having an animated discussion about native wildflowers and herbs.

An hour later, when Evelyn and I set out the dinner dishes, all attention shifted to the meal. And what a meal it was. Meatloaf spiced to perfection, gravy to die for, buttery mashed potatoes, green beans from Evelyn's own rambling garden, tomatoes from her sister's hoop house, and a reasonably fresh baguette Bixie had liberated from the local grocery store. A veritable feast of comfort food.

After the initial round of gorging had subsided and we were picking at second helpings, the table talk started up again. At first, it was all very predictable and safe. The weather. The tourist hordes. The annual UP firefighters' competition. Best routes for avoiding the worst of summer construction traffic. But, inevitably, talk turned to Ben Roberts and the ongoing investigation. Even in death, Ben managed to be the center of attention. Just the way he liked it.

It was Charles who, once again, dropped a conversational bomb into the gossipy banter. It seemed to be a habit with him. The topic had shifted to speculation on exactly how Ben died, the details, the mechanics of it. What killed him? Was it, as Bixie and I suspected, penicillin? If so, how it was administered? And when?

As I began stacking dinner plates and clearing the table, Charles picked up his coffee cup, added a dollop of cream, and in an offhand voice said, "At the casino this morning, I overheard a group of people talking about the murder. One of them said that what killed Ben was amoxicillin, and that it had been injected into the wine he was drinking. Hypodermic needle. Straight through the cork."

If Andrew's reaction time had been half a second slower, the plates I was holding would have crashed onto the tabletop. Taking the stack out of my hands, he placed it carefully in front of him.

"Amoxicillin?" Bixie wondered out loud.

"It's one of the drugs in the penicillin class," I answered automatically. Four pairs of eyes gazed at me. "I thought everyone knew that." More gazing. "I can't help it. My mother was a nurse. She loved talking about drugs, new treatments, surgical techniques. I kind of enjoyed it, except for the gory bits about wound care. I was always reading her *Merck Manual*."

Andrew turned to Charles. All business. "Who were these people you overheard? As far as I know, the police haven't yet released any findings from the path lab in Marquette."

Charles shrugged. "There was a big group standing near the door of the break room, not far from the coffee machine. Maybe nine or ten people. A croupier, a security guard, one or two cleaning staff, one of the cashiers from the gift shop, a few players who were maybe friends of the employees, I don't remember who else. I was in the break room at a table, checking the roster before the evening shift came on. That's when I heard someone say they'd heard from a friend of theirs, whose wife worked for the Marquette Police Department, that the lab guys had been testing all kinds of evidence from Ben Roberts' house. They had his medical records, so they started with those, looking at what he might be allergic to as well as testing for common poisons. They finally discovered the amoxicillin in the wine he was drinking. And they also discovered how it got there."

"Clever, but not original," I said, half to myself. "Whoever killed Ben probably lifted the idea from...I think it was an old *Colombo* episode. Or maybe *Murder She Wrote*. There was also a made-for-TV movie that featured the same method. It's diabolical, really, when you think about it. The murderer doses the liquor, then disappears. The victim dies days, weeks, maybe months later, and the killer is miles or even continents away."

When I snapped out of my reverie, I realized that everyone was staring at me again.

"Is that a sort of hobby of yours?" Charles asked. "Collecting methods for murder? Ways to kill people?"

Evelyn answered for me. "It's mysteries that are her hobby. Ever since she was a little girl, when other kids were watching cartoons, Karin was watching reruns of the Alfred Hitchcock show or digging through the attic, looking for her mother's old Nancy Drew books."

Andrew was still clearly troubled by the fuzziness of the source and, no doubt, by the fact that if this was true and not just water-cooler gossip, there had been a serious leak, a breach of police protocol. To divert himself from whatever he was thinking or suspecting, he picked up the dirty dinner plates and headed to the kitchen. "I'm not much of a chef, but I'm great at clean-up detail. Where's your dishwasher, Evelyn? And I'll need a dishpan and some scouring pads for the pots and pans."

With a smile I didn't quite trust, Evelyn told me to sit back down, ordered Bixie and Charles to do the same, and followed along behind Andrew with another stack of dirty dishes. I could only wonder what they'd find to talk about.

Those musings were cut short when my phone sounded. I checked the screen. Roger. It might have been sheer curiosity or the fact that Ben's murder was top of mind. Whatever the reason, and even though I probably shouldn't have, I excused myself, went into the hallway, and took the call.

"Roger," I half whispered into the receiver, not wanting Bixie or Andrew to hear me say the name. "Whatever it is, I can't talk now. I'm at a dinner with family friends."

"Well, darlin', friends notwithstanding, you're going to want to drop whatever you're doing and speed over to my side."

"I doubt that very much. But give it your best shot. What's up?"

"What's up is an invitation from Meredith Wood, who's in dire need of comfort and consolation, for drinks at the Roam Inn bar. When Meredith heard you were in town, she was thrilled. A friendly face from the past. Someone to remind her of home and happier times. A break from hostile strangers. I'm sure she has all kinds of things she's just aching to share. Oh, and I should probably mention that at least one of Ben's grieving children may be joining us. But of course, since you've got better things to do, I'll make your excuses and..."

"When?"

"Half an hour from now."

Go? Or not? It would mean lying to friends. Interrupting a pleasant evening. Getting involved when I should keep my distance. It might not yield a single new shred of information. And if by some remote chance Meredith or one of the kids had killed Ben, I could be putting myself in danger. Who in their right mind would do that?

"I'll be there."

Chapter Twenty-Five

I only lie on rare occasions. Honestly. But on those occasions, I take pride in my ability to craft highly creative yet entirely plausible white lies on the spur of the moment.

This one was going to be tough. Given the audience—the fact that every one of them knew me in different ways and to different degrees, and that probably no one in the world knew me better than Evelyn—creativity was out. The situation called for something simple and mundane.

Ah yes. A headache. Classic. And generally believable, depending on the liar's acting ability.

When I explained to Evelyn that one of my rare migraines had started, she was all motherly concern. Would it help to lie down in the guest bedroom? No? Well then, I should go back to the cottage immediately. Take care of myself. And did I have Tylenol, or should she send a bottle with me?

I was halfway to the door, keys out, when Andrew appeared in the kitchen archway, wiping his hands on a towel. Trouble.

"Lousy thing, headaches," he said, his voice dripping with false sympathy. "But at least your timing is good. I just finished up." With a smile, he handed the towel to Evelyn, walked over to me with a gotcha look flashing in his eyes, and gently pulled the car keys out of my hand. "You shouldn't be driving with a migraine. I'll take you back to the cottage."

"Oh. No. I'll be fine. There's no need. It's just a short drive." While I spluttered, he turned his head toward the living room, where Charles and Bixie were still in deep conversation at close quarters. "Bix, Karin's not feeling well. I'm taking her back to the cottage. No need for you to come with. I've got this."

Bixie turned to us with the dazed look of a sleeper roused from a REM state. "Oh. Alright, if you're sure. I'll probably be leaving soon myself." Not from the look on Charles' face, she wouldn't.

Evelyn put her arm around me as she walked us to the door and brushed my cheek with a light kiss. "If the Tylenol doesn't work, give me a call. I'll send some willow bark home with Bixie. And Andrew," she fixed her big, earnest eyes on his face, "take good care of our girl." Our girl? "And let me know if you need anything."

"Don't worry." Andrew smiled down at her. "I'll make sure she doesn't get into any trouble." If Evelyn thought that last comment was a bit off, she was too polite to say so.

When we were settled in the car, Andrew slipped the key into the ignition and glanced over at me. "Where to?"

I crossed my arms and stared straight ahead at the solar-powered lights lining the long gravel driveway. "The cottage, of course. Where else?"

He leaned his head against the driver's window. "No, I mean, where are we really going?"

"Where else would we be going except the cottage? I've got a headache, and you're supposed to be ministering to my needs."

"Ministering to your needs," he mused. "Normally, that idea would present some interesting possibilities." I shot him a quick, confused look. Who was this man? A döppelganger? An evil twin? He certainly wasn't the Andrew I knew. Although, I reminded myself, the Andrew I knew, or had known, was married. "However, you don't have a headache. You have a plan. I want to know what it is. And we're going to sit here until you tell me. Or until Evelyn gets so worried by the fact that this car hasn't moved that she comes out to check on your condition. It's entirely up to you."

"How dare you ambush me like this? How…

With one hand gripping my headrest, he leaned in so close I could feel his breath. "This is why I'm here, Karin. This is why I drove four hundred-plus miles. This is why I arranged to stay in that god-forsaken cottage on Lost Lake. This is why I'm sleeping on an Army surplus cot. To make sure you and my sister don't get in over your heads. Now, for the last time, where are we going?"

Options. Options. There had to be options. A quick scan of my addled, angry brain told me there was only one.

"The Roam Inn. It's a local boutique hotel with a bar."

"Right. And who are we meeting there?"

"Roger." For a few strange seconds, I time-traveled back to early winter and saw myself in the Ann Arbor Police station, one of those grimy little rooms they use for interrogations. Or interviews, as they like to call them. Two plain-clothes officers were tossing rapid-fire questions at me.

Deep, measured breath from Andrew. "Who else?"

"What makes you think...?"

"Who else?"

"Meredith Wood." I paused to clear my throat. "And possibly Ben's kids."

"What the...?" Andrew let out a string of expletives, some of them new to me. Then he leaned back hard against his seat and in a carefully controlled voice said, "Just tell me one thing. How can someone as smart as you do something as stupid as this?"

Everyone has their trigger words. Call me stubborn. Call me naïve. Call me self-centered. Call me a long list of unflattering things, and I probably won't object a whole lot, knowing they contain at least a grain of truth. But don't call me stupid. I got up on the highest horse I could find.

"Okay, lieutenant. Enlighten me. What is stupid about a suspect in a murder case wanting to uncover facts that will make her not a suspect anymore?"

Andrew gave a weary shake of his head. "You really don't get it, do you? What do you suppose the police will think when they discover that you and your reporter boyfriend—because that's how they'll see it—spent a cozy evening talking with the last person to see Ben Roberts alive? Someone who will probably benefit by his death. And not only that, but with one or two of his children who, by the way, have been publicly feuding with their father for years and who also stand to benefit by his death in more ways than one. Do you think that might just possibly raise a few red flags? Trigger some questions? Maybe open up a new line of inquiry?"

I hate it when I make a lousy decision, when I fail to see the obvious and leap before I look. But I hate it even more when someone, some authority, some Andrew type points it out to me.

"Maybe the police won't find out," I said, without a shred of conviction in my voice.

"Of course they'll find out. For one thing, they're going to keep interviewing people, all kinds of people. Turning over rocks. They're also going to be re-interviewing people of interest. Like Meredith. And Ben's kids. And you. And my sister. In the process, they'll get some pieces of the truth. But along with the truth, they'll also get hints and suggestions from people like Meredith and Ben's kids. Who, if they did happen to murder Ben, will be looking for an out. A false trail. A scapegoat. And here you are. Providing them with the perfect goat."

He put the car in gear, navigated the narrow driveway, turned onto Indiantown Road, and headed west toward town. By now, I was so aghast at my, well, okay, I'll admit it, my stupidity, that I could only sit there next to him in shamed silence. But when we drove past the road to the cottage, I had to ask, albeit in a meek voice, "Where are we going?"

Andrew kept his eyes on the road and the endless traffic moving through a lingering North Country twilight. "Where else? The Roam Inn, of course."

Chapter Twenty-Six

For a small, bird-like woman, Meredith is surprisingly heavy. I know this because, at that particular moment, she was draped over me in a state of near collapse, clinging like a barnacle, and I was struggling to keep us both upright.

Andrew and I had been standing in the entryway for maybe four seconds when Meredith spotted us, sprinted across the room, and launched herself at me. Odd, considering that over the years our relationship had never budged beyond friendly nods and casual chitchat.

"Karin," she moaned into my shoulder and tightened her grip. "I'm so glad you're here. Isn't it horrible? I can't believe Ben is gone."

With her thicket of dark hair pressed up against my mouth, the best I could manage by way of reply was, "Muwaduthibzozorry."

Avoiding eye contact with nearby patrons, I made a couple of vain attempts to disconnect. But it was Andrew who, with expert gentleness, separated us and began guiding Meredith back to one of the far tables where Roger sat, drink in hand. Sitting next to him was Ben's dry-eyed son, Devon.

As we approached the table, Roger and Andrew stared at each other like two gunslingers in an old Grade-B Western. Not bothering with introductions, or the hypocrisy of a handshake, Roger shifted his gaze to me. "I didn't expect you to show up with a police escort."

"Police?" The word snapped Meredith out of her semi-hysterics, and Devon's spine seemed to grow a couple of inches. "What's going on?"

Andrew answered in a voice as cold as Roger's. "Your reporter friend here is referring to the fact that I happen to be on the Ann Arbor Police force. What he failed to mention is that I have absolutely no jurisdiction in this case." He pulled out a chair for me, then one for himself, and sat down. "But I also happen to be a friend of Karin's. And I figured she could use some support right about now. This has been a rough time for everyone who knew Ben, and cared about him." He flashed what Bixie refers to as his Grand Seducer smile. It didn't make a degree of difference in Devon's frosty stare, but it seemed to work on Meredith. A fact that did not escape Roger.

"Well played, Lieutenant." He turned to his companions. "By the way, this is Andrew Murray, Bixie's brother. You both remember Bixie, I'm sure. Lieutenant Murray, may I present Meredith Wood and Devon Roberts. Now," he pushed his chair back, "what's everybody drinking?"

Once a fresh vodka martini was sitting in front of her, Meredith stopped sniffling into her cocktail napkin, gave me back the hand she'd been clutching, and took a long swallow. Devon showed no interest whatever in his gin and tonic beyond moving the glass around on its coaster. From the look of those broad shoulders and muscled arms, bronze against the white of his polo shirt, he was still finding plenty of time for tennis, which Ben always insisted was the only thing his son truly loved. And the only thing he was good at.

I put a light hand on Meredith's shoulder. "How are you doing? I can't imagine what it must have been like for you, being there during...while Ben...I mean..."

After another long swig of her martini, the story came tumbling out. How Ben had invited her up for the week because he knew how hard she'd been working on her new Native Arts gallery, opening in September, which was practically no time at all, and wasn't that thoughtful, so like him.

More sniffling, more cocktail napkins.

She told us how, on that last day—deep shaky breath here—how on that day, around noon, they'd taken his boat over to Marquette, where Ben was meeting with his partners to work on strategies for pushing through their latest development. Maybe we'd heard about it, the luxury condos on Sand Point Road. How she'd spent the time shopping and checking out the new cafés and bookstores downtown. How they'd had dinner in Marquette, at that bistro, the one in the renovated movie theater, and then sailed back to Munising. How they'd decided to end the day with a soak in the hot tub. How Ben, feeling more optimistic after the meeting, opened a bottle of wine, and how they'd toasted to the success of his new project. But how, suddenly, after a couple of glasses, Ben was choking and grabbing at his throat and gasping for air.

Another surge of tears, another scramble for cocktail napkins. Pats on the back from me, along with murmurs about what an awful ordeal it must have been. Although the tears were real enough, Meredith was looking remarkably good for a woman supposedly prostrate with grief. Waterproof eye makeup probably helped. Across the table, Devon watched us both with a reptilian focus. Unreadable. Inscrutable. Andrew sipped at his watered-down scotch and scanned the room to gauge how much attention we were attracting.

Fortunately, the place was packed with out-of-town revelers. If there were any locals on the premises, I didn't see them from where I sat. And no one seemed to be taking much notice of the emotional pyrotechnics at our table.

When Meredith's sobs had quieted, I asked the question that had been prancing around my brain. "But Ben must have kept an EpiPen in the house somewhere, no?"

"Of course." Meredith dabbed at the tears that had begun drying on her cheeks and blew her nose daintily on a couple of napkins. "If he remembered, he'd put one in the glove compartment of whatever he happened to be driving. But he often forgot. Usually, he stuffed one into a jacket pocket or a fanny pack, along with a few Benadryl tablets. And generally there was one in the master bath." She let out a shaky breath.

"So you gave him an injection," Roger chimed in.

"No," Meredith's eyes widened and filled to overflowing. If this was an act, it was Oscar-worthy. "No," she repeated. "I checked the pockets of the robe he'd been wearing. Nothing. So I ran upstairs to the master bath. Nothing there either. I looked in every bathroom, pulled open every door of every medicine cabinet. I looked under the sinks. I yanked open the drawers of all the bedside tables. There were no EpiPens anywhere. Finally,

I found the clothes he'd worn earlier in the day. They were in his closet, in a laundry basket. But if he'd been carrying an EpiPen, he took it out before he undressed because it wasn't there now. I knew time was running out, so I called 911. Only it was too late. When I got back to the hot tub..." She broke down in a series of gasping sobs. "Ben...was...he was..."

What I *said* was, "How horrible for you." What I *thought* was, "Either you didn't lift a finger to save him. Or someone else was very thorough, knew Ben's habits very well, and made every one of those EpiPens disappear."

An unexpected wave of pity for Ben washed over me, followed by a smaller wave for Meredith. Odds are, she really was fond of the guy.

Roger was unmoved. Ever vigilant for the smallest lead, he went into full-bore reporter mode and shifted the topic abruptly. "Strategies. You said that Ben and his partners were meeting to discuss strategies. To push through the development. What did you mean by that? Was there a problem?"

"You could say that." The sound of Devon's voice startled everyone. "But it's on the way to being solved." He sat back in his chair. "Sand Point is part of the Pictured Rocks National Lakeshore Park. The land technically belongs to the federal government, which means that all seventy-three thousand acres fall under the jurisdiction of the Department of the Interior. Specifically, the Bureau of Land Management."

"So," Andrew broke in, "what does that mean for developers like Ben and his partners?"

"In this case," Devon was using his MBA voice now, "it meant that they had to submit detailed plans and an environmental impact statement to the Bureau of Land Management. Which we had done. No problem. Things were looking good for the project."

"Except for what?" Roger demanded. It suddenly occurred to me that he must have a digital recorder switched on and stashed in one of the many pockets of his travel vest. "You've already told us there was a glitch."

Devon nodded. "It was the Sault Saint Marie Chippewa Council. They'd been lobbying the feds hard, insisting that the land had been a burial site for the Grand Island tribe. They said it hadn't been fully excavated and that putting up condos, or anything, would amount to cultural desecration. For a while, it looked like they were winning. But my dad came up with a plan that seemed to satisfy the feds. Even though the Indians were still pretty upset."

He looked down at his untouched drink. "I tried to convince him that we should agree to a delay so the artifacts could be removed in an organized, supervised way. It would have been good for community relations."

"And it would have generated good press," Roger added cynically. "But I suppose your father was having none of it."

Before Devon could answer, Andrew jumped into the conversation. "You used the word 'we' in connection with the project," he said. "So you're part of the investor group?"

"Hardly." The flash of anger vanished so fast, I couldn't be sure I'd really seen it. "Dad was a firm believer in everyone making their own way in the world. Just like he did. In order to qualify as an investor, I'd have to come up with, well, let's just say a lot more than most of us can scrape together. So, no, I wasn't in the investor pool. I was a consultant on the project. Well paid. But just a consultant."

"It wasn't right, leaving you out of the deal," Meredith interrupted. "I told your father that many times. Once those condos are up and running, they're going to be a huge money-maker."

"You're absolutely correct." Devon reached for his glass and held it up in a kind of mock salute. "Everyone involved with that project is going to make a killing."

If they hadn't already.

Chapter Twenty-Seven

Outside, the evening sky was a perfect trifecta. Above the last shimmering sliver of sunset, a crescent moon shared the dusky horizon with Venus. An hour from now, anyone who happened to glance upward would see the sky dome spattered with hundreds or—depending on their distance from town—thousands of stars and planets, most of them usually vanquished by light pollution. As I leaned my head back to take it in, a soothing lake breeze brushed against my skin.

I only bother to tell you this, to describe this uncharacteristic reverie, this star-gazey state of mind, as a way of explaining my actions or, more precisely, inactions in the moments that followed.

We were just a few feet from the car, directly under a streetlight, when Andrew half-turned and darted a glance at the entryway to the inn. Then, without a word, without a pause, without a signal or a nanosecond's warning, he pulled me close, tipped my chin up gently, and gave me a long, lingering, toe-curling, take-your-breath-away kiss. A movie kiss.

I was too shocked and amazed to resist. And so out of practice that, for him, it must have been like making out with a mannequin.

When he finally pulled away, and before I could catch my breath, he whispered against my cheek. "We have an audience, so save the tirade for later. This was all in the line of duty."

Breathing hard and fighting down a surge of outrage, along with a few other emotions better left unexamined and unnamed, I slanted my eyes toward the entryway.

"You did this for Roger's benefit?" I hissed.

Andrew opened the passenger door and held it for me. "Of course. What other reason would I have? The man is a predator. Someone has to protect you and Bixie from yourselves. And others. It's part of my job as your self-appointed guardian."

"And this little scene achieved what exactly?" I didn't bother whispering, now that Roger had disappeared into the building.

Andrew settled himself behind the steering wheel and smoothed his shirt. "It laid out the ground rules." He started the engine.

"Ground rules?" I pushed the hair off my damp forehead and tried to get my bearings. "So it was like, what, putting up a No Trespassing sign? Or maybe, Private Property Keep Out? Of all the sexist, macho, outrageous, inexcusable, arrogant, presumptuous…"

Andrew made a smooth right turn onto the highway. "More like a way of announcing that you're under police protection, of a sort. Roger has a spotty record when it comes to his treatment of women." He rolled down his window, and suddenly the car was filled with balmy night air. "Look, there are a lot of other things we could and should be talking about, all of them relating to Ben's murder. And there are a lot of things I need to think through. So, how about we discuss this later?"

I stared straight ahead at the oncoming headlights and made my voice as steely as possible. "Oh, yes. We will discuss this."

Anything else I might have said was forestalled by the pinging of my phone. "Hey, Evelyn." I tried to make my voice sound like it belonged to someone with a bad headache. No easy matter when you've been soaring in the higher octaves of human emotion.

"How am I?" I repeated and stared hard at Andrew's profile. "A little better, thanks. The pain seems to have shifted. I'll get over it." Evelyn's voice was having its usual calming effect on me. "Tell you what. Let's meet tomorrow for breakfast at the Navigator. Or just coffee if you like. You pick the time. There are some things I need to talk to you about. Oh sure. I'll be fine by then." Another dagger glance at Andrew. "Certainly much better than I am right now. G'night."

"I like Evelyn," Andrew spoke into the darkness. "She's what my mother would call good people. You're lucky to have her as a friend."

"Yeah. With Evelyn, at least, there are no surprises. I always know what to expect. Which is more than I can say for some of my friends."

I had more to say, but we'd just pulled into the cottage parking lot and the interior lights were on.

Inside, Bixie was curled up on the couch with one of our landlady's crocheted afghans, watching the eleven o'clock news. For a moment, the look on her face took me back to my high school beer party days. It was the look my mother wore when she flicked on the hallway light and caught me, shoes off, doing a slightly drunken tip-toe up the steps. It was a look that said, "Start explaining. Now."

So we did. And whether it was Bixie's shameless curiosity about Ben's murder, or the fact that Charles was working some erotic magic on her nervous system, she listened quietly, intently. Although midway through, she couldn't resist guilt-tripping us by making puppy eyes and saying, "I wish you two didn't feel that you had to lie to me. Why didn't you just take me aside for a minute, at Evelyn's, and explain what you were planning to do?"

"Well, Bix," Andrew tried not to smile, "you and Charles were having a pretty intense conversation, and it didn't seem like a good time to break in."

"And," I added, trying to make up for my earlier lack of honesty, "I didn't want Evelyn or Charles to know, or to start speculating. I didn't want it to get around that I was prying into Ben's murder. I just wanted to find out what I could, quietly, from Meredith and maybe Devon and Audrey. But of course I was going to tell you everything when I got back." Of course. Maybe. Possibly.

"Speaking of Audrey, why wasn't she there?" Bixie wanted to know. "She was always a lot closer to her father than Devon. The quintessential daddy's girl."

"I asked about that right before we left. According to Meredith, Audrey had to fly back to Chicago this morning. She's working as an assistant curator at the Art Institute. Her department—Native Arts of the Americas, something like that—has a big exhibit opening tomorrow, and she needs to be there. And get this. The exhibit is focused on tribes of the Great Lakes. Michigan and Illinois, in particular. So that means the Potawatomi, the Odawa…"

Bixie finished the list for me. "And the Ojibwe." She sipped her tea with a thoughtful look. "Interesting, the way native art connections keep coming up."

"Isn't it, though?" I agreed. "With a little prodding, Meredith admitted that Audrey has been consulting with her on the new gallery she's opening. For some reason, she's got really high hopes for this place, in terms of money. So that's another connection. And then," I hesitated for a moment, "there's also Charles' collection of artifacts. And all the upset about Ben digging up items from the Ojibwe burial site to make way for his condo development."

Cued by the look on Bixie's face, I stopped talking. After a few empty seconds, Andrew jumped in. "So what are you two planning for tomorrow? I'm having lunch in Marquette with an old buddy of mine from the police academy. He's been stationed up here for the last five years or so. I thought I'd leave early and spend some time checking out the town."

"I'm meeting Evelyn for breakfast at the Navigator," I said, "where I plan to make a full confession." Seeing the look on Andrew's face, I added, "Without going into too much detail. What about you, Bix?"

From the way she started fidgeting with the afghan, pulling at it, folding it, patting it, draping it over the arm of the couch, I could guess the answer. "Charles volunteered to take me on a tour of Grand Island. One of his friends has a cottage there, so we'll be able to get off the official road around the outer rim and do some exploring. But right now," she gave the afghan one final pat, "I'm going to take a shower and go to bed."

Without so much as glancing at either of us, she turned and walked toward her bedroom. At the door, she stopped and pivoted. "Oh, by the way, Andrew, that shade of lipstick looks good on you. That's your color, isn't it, Karin?"

Chapter Twenty-Eight

Bixie's door and my mouth closed at exactly the same moment. Andrew swiped a hand across his lips and looked down at the light smear of color on his fingers. "For someone who lives in her own world most of the time," he mused, "my sister doesn't miss a single detail in this one. She's like a human drone."

Feeling suddenly weary and desperate for solitude, I picked up my phone and grabbed the neatly folded afghan, ready to head outside. There, between stars and water, I would distract myself with the day's accumulated texts and voice messages, and ponder how to explain to Bixie that what might seem obvious really wasn't, and that appearances could deceive.

Andrew stretched and yawned. "It's been a long day. I'm bone tired, and I still need to unpack. Good night, Karin."

"Just one thing." Chin up, shoulders back, I made myself as tall as I could. "Two things, really. First, I know about you and Helen."

His face tightened. "Roger?"

"Who else? Bixie would never betray your trust." I hurried on. "Anyway, I'm sorry. I can imagine what you're going through." His face told me otherwise, that I didn't have a clue as to what he was feeling, but I plodded on. "So I'm assuming that the scene in the parking lot was related somehow to…"

"That's one thing. What's the other?"

I cleared my throat. "Just so we understand each other. The next time I need protection, the kind of protection you provided in the parking lot, I'll let you know. Until then, you can assume I'm doing just fine without a knight errant."

Andrew held my eyes for a few seconds during which, miraculously, I managed not to flinch, fidget, or wilt. "Understood, my lady." He half-bowed, Lancelot style. Amused. Mocking. Rueful. As I opened the back door and stepped onto the porch, his voice called after me, "I will eagerly await your summons."

Outside, I lowered myself into the Adirondack chair and tented the afghan over my head to ward off marauding insects. Mercifully, the mosquitoes were in short supply. Probably feasting on the thousands of tourists who filled every campsite for miles around.

I was still debating whether it was too late to phone my friend Margaret, who also happens to be the assistant pastor of my church and a fount of mostly good advice, and had just recalled that she was currently somewhere in Ghana heading up a youth mission trip when my phone sounded. It was a local number. The Alger County Police wouldn't be calling this late on a Sunday, using a personal cell phone. Would they? I risked it, and was rewarded by the sound of a voice familiar to Channel Six viewers.

"Sandy!"

"Sorry to be so late getting back to you. The little witch at the front desk likes to delay any messages that she thinks might be personal. What a piece of work. Unfortunately, she's fireproof. The station manager's niece. But at least she got your number right. So, how long are you going to be up here? And when can we get together? I'd love to see you."

"I'd love to see you, too." Brief pause. "For a lot of reasons."

"And I'm guessing that one of them," Sandy's voice took on a wily tone, "has to do with your old boss. I'll bet the local constabulary has been sniffing up that alley, dropping by, asking questions." Some things never change, Sandy's speed-of-light brain being one of them.

Without pausing for breath, she rolled on. The thing about Sandy is, even off-camera, she tends to take up all the airtime. "So are you available for lunch tomorrow? It's supposed to be my day off, we'll see how that goes, and I've got a mad craving for white fish bites from the Vierling. Oh, and you've got to try their spinach artichoke dip. Actually, it's the perfect place for a murder suspect like you. The back tables are so shadowy, you won't need a disguise. What do you say?"

"I say, how about eleven thirty at the Vierling, tomorrow?"

After some serious star-gazing and a one-sided conversation with Terry—God, but I missed the sound of his voice, and his smart, sensible advice, and the feel of his hand holding mine, especially at times like this—I made my way back to the cottage, which was blessedly silent. One hot shower later, I snuggled under my landlady's faded but cozy patchwork quilt and lulled myself to sleep with thoughts of what I might learn from Sandy.

The next morning, I lay in bed until a little after seven, listening to the oddly comforting sounds of a man walking around in the next room and waiting for the equally comforting sounds of that same man closing the front door and driving away. By the time I left for my breakfast date with Evelyn, it was eight thirty. Bixie was evidently having what the Brits call a lie-in. Either that or she was avoiding me.

The Navigator was only half full, no surprise since most tourists either head out at dawn or dawdle over their hotel breakfasts. Evelyn was at one of the window-side tables, and within a few minutes we'd placed our orders and I was rushing through my mini-confession. As I spoke, a small corner of my brain kept thinking how the whispery blue of Evelyn's blouse set off her skin tones and shimmering waterfall of black hair. Even as a kid, it used to puzzle me how my adored babysitter could be so unconcerned with her looks and so unaware of her own beauty.

She spoke now over the rim of her lifted coffee cup. "Do you really think it's wise to go poking around, investigating on your own? Didn't you learn anything from that nasty episode in Ann Arbor...when was it? Last September?" Still holding my eyes, she took a sip of coffee. "Sometimes I think you still need a babysitter. Leave it to the police, Karin."

I looked out the window at the tour boats tethered to the docks on the placid, mirror-like surface of the lake. "That's exactly what Andrew would say."

"Since we're on that subject, what about Andrew?" Evelyn smiled as the server laid out our identical plates of scrambled eggs, bacon, and toast with strawberry jam on the side.

"And don't tell me there's nothing going on between you two. I can read you too well."

I picked up my fork, stared at my plate, and willed myself not to cry. "There isn't anything between Andrew and me. And there won't be. Because," my voice wavered, betraying me. "Because I'm still very married and always will be. When Terry died, he took my future with him."

Evelyn reached over and placed her hand on top of mine. "Maybe you and Terry need to have a talk about that. He loves you. And just like always, he wants you to be happy." She pulled her hand away and took a few bites of her jammy toast. "Also, Terry knows that the human heart is expandable, and that he'll always have a place in yours, even if you make room there for someone else."

I took advantage of the moment to switch topics. "If you want to talk about romance, I'm much more interested in what's brewing between Bixie and Charles. Truth is, I find Charles intriguing. But I know almost nothing about him." I slowed down, aware that I was about to broach a delicate subject. "Except that he seems passionately devoted to the idea of protecting Ojibwe culture and history."

Evelyn looked up from her scrambled eggs. "He is."

"Which makes me wonder, just *how* devoted? He told Bixie and me about the way Ben's construction crew had treated the remains from the burial ground. How artifacts and bones kept disappearing. He was still furious about that. And then..."

"Are you asking me whether I think Charles could have killed Ben?"

I raised my hands. "Don't get mad."

"I'm not." Evelyn shoved her plate away. "Not much anyway. And yeah, okay, if I take a few steps back, I can see how you might think that Charles... that the thought might have occurred to him. But he would never carry through on it. Never." She gave me one of her soul stares. "I know that, in the deepest part of me."

"What about his relatives? His friends? Are any of them what you might call cultural activists?"

"You mean, like, radicals? People who are trying to bring back the old Red Power Movement?" Evelyn put down her fresh cup of coffee hard enough that half of it slopped onto the table. "Where are you going with this?"

She put her napkin down to sop up the mess. "Alright. Yes. Charles has a lot of friends. And some of them are passionate about our tribal culture. But we're all focused on other, more immediate projects. After years, we finally have a community center. Now we're working on services for tribal members. Health care. Job training. Rehab. That's where our energy is going."

I managed to stop myself from pointing out that, while Evelyn might have her eyes on the prize, there could very well be a fringe group with more extreme views. Wisely, for a change, I left things as they were. After forty-five minutes of harmless gossip, we hugged goodbye and agreed to see each other again soon.

When I got to the parking lot, I called Bixie and left a voicemail, asking her to find out from Charles if anything valuable had been stolen from the Sand Point construction sites. Especially from Ben's property. If so, I added, we might be able to link those thefts with Meredith or even Audrey. Somehow. After that, I headed west on M-28 and pulled into the sandy parking area of Shelter Bay. There, I spent the next hour in nostalgic bliss, looking for agates, skipping rocks, and reliving childhood summers.

By eleven thirty, I was seated at a table in the Vierling, waiting for Sandy. My eyes were just beginning to adjust to the filtered light when the hostess walked by with two men in tow. One of them was a stranger, although, given the holster bulge beneath his suit jacket, he had to be a cop. Had to be. Since the man with him was none other than my very own, not entirely welcome house guest.

Chapter Twenty-Nine

When his eyes landed on me, Andrew stopped mid-stride, grabbed his friend's arm, leaned toward the hostess, and pointed to a table at the back of the room. Far enough to prevent eavesdropping, but close enough that we were still in clear sight of each other. Close enough that his lunch companion would be sure to recognize Sandy, who at that moment was scanning the room, silhouetted by the brilliant light flowing around her from the entryway.

I was right. Andrew's police buddy spotted her not long after I did, raised his hand in greeting, and got a professional, all-purpose smile in return.

After a quick hug, she lowered herself into the seat directly across from me. So like her, I thought. While most women I know would choose the chair next to mine, Sandy, ever the reporter, was always more comfortable sitting directly across from people. Interview style. I half expected her to whip out a notepad and digital recorder. Instead, she tossed back her curtain of white-blonde hair, dropped her designer hobo bag on the seat between us, planted her elbows on the table, and said, "God but it's good to see you. It's been, what, a year? And you're just as slim and beautiful as ever. You'll have to tell me how you do it. The slim part anyway."

"Clean living and a fast metabolism." Hoping that a glass of wine might slow down her hyperspeed chatter, I ordered the house Riesling for both of us. "So who's the guy who just waved at you? One of your admirers?"

"Hardly," she unwrapped a pat of butter and reached for a breadstick. "He's a detective with the Marquette Police. Name of Paul Wyndham. Used to work downstate. Lansing, I think. I've interviewed him a few times, usually about drug busts, there are so many up here, and once about a kidnapping. Oh, and a suicide not long ago. On the surface, he always seems cooperative and helpful. But afterwards, I realize that he's given me nothing in the way of facts or real news. What he's best at is dodging questions and routing reporters to the police PR department." She reached for a second breadstick. "Now it's your turn. Tell me why that hunky guy with him keeps looking over here. I'd like to think it's me, but I'm guessing not."

"Could be you." I sampled the Riesling. "Or it could be the fact that he's Bixie's brother, Andrew. Otherwise known as Lieutenant Murray of the Ann Arbor Police."

"And he's up here because...?

"Because he's determined to keep his sister and me from being hauled away in handcuffs. He's also determined to keep us from meddling in the investigation. Although, in light of who he's having lunch with, it's obvious he's doing some meddling himself." Another sip of Riesling. I was going to have to ration myself. This stuff was habit-forming. "That's pretty much it. Except for the fact that I have no intention of backing off. In fact, I'm hoping that you and I can do a little meddling together."

Sandy put down her nearly empty glass and leaned toward me with eyes that seemed to send off sparks. "Oh yum. This is going to be a fabulous lunch. We have so much to talk about. Starting with, is Andrew married?"

Uh, not exactly." I fumbled for words, feeling oddly off balance. "Not for much longer. In any case, it shouldn't matter to a happily married woman like you."

"Oh, I don't know about that. As my grandma told me on the day of my wedding, 'Don't forget that the ring is around your finger, not your eyes.'" She handed me one of the menus. "Here. Let's order, and then we can get down to some serious meddling."

For the next hour, we feasted on white fish bites, avocado salads, and non-stop conversation. By the time two plates of cheesecake arrived, smothered in wild blueberry sauce, I knew considerably more about the investigation than I had this morning.

I knew, for instance, that Ben's partners in the condo venture were all longtime real estate investors, most of them focused on the state's more exclusive resort towns. Harbor Springs. Traverse City. Saugatuck. Charlevoix. And now Munising and Marquette. I also knew that they were all heavily invested in the condo project and that they relied on Ben's business acumen, deep pockets, local business networks, and ruthless but effective management skills, making it highly unlikely that any of them would have killed their golden boy. I learned that the Munising police were focusing mainly on family members—not only Ben's kids and ex-wives but his estranged sister as well.

Not surprisingly, I also learned that as the last person to see him alive, Meredith Wood held a special place on their suspect list. But they were also looking at all the enemies Ben had made among the locals.

I contributed a fair share of information myself. What I didn't speak of, what I was careful to avoid, was any mention of the hatred of Ben that ran so deep in the Ojibwe tribe.

"Honestly," I said, fork poised over the cheesecake, "Ben has always been so successful in making enemies, downstate and now upstate, that there must be dozens of people who are glad he's dead. It's hard to see how the police are going to work their way through such a long suspect list."

Sandy used her dessert fork to chase the few remaining clumps of cheesecake around the plate aimlessly. "Yes. And much as I hate to point it out, that long suspect list also includes you and Bixie. You especially, since you were at his open house. And whoever killed Ben either gave him a bottle of wine that had been pre-poisoned, or had access to his home at some point, long enough to doctor at least one of his bottles." She glanced at me apologetically.

"But," I pointed out, "that same person also had to have access to penicillin. Or amoxicillin, same thing."

"Oh, for God's sake, Karin." Sandy shook her head at my ignorance. "Anyone with a pet, a cat, a dog, whatever, can easily get penicillin from a vet. Or even order the stuff online."

"Really? How do you know that?"

"I know that because I have a brother-in-law who's fixated on dogs and has a minimum of four at any given time."

I leaned back in my chair, resisted the urge to undo the top button of my jeans, and wished I hadn't eaten so much. "Okay. As an ace reporter who knows everything there is to know about the local area and the local people and the local law, what do your instincts tell you? Any sense of where this is going?"

"Well, it's early days yet, and there's still a lot we don't know," Sandy ruminated, staring dreamily at a spot just above my head. "The murderer could be almost anyone. A business rival. A longtime enemy hiding in plain sight. Some poor sod who got sideswiped by Ben's greed. A jilted lover. But I'm thinking it's most likely one of Ben's nearest and dearest." She put down her fork. "If we're going to solve this, we need to follow the money."

"We?" I asked.

"Yes. You don't think I'm going to be left out of this, do you? I'll contribute as much as I can to your sleuthing. Within the limits of my contract with the station. You'd be amazed at all the rules and regulations I have to live with. Speaking of which…" Sandy glanced at her watch and jumped up, nearly tipping her chair in the process. "I've got to get back and start prepping for the six o'clock broadcast. That vacation day I mentioned last night fell through. It's just another workday for me, and I completely lost track of time." She tossed three twenties on the table. "My treat. This was totally fun. I'll be in touch."

Glancing across the room, I silently rejoiced to see that Andrew's table was now occupied by three middle-aged women in full tourist regalia. Which meant I had safe passage out of there.

After finishing the last of my coffee, I turned over the bill, added ten dollars to Sandy's already generous tip, slipped on my sunglasses, and ambled out into the sunlight. Basking for a few seconds in the luscious heat, I pulled on my thunderbird cap and was fumbling for the car keys when a touch from behind made me spin around, heart pounding.

Andrew's sunglasses were too dark for me to read his eyes, but his words were crystal clear. "How about we find ourselves a quiet stretch of beach and do a little debriefing?"

Chapter Thirty

By sheer luck, there was one empty parking place in the small sand-covered lot adjacent to Lighthouse Beach. Actually, I'm not sure the beach even has a name. But that's what I've always called it, in honor of the bright red Marquette Harbor Light—perched on a nearby bluff—that's given the place its ambience since 1866.

Back in my college days, this stretch of sand was a favorite hangout for my roommates and me. In the chilly late spring, we'd squirm into our bikinis, load up our bags with Coppertone and cheap sunglasses, find someone with a car, buy ourselves a bottle of third-rate wine, and cluster together on dorm towels under the sheltering dunes. There, we'd while away the afternoon. Gossiping. Giggling. Drinking. Dreaming. Watching ice floes drift by in the lake.

Now Andrew and I sat in silence next to those very same dunes, or their current incarnation, letting the lake breeze ruffle our hair and listening to the hypnotic lap of waves against beach sand. Finally, in a half-asleep voice, Andrew broke the spell. "So what did your reporter friend have to say about the case?"

On the drive over, I'd decided not to waste effort denying the fact that Sandy and I had discussed Ben's murder. Instead, I told him everything I now knew. But only after he grudgingly agreed to share what he'd learned, or as much as he could tell a civilian, about the official investigation and where it was headed.

When I finished, he looked thoughtful. "Of course," he began, "you have to understand my conversation with Paul was strictly by the book." I quirked an eyebrow. "Seriously. He can't discuss details of the case with anyone, including police from other jurisdictions, unless they're involved in the investigation. And I'd never ask him to step over that line."

"So then, what you're saying is that you didn't learn a whole lot more than I did."

"These local reporters know how to dig," he acknowledged. "They've collected a lot of facts. One thing you didn't mention, though, is that the FBI has been called in. But that was a given, since the crime was committed on federal property."

"From what I've heard, there's usually not much love lost between local police and federal agents." I flashed on scenes from my favorite cop shows. "Is that true?"

"Let's just say they co-exist. In this case, the feds appear to be giving the local police a lot of room to maneuver. Probably because the Munising crew has a good record with murder investigations."

I looked into Andrew's face, grateful to whoever had invented sunglasses, the perfect social shield. "Well then," I said, "what do we do now?"

Picking up a short, thin fragment of driftwood, Andrew traced aimless designs in the patch of sand between us. "We do the only thing we can." His mouth formed the start of a smile. "We do what everyone else does. We take in the sights. Visit waterfalls. Hang out at beaches. Hike trails. Go on overcrowded boat cruises. Take too many photos. Of course," he rubbed loose sand off his hands, "since this is my first time in the True North—that's what you call it, isn't it?—I'm appointing you my official tour guide."

I hadn't seen that coming. Registering my surprise, he went on. "It's not a bad arrangement, really, when you think about it. I get the benefit of your local expertise. You get to revisit your favorite spots. And you also get free meals, although the way you eat, that part of the deal could set me back considerably."

He filled the small silence that followed with a look that would have left most women a molten mass right there on the sand, then leaned toward me. "And I promise to be on my best behavior." I could feel my defenses weakening. "What do you say? How about it?"

I looked into his eyes, or what I could see of them behind the dark lens, and took a few seconds to argue with myself. Yes. No. Maybe. Oh, what the heck. When could I ever resist showing off my home turf? I nodded. "Okay. You've just hired yourself a tour guide."

I stood up and brushed a quantity of sand off my jeans. Following my example, Andrew got to his feet and shook his jacket, which had been doubling as a beach towel. "So, where to? What's on the agenda?"

"Well, every major guidebook attraction is going to be overrun with tourists. Guaranteed. So, unless you like crowds, I suggest we head for some out-of-the-way places. Get off the beaten track."

"Off the beaten track sounds good," he swung the jacket over his shoulder as we trudged up the dunes to the car. "I'm all yours."

Now there was a thought.

Our first stop was downtown Marquette for a short walking tour. I pointed out the ornate buildings made from locally quarried red sandstone, most of them constructed in the late eighteen-hundreds. Old City Hall. The Savings Bank. Buildings that most tourists look at without really seeing. Then we took a four-block detour to St. Peter's Cathedral, where I insisted on lighting a candle and visiting the basement crypt of Bishop Frederic Baraga, better known as the snowshoe priest.

Next stop was the Superior Dome, all fourteen stories and five acres of it. "Not only the world's largest wooden dome," I pointed out as we walked the indoor track, "but probably the country's quirkiest football stadium."

Finally, I pointed the car north. As we glided along County Road 550, Andrew seemed content to sit back and watch the landscape flow by. But when we got to Big Bay and pulled up to the Thunder Bay Inn, his eyes popped. "Whoa. Wait a sec. Wasn't this the setting for the movie…"

"*Anatomy of a Murder*," I finished for him. "Yup. Back in nineteen fifty-two. Directed by Otto Preminger. Starring Jimmy Stewart."

"And Lee Remick," he added.

"Very good," I nodded approvingly as I parked the car in the mostly empty lot. The place had been renovated a while back, and its smooth high walls, elegant pillars, and meticulously painted red shutters looked positively palatial—and a little out of place—in the backwater setting. "Come on in. This is where the cast stayed. You can buy me a drink in the Duke's Grill."

Since my last visit, the bar area had been transformed from its original nineteen-forties kitschy clutter to an open, airy space. The only thing that hadn't changed was the grand piano in the corner. Andrew and I sat at the table nearest the piano, and a tanned, smiling man who looked more like an owner than a server took our drink orders. A beer for Andrew, mineral water for me.

I looked around, let out a deep sigh, and then realized that Andrew was staring not at the surroundings but at me. Probably wondering if I'd become unmoored, dragging him on such a bizarre tour.

"Back in my college days," I explained, "John Voelker, the man who wrote the novel that inspired the movie, was ancient but still alive. Being a little celebrity-crazed, I'd convince whatever guy I was dating at the time to take me out here, to this bar. We'd usually find Judge Voelker right there." I turned around in my captain's chair and pointed to the piano. "Always in a business suit. Always draped over the piano. Always with a drink in his hand. Reliving the glory days and telling stories about the cast and crew."

Andrew raised his beer. "Here's to Judge Voelker." I touched my glass to his, took a long, satisfying swallow, and realized how thirsty I was.

After polishing off most of his beer, Andrew wandered off to examine the black-and-white movie stills lining the hallway. I took out my phone and dialed Bixie. When she picked up, I told her I was just checking in, explained how Andrew and I had surprised each other at the Vierling, and how I'd been playing tour guide for the past few hours.

"Oh, and one more thing," I added. "Just for the record. There is nothing going on between your brother and me. That lipstick episode was just part of a weird little revenge drama, some mano-a-mano thing between Andrew and Roger."

"I don't doubt that for a second," Bixie said. "But do you really *not* see what's going on? Don't you realize what's at the center of the drama?" She paused. "Karin, it's a duel. And who do you suppose they're dueling over?"

Something inside of me started squirming, so I veered onto a more comfortable topic. "Look, the main reason I called was to tell you that I'm thinking about heading over to the gluten-free bakery in Negaunee to pick up some pasties for dinner. Sound okay?"

"Sounds great." Amazing, how two simple words like *gluten* and *free*, in close proximity, could cause such a sea change in her mood. "Make mine all vegetable." As if I'd dare order anything else for her. "Oh, and you better get an extra pasty, probably beef, for Charles. He's agreed to tell us what he knows about the artifacts the construction crew dug up at Ben's site. You know, the items that disappeared. It seems they've been turning up in some interesting places lately."

Chapter Thirty-One

"**S**o you're saying that the checked items on this list have turned up at a gallery downstate?" I put down my fork, scrubbed my fingers with a paper napkin, and, with Bixie crowding in next to me, picked up the piece of paper that Charles had just placed in the middle of the table. Andrew took a quick bite of his pasty, chased it down with beer, and leaned in on my other side.

Heads together, we scanned the typed list:

- Courting flute
- Rattle drum
- Pogamoggan
- Tobacco dish
- Carved wood deer call
- Ceremonial pipe
- Ball head club
- Arrows
- Beaded moccasin fragments
- Fish net float
- Slingshot

Nearly every one of the items had a check mark next to it. "What's a pogamoggan?" Bixie wanted to know.

"A hatchet," Charlie answered. "And yes, like I said, those items were on display and being offered for sale."

I returned the list to its original spot in the center of the kitchen table, being careful to avoid pasty crumbs, catsup spills, and the wet rings created by assorted glasses and bottles.

"But…" Bixie wondered aloud, "what makes you think the artifacts that were spotted downstate are the same, and not just similar?

"Couple of reasons." Charles pushed his empty plate to one side. "More than a couple, actually. First, the guy who brought them to our attention is a serious collector. He's studied Ojibwe culture. He spends every summer up here, has for years, and he's even volunteered for archaeological digs on Grand Island. That's how I met him. Second, he's a good friend of one of the tribal council members, Nick Leveque. That's how he learned about the thefts at Ben's place. And third, when he saw the items the gallery owner was so excited about, he had the presence of mind to take some photos and send them to Nick. Who, in turn, showed them to the tribal members who'd been working at the site."

I stood up and walked my plate and silverware over to the kitchen sink. It's a habit. Part OCD and part what my Aunt Saimi would call good home training. Once there, I picked up a half-empty bottle of wine. "Anybody want a refill? Wine? Beer? Charles, do you want your water topped off?"

I refilled Bixie's wine glass, did the same for mine, and was just putting a fresh beer next to Andrew's plate when he looked over at Charles and said, hesitatingly, in a walking-on-eggs sort of way, "No offense. But based on the little I know about the subject, I didn't think that Great Lakes tribal artifacts were all that valuable. On the open market, I mean. At least not compared to items from the Pueblo tribes."

"That used to be true." Charles picked up the list as he spoke. "But in the last ten years or so, there's been an explosion of interest in all the Great Lakes tribes. Not sure why, but the price for Chippewa artifacts has increased, big-time. I'm talking maybe tenfold. And the market keeps growing. The same thing is true for Native American artifacts in general, across the country."

"So the demand is there," he went on. "And keep in mind that all of these," he tapped the list, "came from grave sites. They're what the experts call funerary items. They were placed there deliberately and carefully, and left

138

undisturbed. So when they're dug up, they're generally intact, or at least in much better condition than daily artifacts discovered at settlements. Better condition, higher prices."

I was about to turn the conversation back to the facts of the case, but Bixie beat me to it. "Exactly where is this gallery that had the items up for sale?"

"Grosse Pointe. The gallery isn't officially open yet, at least not to the public, and won't be for a couple of months. The artifacts were on display as part of a special preview party. And here's the really interesting thing. The owner..."

"Wait!" Andrew interrupted. "Don't say it. Let me guess." He leaned back in his chair with a satisfied smile. "The owner is none other than Meredith Wood."

"Jackpot," Charlie grinned back at him. "Care to make any other guesses, or should I say deductions?"

"If I did, they'd be pretty obvious," Andrew answered. "One thing, though. There must be laws governing ownership of these funerary items. Federal laws, I'd assume. And so gallery owners and collectors would need to be very cautious about toeing the line. True?"

Something in my brain clicked, and I suddenly remembered once talking about this very subject with Evelyn. "NAGPAR," I burst out, ignoring the baffled looks from Bixie and Andrew. "Now let's see if I get this right. Native American Graves Protection..." I faltered.

"And Repatriation Act," Charles finished for me. "It's a good law, and a real step forward for us. But it's complicated."

"Yeah," I went on. "I remember Evelyn calling me when it finally passed years ago. She was thrilled. Basically, the law protects tribes from grave robbers."

"So then how is it," Bixie puzzled, "that Meredith would have the audacity to sell grave artifacts to knowledgeable collectors, who are certainly aware of the law? And to do it at a public gala, no less? She might be greedy and brazen, but she's not stupid."

My phone rang. I ignored it, wanting to hear what Charles had to say. "Like I told you, the law is complicated. Even worse, it has a major loophole."

We all waited expectantly as he reached toward the plate of chocolate chip cookies I'd put on the table. "It doesn't cover non-funerary items found on private property. That is to say, items found near a grave but not placed there as part of a burial rite."

Following his example, I reached for a cookie and, shame on me, took the largest instead of the nearest. "But how could anyone prove that either way?" I asked. "I mean, someone could claim that even though the item was found near a gravesite, it had nothing to do with the actual burial. They could say it was part of another ceremony, at another time, that wasn't related to honoring the dead. It's just one person's word against another's." I bit into the buttery, chocolaty dough and nearly lost my train of thought. "How convenient for people like Meredith. And Ben."

"Well, loophole or not," Andrew said, "I'm sure the authorities will be eager to talk with Meredith about her acquisitions."

In the silence that followed, my phone jangled again. Irritated, I stalked across the room, fumbled through my purse, and managed to answer just before the call went to voicemail.

"I'm glad you picked up this time!"

"Sandy. What's going on?"

"In case you haven't been keeping up with the local news, I thought you'd want to know." In the background, I could hear the din of the Marquette newsroom. I had to strain to make out what she was saying. "Early this morning, Meredith Wood was discovered unconscious in her hotel room. Possible drug overdose. Maybe accidental. Maybe not."

"What? But how…"

"I can't talk now. We've been trying to pry details out of local police and hospital officials all day. Not to mention the hotel staff. We're just now putting the finishing touches on the story for the ten o'clock news. Be sure to tune in."

I didn't move for maybe half a minute. Just stood there, one knee braced against the couch, listening to the silence on the other end.

After a brief tussle with my conscience, I scrolled through my phone files, located Roger's number, and headed toward the back door. "Bad connection,"

CHAPTER THIRTY-ONE

I called out. "Be back in a minute." Thankfully, no one took any notice.

Four somewhat uncomfortable minutes later, I stepped back into the cottage just in time to hear Bixie say, "Okay, granted, it's clear Meredith is involved in this. But Ben could have lied to her about the provenance, about how and where the artifacts were found. It's entirely possible."

"Maybe less possible than you think," I said from the doorway. "That was Sandy on the phone." When I told them the news about Meredith overdosing, Bixie gasped, and Charles lifted his eyebrows.

Andrew showed no surprise whatever. Arms crossed and voice nonchalant, he pinned me down with his eyes. "And what did Roger have to say about all this?" When it became clear which of us was going to win the staring contest that ensued, I sat down at the table.

"He didn't know much more than Sandy," I said. "But he did promise to call me when the details surfaced. Right now, he's thinking what everyone else is, that Meredith tried to commit suicide either because she was racked with guilt or because she was afraid to face the consequences once the police started connecting all the dots." I picked up the abandoned cookie on my plate. "What about you? What do you think?"

Andrew moved the empty beer glass around on his placemat in an absentminded way. "I think the police will be very eager to have a long talk with Meredith, when and if she recovers." He looked at each one of us in turn. "I also think they'll consider the possibility that her supposed suicide attempt was arranged by someone else. The someone who actually murdered Ben, and who may have no qualms whatever about murdering again."

Chapter Thirty-Two

"**M**ind if I join you?" Andrew's voice fell like a pebble on a still pond, breaking into my nocturnal solitude.

"Be my guest." I withdrew a little deeper into the old Army blanket that served as my combination shawl and pup tent. "It's a big lake." As I shifted my weight, the ancient Adirondack chair groaned. Andrew maneuvered his long frame into the rickety lounge chair next to me, and we let the night sounds settle around us. The distant hoot of a grey owl. The thrum of frogs and crickets. The gentle shooshing of water on sand. The occasional purr of a passing car.

"Sorry to intrude. But it was starting to feel crowded in there."

"Yeah," I answered with a yawn. "I know what you mean. It's as if there's an invisible *Do Not Disturb* sign hovering over those two." I rearranged the folds of the blanket. "So what do you think of Charles?"

"What do I think of him?" Andrew seemed genuinely surprised at the question. "Well, based on two brief encounters over a period of twenty-four hours, he seems like a decent enough guy. Smart. Serious. Quiet. Witty, without being a pain in the ass about it. Good looking, not that it matters. Remote, which probably amps up his appeal for my sister." He folded his arms behind his head, and the chair creaked in warning. "But if police work has taught me anything, it's not to make snap judgments or be too quick about trusting someone. Ask me again three months from now. If he lasts that long."

I smiled into the darkness. "Your sister is hell on men, isn't she? As soon as there's a whiff of anything serious, she's gone. I've lost count of all the rejects."

Andrew let out a short laugh. "I remember talking with a shrink she dated for a while. Nice enough guy, but totally besotted with her. He told me my sister had some commitment issues, but that they'd worked through them. A week later, he was history." He reached for his jacket and draped it over his chest to ward off the evening chill. "But I always figured that when she finally did fall for someone, she'd fall hard. It seems to be a family trait."

He took a deep breath and let it out slowly. "So what's the plan for tomorrow?"

"Well," I stretched out the word to two or three syllables. "I was thinking that we might do a little…"

"If the next word is 'investigating,' the answer is no."

"Of course not," I lied, trying to sound offended, trying not to be daunted by Andrew's apparent ability to read my mind. "I was going to say that I thought you might like to see Au Train Falls. It's just far enough from town, and the trail is just long enough, that the crowds are usually light. And the falls are spectacular, in a quiet sort of way. I know Bixie would like it." And I planned to make sure she saw it. With us. I was feeling the need for some social insulation. "Also, Trenary isn't far from there. It's been years since I've seen the old family farm. And I'll bet you've never had Trenary Toast."

Andrew sat upright, having temporarily given up the search for comfort. "Okay by me. And Bixie will probably tag along. After you went outside, Charles mentioned that the local police have asked him to come in for questioning tomorrow. So she'll have some free time."

I jolted upright so fast that a splinter of wood grazed my bum. "Questioning? What for? He didn't have any direct dealings with Ben."

"Oh, but he did." Andrew leaned back in the chaise. "About a month ago, Ben was in the casino with some of his high-roller friends. Charles happened to be on the floor at the time. Good-sized crowd. Lots of witnesses. He said Ben was drunk and started bragging in a loud voice about how effortless it was for him to make money, how most people struggled to get a few dollars, but that was because they were too stupid to spot an opportunity when it cropped up. And how sometimes it literally did just that. Cropped up. All you had to do was grab it. Of course, Ben could have been talking about anything. But Charles assumed he was referring to the artifacts that were dug up when his house was being built."

I looked over at Andrew, his profile outlined by the light of a three-quarters moon. I wondered what it would be like to wake in the middle of the night next to that profile. Then, shocked at myself, I wondered what dark, depraved part of my brain had released such a treasonous thought. Back to the subject at hand. "Don't tell me he confronted Ben about that. Right there? In front of everyone?"

"Afraid so. Charles accused Ben of stealing the Ojibwe's cultural heritage. Breaking the law. And he threatened him. Not directly. But he remembers telling Ben that there would be justice. Then he mentioned something about a wedneego or a wedge-I-don't-know-what. I didn't understand what he was saying."

"A wendigo," I said, and felt a shiver slide down my spine. "It's the Native American version of a goblin. Or a zombie. A wendigo is usually a monster that punishes evildoers. But the Chippewa have a different take on it. They believe that human beings who have done a great wrong are sometimes turned into wendigos as punishment."

"Uh-huh," Andrew stifled a yawn. "I've come across a few of those in my years on the force. But we have other names for them. Like felons."

We sat there, silent, thinking our own thoughts. After a few minutes, when sleep had made Andrew's breathing slow and steady, I eased myself up from the chair and went back to the cottage.

Bixie was at the front door, watching Charles drive away. "Andrew's asleep," I explained. "I didn't want to disturb him." I gave a backward glance through the kitchen window. "I just hope the mosquitoes don't devour him."

"He'll be fine." Bixie half-collapsed onto the couch, undid her ponytail, let her white-blonde hair fan out over the cushion, and closed her eyes. "For some reason, he's always been impervious to insect bites. It's me they can't resist. Besides, you're right. He needs to rest."

After a few seconds, she opened one eye slightly and focused it on me. "Did Andrew tell you that the police want to question Charles?"

I nodded and settled myself in the faded armchair on the other side of the coffee table. Bixie went on. "I don't like the fact that they're focusing on him now."

I curled up in the chair and tried but failed to keep my eyes open. "Like it or not, there's nothing we can do but wait and see what happens. Your brother has finally convinced me of that."

"I'm not so sure he's right."

My eyes popped open. "Explain."

Bixie sat up. "We could turn over some rocks. You know all kinds of people in this town. People who know people. So if we make a few inquiries about Meredith's movements, we're bound to learn something."

"And the police are bound to hear about it." I couldn't be sure what irritated me more: the fact that I was now wide awake or the fact that Bixie had learned absolutely nothing from our last disastrous adventure. "That's a terrible idea."

It's true that I'd entertained the very same idea myself earlier in the evening. But churning up hidden facts with a pro like Andrew or a source like Sandy was a whole lot different than stumbling around for clues in public and setting off trip wires with Bixie.

Ignoring the Medusa stare she was leveling at me, I plowed on. "Look, I know you're fond of Charles, but try to remember that you're also fond of Andrew and me. And both of us were seen, in public, keeping company with Meredith the night before she tried to kill herself. Or before someone tried to make it look that way. I'm already a person of interest. Do you really think it's a good idea to risk drawing even more attention to myself? And your brother?"

Looking more animated than she had in days, looking in fact like the old Bixie, she dismissed my arguments with a patronizing wave of one elegant hand. "You're just tired now. Take a shower. Get some sleep. We'll talk about it in the morning."

"Right," I rasped. "Let's ask Andrew what he thinks of your idea over a bowl of Cheerios."

She stood up and walked toward her bedroom. "Don't worry about

Andrew," she tossed the words over her shoulder and stepped through the doorway. "We'll figure out a way to do some snooping on our own."

Staring at the closed door, I spoke in a whisper to the empty room. "Yeah. That's what I'm afraid of. "

Chapter Thirty-Three

"Are you sure there's a parking lot ahead?" Andrew gripped the steering wheel with both hands as he navigated a series of bone-jarring potholes. "We don't seem to be getting anywhere except lost."

"Agreed," Bixie piped up from the back seat. "This is like being in one of those creepy German fairytales where travelers enter a forest and then discover that the trees…"

"Of course I'm sure. Look." I pointed at a rust-rimmed metal sign. "It's half a mile to the main parking area of the falls."

When we arrived, only three of the dozen or so parking slots were filled. As usual, most tourists were off doing more predictable things. Crowding onto the viewing platforms at Munising Falls. Snapping photos from the Miner's Castle overlook. Paddling kayaks in the bay. Queuing up for the morning cruises.

After we'd trekked down the quarter-mile trail to the upper falls viewing area, I settled myself on a flat-topped boulder and hoped that Andrew would decide to continue on. Instead, it was Bixie who—after taking in the wide cascades—forged ahead down the footpath to the lower falls.

Andrew seated himself on a massive tree trunk near me and called after his sister. "Be careful. Got your phone?"

Without turning around, Bixie waved her precious new toy. "I'll be fine. Call me when you're ready to leave."

"Don't wander too far," I yelled at her retreating back. "There are dead zones out there. Get much deeper into those woods and your phone will be useless." She gave another casual wave, prompting me to shout. "I'm not kidding. If you aren't back in half an hour, we're sending out a search party."

Watching Bixie, I thought about all the tourists who have no respect for the wilderness, no understanding of how treacherous, how murderous, raw nature can be. I thought about tourists who get lost in the woods and die from exposure or, if they're lucky, are rescued by search crews. Tourists who fall off cliffs in pursuit of the perfect photo. Who take their kayaks out into the fierce open waters of our inland ocean and drown. Tourists, dozens of them every year, who ignore warnings about deadly currents and rip tides, who venture into Superior as if it were a backyard pool or a placid, well-behaved little inland lake and get in over their heads. Literally. Such stupid ways to die.

Gradually, the roar of the falls drew me back into the moment. Swollen by heavy spring rains, the water was wider and wilder than it would be a month from now, when hot, dry days had taken their toll. The upper cascades spanning the river tumbled over a natural staircase of limestone ledges. Somehow, you never develop immunity to that kind of beauty, no matter how many times you've seen it.

The effect wasn't lost on Andrew. Eyes riveted on the falls, he said simply, "I see what you mean about this being spectacular. But you were wrong about the quiet part."

"This has always been one of my favorite spots," I said. "Terry's, too."

Andrew turned toward me. "So he liked it up here."

"Oh, he didn't just like it." I forced my eyes to focus on the falls. "He loved it. The whole way of life. It was one of the many things that bonded us to each other."

"Bonded." Andrew repeated the word.

"Right. Bonded. You know. After all, you and Helen were married for, what, twenty years?"

His face took on a hard, chiseled look. "Correction. Helen and I were *together* for twenty years. We were *married* for maybe ten of them."

I stared at him.

"Surprised?" He stood up, rolled the stiffness out of his neck, and gave a luxuriant stretch.

"Uh…yes…" I dithered. "You two always seemed like the perfect couple."

"Perfect, huh?" He tossed a stick into the river, and we watched it bob up and down on the current. "Tell me," he said, his eyes still on the water. "What do you think of Helen? What are your impressions? Be honest." He grinned. "Don't forget, I'm a cop. I'll know if you're lying."

"I can't…"

"No, go ahead," he insisted. "Please. I want to know. Nothing you say will offend me."

I could tell that, for whatever reason, he wasn't going to let up on this. Might as well humor him. "Okay then. For starters, Helen is stunningly beautiful. But outside-beautiful, not inside-beautiful. And probably high maintenance." His eyebrows quirked up. "She always seems cold in a remote, look-but-don't-touch kind of way. Unreachable. Off-putting, I suppose."

To my surprise, I was enjoying this. It was like being back in a college lit class, dissecting characters and plots. "She likes to take charge of situations." I thought back to how Bixie fell apart when her friend Dana Lewis was murdered last fall, and how Helen insisted on looking after her. "And she's good at it. Organized. Efficient. But the thing that's always struck me most is her perfectionism. She can't seem to tolerate anyone or anything that doesn't meet her standards."

Andrew stared at me intently. I looked back at him, more irritated than intimidated, ready for a confrontation. Which, when I thought about it, was our usual way of interacting. "You told me to be honest," I reminded him.

His face softened. "Right on every count. Especially the perfectionism." He reached down and picked up a broken cardinal flower. "With Helen, everything had to be perfect. Or at least appear that way. Perfect house. Perfect car. Perfect neighborhood. Perfect friends. Perfect kids, if you didn't look too closely. The only thing in her life that wasn't perfect was me."

He stopped. I waited.

"God knows I tried. Especially those first years. But I don't do perfect. I never measured up. Everything about me was wrong. I was in the wrong career. Had the wrong taste in clothes. Certainly, the wrong taste in friends.

I chose the wrong hobbies. Played the wrong sports. Liked the wrong music. Watched the wrong films."

He tossed the cardinal flower onto the riverbank. "Finally, I had enough of trying and failing. I was ready to call it quits. By then, of course, there were the kids to think about. Believe it or not, Helen is a pretty good mother. And despite the fact that they can both be a royal pain in the ass, I love them. So thinking it was best for them, I stuck around. And Helen and I lived our separate lives, together."

"Andrew," I broke into his monologue, willing him to stop.

He went on as if I wasn't there. "And since life with me didn't meet her expectations, she did what any self-respecting perfectionist would do."

I held my breath, not liking where this was going.

"She looked elsewhere."

A flash of heat flooded my face. Where was Bixie? She needed to come back and interrupt this whatever-it-was. Now.

Andrew turned his gaze to the roiling water along the base of the falls. "At first, it was just harmless flirtations. Her tennis coach. Some guy who served on a committee with her. But then, about five years ago, she had an affair. Oh, she denied it. But all the signs were there. Of course, I couldn't object too much, since I'd done the same thing." He craned his neck back and looked skyward, as if speaking to some unseen presence. "What a colossal mistake that was. Anyway, that's when I realized I didn't really care. And that I hadn't, for years."

He scanned the sandy soil, picked up two small flat stones, and transferred one of the rocks to his right hand. Then he angled his arm until it was horizontal to the ground and sent the stone flying. I watched as it skipped just once across the surface before disappearing. "The thing with her personal trainer. I found out about it a few months ago. And all I felt was disgust."

Pulling back his arm, he sent the second stone on the same one-bounce journey as the first. "Calling a divorce attorney was one of the best things I've ever done. I'm just sorry it took me so long."

Absentmindedly, he picked up two more rocks. "The kids aren't happy about it, of course, but they're old enough now to handle it. To tell you the truth, neither of them was all that surprised."

Since Terry's death, I've worked very hard to keep my emotional life flat and placid. Oh, I'm fine with the simple, predictable stuff of life. But when big feelings come up and start churning and catalyzing into something complicated, something I may not be able to control, I panic. Only there was no reason to panic now, I told myself, since none of this involved me.

"Two things," I said. "First, don't beat yourself up for not leaving sooner. We humans have an amazing capacity for living with pain. After a while, it starts to seem normal. And besides, you had work and kids to fill up your life."

Keeping his gaze on the turbulent ore-colored river, he nodded.

"The second thing is a question." I paused. "Why have you told me all this?"

He turned to face me. "I think you know." Even though he stood absolutely still, I had the weird impression that he was moving toward me.

"Hi, guys." For once, Bixie's timing was impeccable. The notes of a cavalry trumpet couldn't have sounded any sweeter. "You should have come along. It's gorgeous down there at the lower falls."

She sat down next to me on the boulder. "So what have you been doing?"

I stood up, slightly breathless. "Your brother and I have been talking about the fine art of skipping stones. Comparing techniques."

I turned to Andrew. "May I?" Without waiting for an answer, I reached over and liberated one of the rocks in his open hand. Hefting it lightly and holding my arm precisely the way my Uncle Jerome taught me, I jettisoned the stone toward the calmest section of the river and had the satisfaction of seeing it bounce five times before disappearing.

Andrew stared at the ripples where the stone had ended its water dance and shook his head. "You are full of surprises, lady."

I looked him straight in the eyes. "But not as many as you."

Chapter Thirty-Four

With its fresh coat of sky blue paint, the Trenary Bakery stood out even more than usual among the tired buildings that populated the tiny downtown. Inside, though, it was the same comforting place as always. The oven-warmed air was saturated with delicious smells. The glass cases were lined with fresh-baked cookies, muffins, brownies, bagels, and buns. The shelves were stacked with loaves of bread: white and whole wheat and Limpa rye and the twice-baked Finnish dunking toast that has become the bakery's claim to fame.

A cheerful, motherly-looking woman behind the counter took our orders. While we waited, Andrew went outside to check his voicemails. Inside, Bixie and I worked our way through the shelves of tourist swag, most of it having to do with Trenary Toast.

About forty minutes later, as we were finishing our sandwiches, my phone sounded. Thinking it was Sandy, I excused myself, walked toward the entryway, and pushed the answer button without glancing at the number. Which explains why the sound of Roger's voice gave me such a jolt.

"Do not hang up. This is important."

I looked across the street at a wildly colorful mural that covered the entire surface of what had once been a grocery store. "I'm listening."

"You're going to be getting a call very soon from the Munising Police." My stomach began gyrating in a way that made me regret that second order of home fries. "Meredith tried to commit suicide last night. She's in the hospital now. Probably with a security guard."

"I know about the suicide attempt," I began, "and..."

"What you don't know is that, when the police examined her cell phone, they discovered that one of the last two calls she made was to me." He paused. Something told me to keep still. "And her very last call was to you."

Whatever breath was in my lungs disappeared. I gasped for air. "But...but I never got a call from her. Not that I know of. I mean, I didn't talk to her."

"Nor did I, dear girl. But think back." In moments of crisis, Roger's brogue disappears. A small mercy. "I'm guessing that sometime last night, whether or not you were even aware of it, your phone probably rang. Once. Then the caller hung up. That's what happened to me. The hour was so late, I assumed it was a misdial."

My mind made a useless attempt at rational thought.

"It's possible she did try to call us before overdosing," Roger admitted. "But it's equally possible that someone else made those calls and deliberately cut them short. Just to make sure there was a record for the police to find."

Fighting off the haze of shock, my brain started whirring and spinning again. "So then, what you're suggesting is that..."

"Is that someone is trying to involve us in this mess. Maybe even implicate us in Ben's murder." There was a pinging sound on the line. "I need to get this before I head over to the police station. Talk to you later."

I stood on the sun-warmed sidewalk and waited for my hands to stop shaking before going back into the bakery. In the short time it took me to break the news, Bixie's face morphed from wide-eyed to worried. Andrew listened in silence until I was through, at which point he uttered just one word.

"Shit."

"My thought exactly," I said. "This puts me right back on the suspect list."

Andrew closed his eyes and rubbed his forehead. "This puts us both on the suspect list."

Given the hundreds of mystery novels I've devoured over the years, his comment shouldn't have surprised me. "But you were just along for the ride," I said. "Trying to keep me out of trouble. That should be obvious. Besides, they wouldn't suspect one of their own." That last argument sounded weak. "And you've got absolutely no reason for wanting to see Ben dead, or for hijacking the investigation."

"No reason?" Andrew snapped. "You really think they're going to see it that way?" The woman at the counter looked up from the pastry tray she was unloading. Andrew lowered his voice to an aggravated whisper. "Come on, Karin. Try to think like a cop. From their point of view, it's a classic situation. A generally decent guy on the cusp of a divorce has a major lapse in judgment, turns into a sap, and allows a beautiful, slightly crazed woman to lead him around by his..."

"Andrew!" Bixie's voice cut through the air, silencing her brother and doubtless triggering memories of those occasions when he managed to provoke his usually placid mother into a state of parental rage.

The look he gave his sister was somewhere between simmering and scalding. "To lead him around by his hormones. How's that?"

It was a relief when my phone sounded. Of course, it was The Call from my new friend Lieutenant Bill Harris. After some preliminaries, I agreed to be at the station within the hour. We all filed back into the Bronco and drove away in silence. Halfway to Munising, I realized I'd left my bag of Trenary Toast on the table.

Andrew dropped me off in front of the station with instructions to call him when I was ready to be picked up. Assuming, of course, that Officer Harris decided to release me on my own recognizance. After forty-five minutes of cooling my heels in the lobby, Roger—looking strained and as close to humbled as I'd ever seen him—walked past me on his way to the exit, escorted by a smug Rob Ketola. At the door, he turned around and gave me a thumbs-up and a weak smile.

Ten minutes and one chewed thumbnail later, I was seated at a table outfitted with a fancy recording device and, I assumed, several cameras. The walls were painted a tepid pinkish beige—a color my brother once described as baby puke. It made me wonder if all police station décor in Michigan was mandated by government regulations. I tried to visualize the palette of ugly colors permitted by state guidelines.

When my two interrogators walked in, I decided that each of them posed a different kind of threat. Bill Harris was dangerous because he was so good at camouflaging his formidable intelligence under the guise of a mild-mannered, small-town cop. Whereas Rob Ketola was dangerous because he grossly overestimated just how smart he was.

I'd prepared myself fairly well for the questions, but not for the relentless, wearing repetition.

What reason would Meredith have for calling me, just before attempting to kill herself? Why would she have my cell phone number? And why didn't I call her back? How long had we known each other? Were we close friends? No? Then why was I seen having drinks with her and Ben's son the night before? Why, according to witnesses, did she seem so relieved to see me? How would I describe her relationship with Devon? And Roger? And how did Andrew figure in all this? How would I describe each person's relationship to Ben Roberts? And to each other? What did we talk about? What did she say in particular? How would I characterize her emotional state? Surely she must have given some indication of her intentions? Some hint? Why would she try to kill herself just hours later? Was something said that might have driven her to desperation? Did I know of any possible motive she might have for murdering Ben?

And so it went. On and on. Why and how and who and what and let's go over all that again.

After two hours, we had established that Meredith and I were longtime but casual acquaintances. That she had my phone number because I'd worked on marketing projects for her galleries and, in any case, she was a compulsive social butterfly and probably had the numbers of a thousand people. That I missed her call on the night of her suicide attempt, and she didn't leave a voice message. That although she was a successful businesswoman, she was also unstable, a drama queen. That she and Ben had a very close relationship and that, as far as I knew, her grief was genuine. That the police already had a detailed understanding of my own relationship with Ben, which was nothing more than employee and employer. That, since he championed me at his agency and was responsible for generating a sizable portion of my income, I had every reason to be grateful and no reason whatever to want him dead. That when her phone was checked for prints, they'd probably discover the surface had been wiped clean or smudged by gloves, worn by whoever really made the call.

I told them it was hard to believe my friend Bixie and I were still on the list of suspects. Yes, I conceded, it's true that last year she and I had launched an ill-advised investigation into the death of a good friend of hers. And, yes, the Ann Arbor Police were upset. Justifiably so. But I had no intention of making the same mistake again. And if it appeared otherwise, I was deeply regretful.

Finally, having turned down two offers of coffee, accepted a glass of water, and signed a formal statement, I emerged from the police station with Bill Harris by my side.

As he reached around me to push open the door, he put on one of his genial, deceptive smiles. On a man the size of a professional fullback, wearing a police uniform, the effect was vaguely menacing. As intended.

"A word of advice, Ms. Niemi." I stopped and turned to face him.

"You're treading a very fine line here." There was steel in his eyes. "From now on, if you have an overwhelming urge to investigate something, I strongly advise that you do it with Nero Wolfe. On a beach. And leave the police work to us." He brought his face closer to mine. "Do I make myself clear?"

"Oh, yes." Despite that last glass of water, my throat felt dry. "Absolutely." I swallowed. "Clear."

Chapter Thirty-Five

The city of Munising is built on a narrow crescent of land bordered by Lake Superior on the north and densely wooded hills on the south, the result being that most buildings are within nine or ten blocks of the water. So even though the lake was out of sight, I could feel it and taste it and smell it.

Eyes closed, I took in a few cleansing breaths and, after sending up a quick thank you to whichever of my guardian angels happened to be on duty at the moment, I called Andrew. No answer. Feeling too bone weary to even think about walking back to the cottage, I considered my options. Roger was out of the question. As was Evelyn, since I didn't have the energy for her motherly concern. That left Bixie, who was probably off somewhere with Charles.

Much as I hated to interrupt young love, I dialed her number. Mine was the greater need. Besides, I wouldn't have been standing in the Munising police station parking lot at that moment if it weren't for Bixie's addiction to meddling. Since the penalties for her bad judgment usually fell hardest on me, she at least owed me a ride.

"Karin, where are you?" Her voice was edged with worry, as it should have been.

"They said I was entitled to one phone call…"

"Oh no. Don't tell me they're holding you. On what charge? That's crazy. Why…"

I let her rattle on as minor payback for the last three miserable hours before interrupting. "Actually, I'm a free woman, for the time being. And I need a ride. Andrew volunteered but..."

"Didn't you see him in there? He left for the station more than an hour ago. They wanted to talk with him, and he volunteered to come in rather than have them drop by, which I suppose they were willing to do as a professional courtesy or something. Who knows."

Poor Andrew. Part of the incidental carnage in this little horror show. There he was, somewhere in that building, defending himself from guilt by association when, in truth, he was just being gallant. That'll teach him. I sighed.

"I didn't see him, but they have more than one interrogation room. So I still need a ride. Can you be here in ten minutes?"

It only took her five. Leaning over, she pushed open the passenger door from the inside and searched my face before blurting out the inevitable: "Are you okay?"

"Sure. Never better." I snugged up the seatbelt, rolled down the window, and realized that I was on the verge of tears. Not sad, poor-me tears. Angry tears. Tears of frustration and general pissed-off-ness. The kind of tears that require an empty room and pillows to punch and scream into, and a soothing scotch waiting at the end. All the accoutrements for a proper tantrum. Luxuries I didn't expect to have, until Bixie explained that she was on her way to an early dinner with Charles, so would just drop me off at the cottage.

"If you're okay with being alone, that is," she said. Three small wrinkles appeared on her otherwise flawless forehead, and she darted a look of concern in my direction. "Otherwise, I'll call and cancel."

"No. Don't." Freedom beckoned. I might be able to throw that tantrum after all. "I'm fine. And I'm sure Charles has a lot to tell you about..."

"Isn't that Devon over there?" Bixie interrupted, leaning over the wheel and peering at a platinum colored Jeep Renegade that had just slid into a nearby parking spot. "And that looks like Audrey with him."

"You're right," I said. We watched as brother and sister got out and moved to the sidewalk. One blonde. One brunette. Both beautiful. They spoke briefly. Then, with a glance at his outsized Rolex, which I'd noticed the night before, Devon handed over the keys and headed toward the station.

"Wouldn't you just love to sit in on that interrogation?" Bixie kept her eyes pinned on Devon until he disappeared into the building. "I thought you said Audrey was in Chicago, curating some exhibit."

"She must have caught a morning flight from O'Hare. Or possibly a red-eye last night." Studying Audrey's svelte body, I pondered how it is that some women can slip into a white T-shirt and nondescript jeans and look as if they just stepped off a catwalk during Fashion Week in Manhattan.

Bixie nodded. "That makes sense, considering how close she and Meredith have always been. It's sweet, really, how she dropped everything to rush up here, maybe even jeopardized her career to be with Meredith and help her pull through."

I watched as Audrey started the Jeep and drove away, sun glinting on the flawless new-car finish. "Or maybe," I murmured, half to myself, "maybe she wanted to make sure that Meredith *doesn't* pull through. That she never has a chance to tell her story."

"Oh, Karin."

"Don't Oh-Karin me," I bristled. "Money is everything to those two. They grew up with it. They think they're entitled to it. They're probably desperate to get their hands on their dad's pile. And it's possible they're both in dire financial straits. Last night, Devon talked about how he—and presumably his sister—had been shut out of Ben's big-money condo project on Sand Point Road. He tried to shrug it off. I just hope the police do some serious digging into their finances."

Bixie put the car in gear and pulled out into the stream of traffic. "But killing their father for his money? It just seems too obvious. Too simple."

"Good grief." My patience, what there was of it, snapped. "You want a complicated plot, read a mystery novel. A nice P.D. James. Or maybe Martha Grimes. We're dealing with real people in the real world. And when it comes to murder, there aren't that many key motivators. Love. Hate. Revenge. Power. Money. That's pretty much it."

Bixie turned left onto Sand Point Road without bothering to signal, nearly cutting off an oncoming truck and setting off a chain reaction of car horns.

We drove the rest of the short distance in silence, she completely calm, me gripping the seat belt with white knuckles.

In the cottage parking area, she left the motor running as I got out. "Call if you need me. In the meantime, I suggest a nap and some of that willow bark Evelyn gave you."

Not bothering to answer, I let myself into the cottage and did a zombie shuffle to the bedroom where I dropped my purse on the floor, opened the closet, pulled on Terry's old U.S. Navy sweatshirt, collapsed onto the creaky-springed double bed and laid there, staring at the ceiling and counting the cracks. Eventually, I fell into a hectic half-sleep filled with waking dreams.

Bill Harris was reading me my rights, Roger was handcuffing me, and my mother was standing by my side, trying to tell me something crucially important, when Andrew's voice broke into the scene.

"Karin? Are you here?"

I indulged myself with a low groan. "In the bedroom."

He poked his head around the half-open door. "Are you okay?" That question again.

"Top of the world," I pulled the sweatshirt closer and tugged up the blankets.

He stepped into the room. "Are you really okay?"

"Of course not." I turned on my pillow to face him. "How'd it go for you?"

"Pretty much as expected. They were professional. Chilly. They let me know I was out of line and should know better, but they did it all in code. I ended up feeling like a damn fool, which I deserved."

I sat up on one elbow, feeling a case of the guilts coming on. "Are they going to report you?"

"Well, it all goes into the official record, and it's certain they're in contact with Ann Arbor. But," he put on a grim smile, "it's nothing I can't handle." He looked at me closely for a few seconds. "Have you eaten?"

"No," I shook my head. "I'm not hungry."

He arranged his face into a Dad look, the look he probably used on his kids when they were young, and moved closer until he was standing next to the bed. "You're never not hungry. What's wrong?"

"What's wrong?" My voice was edgy. I propped myself upright. "Oh, I don't know. How about everything? I've been planning this trip for months, working my butt off, beating deadlines so I could have this time away. I love this place. I couldn't wait to get back here. And what happens? I arrive just in time to be here for the murder of someone I know very well. And if that's not bad enough, I'm implicated in the murder and pulled in for questioning. This kind of thing isn't supposed to happen up here. This is my home. This is the one place on the planet where I feel safe. Where I belong. Where..." my voice broke.

Andrew lowered himself onto the bed. "Hey. It's going to be fine. Bill Harris and his team know what they're doing. They're going to find the person who did this, without our help. And you can go back to being home."

I sniffed. "You don't know that." Damn. Two tears escaped and made crooked, hot trails down my cheeks. I reached for a tissue. "Sorry, this is what happens when I get to a point of...what's beyond tired?"

"Exhausted." He took the tissue out of my hand, dabbed at my wet cheeks, and brought his face close to mine. "What you need is..."

The sound of the front door opening made both of us freeze. Brisk footsteps, coming closer.

"Karin, I was so worried that Charles insisted on canceling dinner so I could come back and check on you." The door opened wider. Wide enough to frame Bixie, jacket on, smile fading, eyes narrowing as she took in the bedside tableau. "But it appears my brother has the situation well in hand."

Chapter Thirty-Six

Through the millennia, we humans have contrived all sorts of strategies for forgetting. There's motivated forgetting, better known as suppression and repression, when the mind deliberately buries unwanted memories. In extreme cases, there's amnesia. But the most common form of forgetting is retrieval failure, also called cue-dependent forgetting, because it occurs when no cues related to the memory are available.

In case you're wondering, I know all this because of a marketing campaign I once worked on for a memory loss facility. The therapist heading up the project didn't seem to mind my incessant questions. So I just kept asking.

Retrieval failure was clearly at work on this particular night. There we were, the three of us, having an uneasy dinner at Arby's. Bixie was sulking over a baked potato. Andrew was studying his French Dip. I was struggling to pry open one of those little hermetically sealed packets of chemicals labeled "salad dressing" when, for no apparent reason, I flashed onto a brief phone call with Evelyn the day before.

"Omigosh," I blurted out. "I completely forgot about the powwow. Tomorrow."

"The what?" Andrew asked from behind a paper napkin.

"It's an annual healing powwow," Bixie answered for me as she peeled away the tin foil from her potato. "Somewhere near Christmas. Charles mentioned it. I'm meeting him there."

I threw the dented packet of salad dressing onto the table and pulled a fresh one out of the dispenser. "Well, Evelyn more than mentioned it. She explicitly invited all three of us." I didn't add that she was especially keen on Andrew attending.

"It completely slipped my mind." I put one corner of the new salad dressing packet between my teeth, yanked, and looked over at Andrew. "But you already have plans. Didn't you say you were heading out to Lost Lake to help your friend Tim with repairs on the cottage?"

He put down his cola. "Give me that damn thing." He held out his hand, palm up. "And, no. I agreed to help Tim with the cottage the day after tomorrow. If he even needs help. It all depends on how many of his five thousand cousins are still around." He tore open the packet with one deft motion and handed it back to me. "So I'll be there. After all, how many chances am I going to get to attend a powwow?"

* * *

Thus it was that, at ten-thirty the next morning, Andrew and I found ourselves at Bay Furnace walking across a vast expanse of grass bordering Lake Superior.

The space was dominated by a large fenced-in dance circle—maybe a hundred feet in diameter—with a canopy in the center for the drummers and singers. At one end, the emcee had set up a small stage and sound system. Rows of folding chairs were positioned around the circle, and beyond them, vendors were selling fry bread, sandwiches, soft drinks, coffee, bottled water, dream catchers, grandmother dolls, jewelry, drums, hand-carved pipes, beaded key chains, feathers, and bundles of herbs for smudging.

Everywhere we looked, we saw costumed dancers. There were young men, old men, boys of all ages, many of them in full regalia, handmade fringed trousers, beaded moccasins and vests, arm bands and headdresses. They were slightly outnumbered by the women and girls, most of them wearing colorful embroidered dresses with fringe along the sleeves and hems. Around their necks were beadwork pendants that bounced as they walked.

In the lull before the official start of the dance, while the musicians warmed up and the emcee did a sound check, the dancers congregated in small groups or mingled with the crowd.

I spotted Evelyn standing among the chairs with two costumed women. Feeling my gaze, she spun around and waved us over. When we were within reach, she grasped each of us by one arm. "Aniin. Hello. I'm so glad you both came. Now let me introduce you."

The older woman, Helen, was slightly familiar, a longtime friend of Evelyn's who had traveled from the Sioux to dance. But it was the other, younger woman who captured my attention. Slender, ballerina posture, hair plaited in long braids, she looked out at the world through large almond-colored eyes. What fascinated me most, though, was her dress. Cardinal red, the long skirt trimmed with row upon row of tiny elongated metal funnels. Like bells. Dozens and dozens of bells.

Placing a hand on the young woman's shoulder, Evelyn beamed at me. "Karin Niemi, Gem Waters. I especially wanted you two to meet before the dancing started." She squeezed my hand. "Gem is a jingle dancer. She dances for healing. Each one of the ornaments on her dress represents a person she's dancing for today."

I was startled to hear Andrew's voice break into the conversation and realized I'd forgotten he was standing next to me. "So many people in need of healing," he said. "There must be, what, a hundred or more jingles on your dress?"

Gem nodded. "It's my work. I'm called to it. I'm honored by it." She smiled. "And there are one hundred and seven now. I added two new jingles last night. By request." She looked at Andrew and me in turn. "One for each of you." At that moment, the emcee announced the opening procession. She and Helen turned abruptly. "We have to go now." Gem tossed the words over her shoulder. "Nice to meet you both."

As they hurried away, Andrew and I gave each other a what's-going-on look. But there was no chance to confer. By then, a small group of men had claimed the chairs directly behind us, and Evelyn was making more introductions.

I emerged from my brain fog just in time to hear her say, "...William

Stratton, the new chairman of the Sault Tribe of Chippewa Indians." He gave me a firm, dry handshake and paired it with a warm smile that reached his eyes.

Even before Evelyn's next introduction, I knew that William's companion had to be in the media. Slightly overweight. Haggard. Intelligent face. Seen-it-all-heard-it-all eyes. Small notebook in one hand. Extra pens in the upper pocket of his faded sport coat. "And this is Matthew Johnson," Evelyn said, "the editor and chief reporter for our tribal newspaper." In the brief silence that followed, Matthew offered an infinitesimal nod. "Karin is a writer," Evelyn went on, "and she was born in this area. So you two have a lot in common." Matthew's face told me he doubted that very much.

I reached out my hand, put on a smile, and got a quick handshake and a distracted how-do-you-do in return. I kept the smile in place. Whether or not Matthew Johnson knew it, he was going to be answering a lot of questions from this Anglo before the day was over. And there was no time like the present. I let him settle into his seat and arrange his gear before launching my conversational gambit.

"You know," I ventured, "this has been one of the oddest trips home ever for me." That earned me a noncommittal grunt. "The third night my friend Bixie and I were here, Ben Roberts died. We'd both worked for Ben when he had an ad agency in Ann Arbor. His death was a huge shock. But then to learn he was murdered." Silence. "Since Munising is part of your beat, you've probably been reporting on the story, no?"

"A little," he said in a gravelly voice. "Ben didn't have a lot to do with the tribe. Or Native American culture."

"Oh really?" I forged on. "That's not what I heard. I know that his good friend Meredith Wood has a Native Arts gallery downstate. Also, I heard through the local gossip mill that Ojibwe artifacts were discovered on Ben's property, some of them possibly having to do with burials. There must have been a lot of upset over that."

More silence. He had to have a button somewhere, and I was determined to find it and push it. Preferably before Evelyn stopped glad-handing and tuned into our conversation.

165

"I also heard that members of the construction crew working on Ben's house were convinced that some of the artifacts, a lot of them in fact, went missing. Do you know anything more about that?"

"You're pretty well informed, aren't you?" He spoke in the voice of a man who wanted nothing so much as to end the conversation he was in, permanently. "Let's just say I'm looking into it. As is the FBI. And the local police. And the Tribal Police. And the National Park security team."

"An accusation that serious—and, knowing Ben, probably true—must have ignited all kinds of bad feelings within the tribe."

"Bad feelings? Sure. What else would you expect?" His voice had a sharp edge. "How would you feel if someone disturbed the graveyard of your ancestors?" He pulled an eyeglass case from one of his sagging jacket pockets and slipped on a pair of aviator sunglasses. Then he cocked his head toward the other side of the circle, dense with spectators. "Tell you what. If you're so curious, I see half a dozen guys over there who worked construction on Ben's house. Some of them have also signed on to work on that new luxury condo development." He brought his face close to mine. "I'll be glad to introduce you."

I pulled back instinctively, sensing danger real or imagined. Was he threatening me?

He stood up. "In fact, I'll go talk to a few of them right now. Let them know how interested you are in the goings-on at Ben's place. I'm sure they'll be happy to rake up all those, what did you call them, bad feelings."

"No, don't bother." I spoke too quickly, and he knew I'd heard the message beneath his words. The warning. "It was just idle curiosity. None of my business really."

"No bother." He picked up his battered briefcase. "But you know, in my line of work, I've found it's best to let some stories reveal themselves rather than digging too deep too soon. The truth comes out eventually, if it's for the best. And it's often good to be at a safe distance when it does."

He stared at me for what seemed like a long time, but was probably only four or five seconds. "Nice to meet you, Ms. Niemi." Swinging his briefcase strap over one shoulder, he nodded, paused, and then spoke one word in a low, gravelly tone.

"Ayaangwaamizin."

As Matthew walked away, I heard Andrew's voice behind me. "You just won't let go of this, will you? That last thing he said. What does it mean?"

I kept my eyes on Matthew as he trudged to the other side of the dance circle, and started feeling twitchy when he stopped to chat with a short, heavily muscled man. They both looked my way.

"It means 'Be careful.'"

Chapter Thirty-Seven

Surveillance is my forté. After Andrew wandered off, I became so engrossed in watching Matthew and his bulky friend, who had been joined by two other equally bulky friends, that the sound of my phone nearly caused me to tip backwards in my folding chair.

It was Paul, calling to tell me he'd heard the news about Meredith. "The poor dear," he cooed. "How awful for her. Although she always did have what you might call precarious tendencies." He took a deep, satisfying breath, being subject to no such tendencies himself. "But what I really called about was to tell you that, since you don't want my company up there," I could hear the pout in his voice, "I've been doing some digging on my own, asking around about Meredith's sources for her Native American merchandise."

"I'm all ears." I stood up to give myself a better view of Matthew Johnson and company.

"Well, I happened to be talking with Gloria DeRoche. I'm sure you've met Gloria." I hadn't, of course. Paul moves in the world of beautiful people and rich folk who adore—and, more importantly, buy—his handcrafted furniture. He's forever name-dropping, and I've found it saves a lot of time to let him assume I know whoever it is he's dishing about.

Without waiting for an answer, he went on. "The word is that she and Ben had a fling some years ago and, somehow, they managed to stay friends. Very close friends. She and her husband—by the way, rumor has it he swings both ways—anyway, the two of them used to see Ben socially on a pretty regular basis. And in fact...well, never mind." Paul did a course correction, leaving me curious as to what arrangement might have existed between

Gloria, her husband, and Ben.

"Gloria told me, in the strictest confidence, of course, that Ben was supplying Meredith with a lot of artifacts directly from up north." Suspicion validated. Thank you, Gloria. "Which made me wonder if Audrey knew about their arrangement. I mean, she's been consulting with Meredith for years. Authenticating objects. Advising her on their value. Giving Meredith enough background for her to sound like she actually knows what she's talking about when she chats up customers."

He stopped for a quick breath. "I mean, what Ben was doing had to be a federal crime, no? And wouldn't that make Audrey an accessory? Or something?"

I took off my firebird cap and let the lake breeze cool my face. "It should be a crime," I agreed. "But evidently, the law is murky. There are all sorts of loopholes and exceptions."

Paul let out an exasperated sigh. "Well, this was way bigger than a loophole. From the sound of it, these handoffs were on the scale of grand theft. So the question is, do you think that the fear of being discovered might have driven Meredith to suicide? It's hard to believe, since she's always been so impervious to gossip and social shaming. Of course, she'd have to be, wouldn't she, hanging out with Ben all these years?"

I mouthed a thank-you as Andrew handed me an iced tea foraged from one of the booths. On the other end of the line, I could hear Paul munching on something. I suddenly wished I were in his impeccably decorated country kitchen, sitting down to a slice of his German chocolate cake and a long, delicious gossip.

"No, I don't think anything drove Meredith to try to kill herself," I said. "I think someone is trying to make us all *believe* that Meredith attempted suicide because she was overcome with guilt after killing Ben."

There was a gasp on Paul's end. "What? Meredith kill Ben? That's absurd. Cheating, yes. Lying, yes. Overcharging customers, sure. Maybe even a little low-key bribery, that I'd believe. But murder? She's simply not capable of it."

Glancing to my left, I could see Charles' tall, straight figure approaching from the road. On the lakeside, the opposite direction, Matthew and his friend were also heading my way. "I happen to agree," I said. "But I can't talk now. I'm at a powwow and things are about to get interesting."

"A what?"

"A healing powwow. I'll tell you about it another time. There's someone I have to talk to right now, whether or not I want to. Give David a hug for me."

When Charles reached our little circle, Bixie wrapped her arm around his waist. The gesture seemed to surprise Andrew even more than it did me.

"Beautiful day for a powwow," Charles said. He took off his Stetson—that man certainly knew his hats—and wiped his forehead with the back of one sleeve. "But heads up. Bill Harris arrived about the same time I did. I saw him parking his police cruiser. He was on the phone, but he'll probably be here in a couple of minutes."

Evelyn gave me a gentle nudge. "No worries. It's not about you, Karin, hard as that is to believe. It's part of the police department's community outreach. You know, goodwill and all that. Besides, Bill is married to a member of the tribe."

I turned to Charles, who was sipping at a travel mug Bixie had handed him. "If you don't mind my asking, why did the police call you in for questioning yesterday?"

His voice was cool and nerveless. "Oh, for all the obvious reasons. I'm an Ojibwe. Known as a collector of native artifacts. I'm also what you might call an advocate and what some people consider a pain in the ass. A troublemaker. I have a wide network of Ojibwe friends. And I'm the one who overheard the rumor about how Ben was murdered." He took a swallow of what I guessed was coffee. Somehow, I couldn't quite imagine him sipping contentedly at one of Bixie's herbal teas.

Just then, Bill Harris sauntered by, scanned our little group, nodded, and touched two fingers to the bill of his police insignia cap. I looked him up and down. Blue jeans. Running shoes. Badge displayed on a white shirt. His semi-off-duty look, I supposed. We all responded with nods and, in Evelyn's case, a smile.

170

Charles was the first to break the silence that followed. "Oh yeah, I almost forgot. Rumor has it that Meredith is going to be alright."

Alternating waves of relief and curiosity swept over me. "If it's true, that's great," I burst out. "I wonder if she can have visitors. I'd like to..."

"Don't even think about it." Heads turned as Andrew's voice whipped through the air. "She's probably still under police guard. Any visitors, if they're allowed, will be closely monitored. You turn up at the hospital, and you're going to stay on their radar screen."

At that point, Evelyn decided to pile on. "Really, Karin," she said in that scolding voice I remember so well from childhood, "that poor woman deserves to be left in peace. You probably just want to pump her for information." I tried to summon a look of outrage, but couldn't quite manage it.

Hands firmly on her hips, she let her eyes travel back and forth from Andrew's face to mine. "Besides, the Creator has blessed us with a beautiful day. There's a healer over there dancing for you two, and you should respect her enough to pay attention."

She nodded toward the dancers circling in time with the chants and drums. "The dance Gem is doing came down to the Anishinaabe through the dream of an Ojibwe brave, long ago. His wife learned the dance from that dream. Since then, generations of women have taught it to each other." She paused. "Look at Gem. She never turns or circles. She always dances forward, moving fast. It's hard, what she's choosing to do, hour after hour, for you and Andrew. So watch her. Show some gratitude. Let yourself feel the healing."

Evelyn's little talks never fail to whip me into shape. I immediately became an obedient nine-year-old again. Amazingly enough, her words seemed to have the same effect on Andrew.

"You're right, of course," he said. He put a hand on my back and, quietly, without another word, he and I walked over to the wire fence and gave our full attention to the dancers. Minutes went by. Gradually, the drumming, the chanting, the continuous rhythmic stepping and rocking began to work their way into my overheated brain.

Gem's concentration was complete and fierce. The summer sun seemed to set fire to the metallic bells on her skirt, giving the impression that she step-danced on a cloud of light. She never once glanced at either of us. Even so, I felt a deep connection, almost as if I were dancing alongside her.

Healing. She was dancing for my healing. For Andrew's healing. But healing from what? And for what? A sudden bout of dizziness sent me reeling against Andrew. He gripped my arms, asked if I was alright, and, when I didn't answer, guided me to a nearby chair, not letting go while he sat down next to me.

As he held me, the dizziness faded, and the world that had been in retreat came back into focus. I looked at him. It must have been a trick of the sun, but his face seemed to be lit from within. It reminded me of a portrait by Raphael I once saw at the Met. He really was beautiful. Did he know it, I wondered?

"I'm fine," I said and meant it. By the time I'd finished the bottle of water he brought back from one of the vendors, I felt like myself again. Only stronger. My thoughts more clear and certain.

Staring at the dancers, I experienced what old-time authors would probably call a moment of reckoning. I realized that now it wasn't a game. It wasn't a live version of Clue. It wasn't me just following Bixie's lead, playing at being girl detectives. It wasn't mere curiosity, not anymore.

This was personal. And serious.

Suddenly, I wanted to know. Really, deeply, absolutely, I wanted to know who killed Ben. More than that, I deserved to know. And even though the circle of suspects was too large for me to take on, even though the case could only be solved by the police with their vast resources and manpower, I owed it to myself to at least rule out all the people in my circle of acquaintance.

And that's exactly what I intended to do.

Chapter Thirty-Eight

Might as well start now.

Excusing myself, I headed off in the direction of the porta-johns, down a path lined with shredded cedar mulch. Sitting on a stump next to the women's toilet, I pecked out Paul's number. No answer. I left a message.

"Paul. One thing I forgot to mention. I need you to do me a favor, please. Find out everything you can about Devon and Audrey Roberts' finances. And while you're at it, ask about Meredith as well. See if any of them have serious money problems. Turn over some rocks. But do it discreetly, okay? Without raising any suspicions. Thanks." I breathed in the heady scent of pine needles. "Oh, and be careful. Very careful."

Turning my face up to the sun, eyes closed, I took a series of deep breaths, feeling calmer with each one.

"Are you alright?" I opened my eyes. The person asking the question was a large, kind-looking woman in a cheap, flowered blouse. Her wide face was filled with concern. With the sun forming a halo behind her, she could have been an oversized angel.

"I'm fine," I said, smiling. "Better than I've been in quite a while, actually. Thanks for asking."

Smile still in place, I headed back to the powwow, stopping in the forest shadows at the end of the path to scan the crowd. Evelyn was in animated conversation with Matthew Johnson and another man, mid-height, stocky, wearing a T-shirt, jeans, and a brown vest with something on it that gleamed in the noonday sun.

Spotting me at the edge of the clearing, she waved me over. Dear God, what had I set in motion? I can be such an idiot sometimes. A ripple of anxiety threatened to overwhelm the burst of determination set off by my powwow epiphany. Returning Evelyn's wave, I made a detour to where Andrew was standing, still engrossed in the dance. When I touched his shoulder, he gave a start, like a sleeper awakened mid-dream.

"Evelyn has someone she apparently wants us to meet," I said. "And if that thing gleaming on his vest is a badge, he's one of your brethren. Professionally speaking."

I've never been good at apologies. Blame my Finnish parents. In our house, the words "I'm sorry" were never spoken, and emotions in general were communicated telepathically, if at all. Still, as we walked around the perimeter, foot-dragging our way toward Evelyn and her companions, I felt compelled to offer, if not an outright apology, then at least an explanation.

"Whoever this guy is, I'm afraid it's my doing," I confessed. "I may have given Matthew Johnson the impression that I was interested in knowing more about the goings on at Ben's place during the construction. You know. The artifacts that were supposedly dug up and then supposedly disappeared." I swallowed so hard it made my throat ache. "And I also may have wondered out loud if any members of the tribe could have been so enraged they took the law into their own hands."

"You *may* have?" Andrew pulled down his sunglasses and shifted his eyes my way. "Why am I not surprised?"

As we got closer, I could see that the gleaming object was indeed a badge. Evelyn drew us into their little circle and introduced the newcomer as Jonathan LaPointe, which she pronounced the French way. "Jonathan is chief of the tribal police," she said, adding, "and Andrew is on the Ann Arbor Police force."

"I've been telling Jon about your interest in the artifacts at Ben's place," Matthew growled in his smoker's voice. "Evelyn explained to us that you worked for Ben and that you've been, uh, helping the Munising Police with their inquiries."

"Did she also explain that I've been questioned by them, not just once

174

but twice? And that I'm a suspect?" Evelyn gave me one of her "behave yourself" looks, which I chose to ignore. Feeling slightly reckless and just a little self-righteous, I kept going. "And did she tell you that someone tried to implicate me in Meredith Wood's supposed suicide attempt, which may actually be a murder attempt? Which is why I want to know more about other people's possible motives for harming Ben?"

Jonathan nodded in a commiserating kind of way, and the furrows in his forehead deepened. "I understand Ben was your friend as well as your employer," he spoke with simple dignity in a low, steady voice. "I'm sorry for your loss." He glanced at Bixie, who had just joined our group with Charles in tow. "Condolences to both of you."

His words threw me off balance. It was the first and only time anyone had acknowledged that Bixie or I might be among those who mourned the death of Ben, at least a little. "Thank you," I said, feeling oddly moved. "Ben wasn't a friend exactly. And he wasn't an easy person to know. But he was important in both of our lives, professionally and to a degree personally."

"Just so you know," Jonathan went on, "even if I could share information with you about the case, which I can't, the Tribal Police have fairly limited domains. Mostly, we deal with domestic abuse, fights, minor crimes, and accidents that involve members of the tribe, on Ojibwe property."

I nodded. "Of course, I understand. It's just that…"

"We're working with the local police and the FBI as well as the park service rangers, as needed," he went on. "But we're not on the front lines, that's for sure." He let his eyes drift toward the crowd and lifted his hand to someone behind me. "Still, it might interest you to know that even before Ben died, we were investigating some other angles in the alleged theft. Actually," he corrected himself, "more than alleged. We've got proof, including eyewitness accounts and receipts from a couple of people who purchased Ojibwe items from Meredith Wood. We're looking at possible options for prosecuting the case."

"Such as?" Andrew asked.

"Let's just say we're consulting on a pretty regular basis with legal professionals. There's some leeway in the federal laws, and these days there's more public support for Native American rights. That works in our favor." There was a brief pause. "Especially if the public isn't inconvenienced too much when those rights are honored."

Charles let out a sharp laugh, and I heard Evelyn whisper, "Ain't that the truth?" Jonathan gave a near-smile, but it was his eyes that told the real story. They looked tired. Not the kind of tired that comes from sleep deprivation or too much overtime. More like the kind of tired you see in the eyes of people who have to face down prejudice, deliberate and incidental, delivered on a daily basis in a constant, offhand, taken-for-granted way.

"That sounds hopeful," Bixie said.

"It does," I agreed. "But there's that old saying about justice delayed being justice denied. Are things moving fast enough to satisfy the members of the tribe?" I looked into Jonathan's weary, sun-strained eyes and resisted an impulse to give him a pat on the shoulder. "Have you given any thought to the possibility that folks might be angry enough to take matters into their own hands?"

That last question seemed to unnerve everyone. It's a gift I have.

During the long silence that followed, Evelyn did one of her classic eye rolls, Charles and Matthew gazed at me in an appraising way that masked God-only-knows-what emotions, Andrew put on his blank cop face, never a good sign, and Bixie stared not at me but at Jonathan, curious to hear his answer.

Sheriff LaPointe kept his cool and with a non-committal shrug said merely, "Of course we've thought about that. But the mode of the crime, the murder weapon if you like, makes it very unlikely that any member of the tribe was involved. Ben didn't have any Ojibwe household help, not cleaners or cooks or gardeners. He had no Ojibwe friends that I know of. Certainly none who would give him a bottle of wine he might consider worth drinking. Construction crew members were never allowed into the house. There were no reported break-ins. All of which leads me to believe that, while a few tribal members might have had, or felt they had, plenty of motive, they wouldn't have had either means or opportunity."

Looking relieved, Evelyn propped one hand on her hip, placed the other hand on my shoulder, and, without attempting to keep the triumphant note out of her voice, said, "Well then, that settles that. Ben wasn't murdered by an Ojibwe."

Jonathan allowed himself the suggestion of a smile. "Looks that way," he agreed. "But over the years I've learned that Yogi Berra was right when he said it ain't over 'til it's over."

The lake was still and windless. From his vest pocket, he pulled out an immaculate handkerchief and used it on the back of his neck. "I've found it's best to keep an open mind. I don't assume anything until a case is solved to my satisfaction." He gave his neck another swipe and looked at each of us in turn. "People are full of surprises."

In the uneasy seconds that followed, we all thought our thoughts. I forced myself to keep quiet as the conversation restarted and drifted on to other, less nerve-wracking topics. After a few minutes, I slipped away, explaining that I needed to call a client in Ann Arbor.

Which was almost the truth.

Chapter Thirty-Nine

Technically, it wasn't a lie. I planned to call Meredith, who does live in Ann Arbor and has been a client. Just not at the moment. Of course, the police had probably confiscated her cell phone, but they couldn't take away the room phone. Or could they?

I made my way to a lonely park bench on the edge of a small bluff about a hundred yards from the powwow and called information, wishing I had Bixie's new super-phone to find the number for me. The hospital operator transferred me to Meredith's room without question or hesitation, making my paranoid self wonder if she was under police orders to forward all calls for monitoring.

After two rings, there was a limp "Hello" on the other end.

"Meredith!" I burst out, then glanced over my shoulder at the distant crowd, wondering how far the sound had carried.

"Karin." Her voice lifted. "What a surprise. You have no idea how good it is to hear from you. I'm going stir crazy in this place."

We talked for a few minutes about her general condition. (Steadily improving.) When she was scheduled to be released. (Possibly tomorrow morning, possibly as soon as this afternoon.) When she'd know for sure. (Whenever someone decided to walk down the hall and deliver the damn paperwork.) Where she'd be staying. (A new room in the Holiday Inn.)

"But," I wondered out loud, "should you be by yourself if you're still feeling…" I searched for a nice, mushy, inoffensive word. "Fragile?"

"Oh, I won't be alone," she assured me. "Audrey is here. She's been spending hours with me every day. She even arranged for personal leave from the Art Institute."

Interesting. "Where's Devon?" I asked.

"He had to go back to South Carolina. Something to do with his work, an emergency of some kind." I'll bet. "But his trip was slightly delayed."

"Why is that?" I asked.

"Because he was the one who discovered me early that morning."

Somewhere in my brain, a little computer screen lit up "Really? How did that happen? If you don't mind talking about it."

She didn't mind at all. In fact, she seemed glad to finally have a sympathetic audience. "After you and Andrew and Roger left the bar, Devon and I went to my room to talk. We had a few drinks. Well, more than a few. That's when he told me he had to be at Marquette Airport the next morning to catch a seven a.m. flight. I remember him leaving my room around midnight. I checked my watch. By then, I could hardly keep my eyes open."

She stopped to take a long breath before going on.

"That's my last clear memory. Later, they told me that for some reason, Devon decided he wanted to say goodbye before he left. So around five a.m., he called. No answer. He waited a few minutes and called again. Two or three more times, in fact." She paused. "I always answer his calls. His and Audrey's. Always. So when he kept getting voicemail, he went down the hall and knocked on my door to make sure I was okay. Still no answer." Her voice wobbled. "Apparently, that's when he really got worried. So worried that he went down to the lobby and convinced the desk manager to unlock the door of my room. And they found me..."

There was a jagged intake of breath. Normally, I would have dived in with some attempt at comfort, but either because of the tempering influence of Evelyn, who has elevated listening to an art form, or my encounters with the local police, who, give credit where it's due, knew how to lay a conversational ambush, I kept silent.

In the background, an alarm went off, the kind of alarm that means a patient is in distress. Very faintly, I could hear staff calling for an emergency cart, stat. Despite the blazing sun, I felt a sudden chill.

When the voices receded, Meredith went on. "Honestly, Karin, it's all so bizarre. None of this makes sense."

"What do you mean?" I asked, assuming she meant that she was shocked and aghast at her actions.

"I have no memory, none whatever, of taking those pills. Of putting them in my drink. In fact, I didn't. I'm certain I didn't. I'd swear to that. But the police don't believe me." She sniffed back tears. "No one believes me. Not the doctors or nurses. Not Devon. Not Audrey. Not Roger. No one."

A few seconds ticked by. I stared at the glistening surface of the lake. Hearing a familiar sound, I lifted my head. Two noisy geese glided overhead in the clear air. Were they mates? Or just a couple of lonely survivors?

"That's not true, Meredith," I told her, fending off the memory of Jonathan LaPointe looking out of those tired eyes of his and warning us all how important it was not to assume anything. "Not true," I repeated, more to convince myself than Meredith. "I believe you. I believe you're telling the truth."

And, I was tempted to add, I'm going to help you prove it. Instead, I promised that Bixie and I would visit her very soon. Then I rang off and thought about how to do that.

It didn't take long to come up with a strategy for breaking free from my bull-headed bodyguard for the rest of the day. It was a plan perfect in its simplicity, provided, of course, that Andrew and the all-seeing, all-knowing Evelyn didn't suss me out.

By the time I made my way back to the group, Jonathan was gone, and Evelyn was explaining the finer points of Ojibwe ceremonial drumming, with an occasional assist from Charles. I moved into the circle next to Bixie, mentally rehearsed my lines, and waited for a lull in the conversation. When it came, I announced in a superbly offhand voice that I had to leave in a few minutes. "My Aunt Saimi is expecting me around three," I explained, "and I just remembered she asked me to pick up a few things for her at the drugstore." Nice touch, I thought.

I inched closer to Bixie, gave her arm a none-too-gentle squeeze, and said, "Bix, do you want to come along? I know Saimi would love to see you again."

Generally, Bixie does a miserable job in situations that call for ad-libbing.

But this time she surprised me, picked up on her cue immediately, and managed to give a halfway convincing performance. Freeing her arm from my grip, she turned on her hundred-watt smile. "Of course. I always enjoy spending time with Saimi." Still smiling, she rubbed her arm. "Should we bring her some of that special blend of coffee she likes?"

Special blend coffee? "Sure," I mumbled. "Whatever." No point in taking this subterfuge too far. All we needed was a plausible cover story.

I glanced at Andrew, whose arched eyebrows and tight smile made it clear he suspected ulterior motives, then at Charles, who was looking mildly puzzled at the sudden turn of events, and then at Evelyn, who thankfully seemed unperturbed. "Charles," I went on, "I hate to ask, but would you mind driving Andrew back to the cottage later so Bixie and I can be on our way?"

Charles was pleased to be of help to his new lady love and her friend. Evelyn was pleased at the thought of me visiting Saimi, who was not one of my favorite aunts. Bill Harris, who'd been eavesdropping during our conversation with Sheriff LaPointe, was likely pleased that we wouldn't be stirring up any more trouble or picking the brains of his fellow lawmen, at least not this afternoon. And Gem was pleased when I went over to the dance circle to offer my thanks, so pleased that she gave me a jingly hug.

In fact, as Bixie and I made our escape, I congratulated myself on the fact that everyone was pleased. And, better yet, no one suspected a thing.

Well, almost no one. As we walked toward the road, I could feel Andrew's eyes following us, step by step, until we rounded a turn in the road and disappeared from sight.

Chapter Forty

Because there was no way I could face the perils of the afternoon without something to eat besides Indian fry bread, and because I wanted to check out the Chicago Art Institute website and learn what I could about Audrey's Native Arts exhibit before we talked with Meredith, our first stop was Falling Rock.

On the way, I explained the plan to Bixie, who was delighted that we were on the case again and even more delighted that I'd finally come around to her way of thinking. As if. After placing our orders, we commandeered one of the larger tables. Then I opened my laptop and we pored over the Art Institute site. As expected, there was a big, splashy segment on the Native Arts exhibit. After scrolling through dozens of photos, I let out a frustrated groan.

"This is pointless." I reached for my iced coffee. "It's unlikely any of the artifacts from Ben's properties are in this exhibit, either as gifts or on loan. And even if they are, we have no way of recognizing them."

Bixie pulled the screen closer and started tapping at the keyboard. "Actually, we do," she beamed as she typed. "I'm sending Charles this link and telling him to see if his friends can spot any of the items that went missing. At least then we'll know whether someone—Ben, Meredith, maybe even Audrey—has been ripping off local Ojibwe relics."

"Great," I said, feeling a small thrill of excitement at the prospect of even a minor breakthrough. Then I reined myself in. "You do realize it's possible that the artifacts have nothing whatever to do with Ben's death, right? They might be totally unrelated. He could have been killed for a dozen different reasons."

Bixie tapped the send key. "Several dozen," she corrected me cheerfully. Still oozing satisfaction, she leaned back in her chair, gave her hair a toss, and smiled. "But even so, I've got a feeling there's some connection."

While I attacked a whitefish salad, Bixie called Charles, who promised to share the site with the men who'd worked on Ben's construction crew and get back to us if they spotted any familiar-looking artifacts.

After lunch, we headed to the local flower shop. There, under Bixie's close supervision, the florist put together a bouquet that would have been perfect for a royal wedding: no less than a dozen roses nestled in with lupine, zinnias, Asian lilies, baby's breath, and every kind of greenery imaginable. Digging through my wallet for my half of the bill, I calculated how many second-hand mysteries I could have bought at Aunt Agatha's Bookstore for the same amount of money. It came to nine books. Including tax.

Cradling the mass of flowers, now artfully trussed up in tissue paper, Bixie shrugged off my cheapskate attitude. "We want a lavish display of affection, right? And we both know that Meredith measures affection—and just about everything else—in terms of cash value."

That seemed a bit harsh. I pointed out that, in her current vulnerable state, Meredith would be overjoyed to see us if we walked in with a wilted cluster of field flowers.

There were no police cars, at least no obvious ones, in the hospital parking lot. We learned why when the crisply efficient nurse at the welcome desk explained that Meredith had been discharged. The route to the Holiday Inn took us back toward Christmas and the powwow, and I fretted over the possibility of crossing paths with Charles and Andrew on their way into town. Traffic was heavy, as usual, so I told Bixie to be on the lookout for Charles' car.

Fifteen minutes later, presumably unseen by Charles and Andrew, we stood in the carefully engineered rustic elegance of the hotel lobby. From the forest green walls to the plaid couches, from the deer antlers above the fireplace to the welcome desk made of fieldstone and varnished pine, the corporate decorators hadn't overlooked a single Up North cliché. After giving us a professional once-over, the cool blonde female behind the desk informed us that Ms. Wood was staying on the third floor, lake view suite number three-oh-seven.

Bixie was right in that Meredith was delighted by the bouquet. But after phoning the concierge for a vase, she set the flowers aside casually and seemed to forget about them. So I was right in that they might as well have been roadside daisies.

Once the mandatory hugs and air kisses were out of the way, I took in the floor plan and noticed open doors leading to two bedrooms. Plenty of space for a live-in nursemaid. As if reading my mind, Meredith said, "Audrey isn't here right now. She's off somewhere running errands." Or, I thought, conspiring with her brother on the phone. "She'll be sorry she missed you."

After liberating three small bottles of Perrier from the mini-fridge, we settled into identical overstuffed armchairs, forest green of course, that looked far more comfortable than they actually were. By way of consolation, the French doors leading to the balcony were open and, from where I sat, Lake Superior was on display in its full glory.

Camouflaging my curiosity with the most empathetic look I could muster, I leaned over and touched Meredith's hand. "Thank God you're alright. You've been through a terrible ordeal." I let a few seconds pass before getting to the point of our visit. "So tell us. What happened that night?"

Meredith used both hands to push back her heavy, dark hair and ponytail it away from her face, as if to clear her head. In spite of a hellish couple of days, she looked beautiful. Even with a bare minimum of make-up and smudges beneath her eyes, her soaring cheekbones and delicate features made me think of catalog models.

"I've already told you," she said in a tight voice. "Devon and I had a few drinks. We talked for maybe two hours. He left around midnight. I went to bed and, next thing I knew, I was waking up groggy as hell in a hospital bed, surrounded by IVs and tubes and wires and digital readouts. And some guy in a police uniform was sitting outside the door."

She sighed and threw back her head, as if directing her next comments to the Almighty. "They told me I'd overdosed on my sleep meds." Her voice cracked. "But I don't remember taking any. By the time Devon left, I was worn out. It had been a long day. So I literally collapsed into bed." She sat upright and gazed at Bixie and me in turn. "That's it. That's all I remember. I kept explaining to everyone who would listen I hadn't taken anything, beyond the drinks I'd had. But the doctors, the nurses, the police, everyone insisted that I'd tried to kill myself."

After a brief silence, Bixie spoke. "During the time you and Devon were in your suite, having drinks and talking, was he ever alone in the living room?" She leaned in toward Meredith. "Did you go to the bathroom? Or into the bedroom? Was he out of your sight at any time?"

Meredith took a few moments to reconstruct the sequence of events. "Well, sure, at one point I went to the bathroom," she said slowly. "And then I took a phone call from a friend and moved out onto the balcony for a little privacy. But why..."

Confusion and anxiety battled for control of Meredith's face. It took a few seconds before she realized what Bixie was implying. When she did, her eyes opened wide in outrage. "Wait a minute. Are you suggesting..."

"I'm not suggesting anything," Bixie said in the kind of mild, reasonable voice that tends to light the fuse of people, like Meredith, who are already well on their way to an outburst. "I'm just trying to figure out who might have had the opportunity to doctor your drink. If you didn't do it, then who did?"

"If you didn't call room service," I jumped in to deflect some of Meredith's growing upset away from Bixie, "and if you got your drinks directly from the mini-bar in the room, well, that narrows down the list of suspects considerably."

By now, Meredith was breathing hard. I guessed that her reaction was fueled by equal parts frustration, fatigue, fear, and whatever meds the hospital staff had dosed her with. "What you're implying is that Devon..." She let the sentence dwindle away into oblivion. "That's ridiculous!"

"Is it?" Bixie asked. "Why?"

Looking angrily first at Bixie and then at me, she stood up. "I don't want to talk about this anymore. I'm tired. I'm afraid I'll have to ask you to leave.

Now."

As she steered us toward the door, I said in a desperate voice, "Just one more question. Please. Do you remember calling Roger or me late that night? It's important."

Stone-faced, she jerked open the door and stepped back. "You need to go. Now."

With one last rueful glance at the water-starved bouquet which, given Meredith's current state of mind, was likely to end up either withered and forgotten where it now lay or upended in the trash, I trailed after Bixie into the hallway.

Back in the lobby, I spotted Audrey heading toward the staircase with a leather tote bag. Even from the rear, her trim figure and designer haircut were unmistakable. With a queasy feeling in the pit of my stomach, I wondered how she'd react when Meredith told her about our visit.

We drove back to the cottage in complete silence. Almost. After the first mile, I did point out that I couldn't ever recall spending forty-two dollars and getting less out of it. In response, Bixie gazed straight ahead at the traffic and murmured, "Let's wait and see what happens. Right now, she's in shock and denial. It's going to take a while for her to think through what we talked about."

By the time I pulled into the cottage parking area, we were both utterly dejected. Andrew was on the back porch, leaning against the rail and drinking something out of a coffee cup.

He watched in silence as we approached, looking like a man at peace with the world. It was out of character for him. And very unnerving. As we approached the steps, he lifted the cup in greeting. "Welcome back."

Studying our faces, he took a sip and savored it for a few seconds before adding: "So, tell me. What did Meredith have to say?"

Chapter Forty-One

I looked at Bixie, expecting at least a spark of defiance, but got a hopeless little shrug instead. Ignoring her defeatist attitude, I rallied. "Why would you think..."

Without losing his equanimity—what was in that coffee mug anyway?—Andrew cut me short. "Why? Because I'm suspicious by nature. Because it's exactly the sort of thing you two would do. And because I know you both better than you'd like to believe." He grinned. "Give it up, Karin. I'll get the truth one way or another."

"Okay, fine," I held up my hands. "Make me one of whatever it is you're drinking, and I'll tell you the whole sordid tale." I started moving toward the cottage door, then stopped. "And if you pour Bixie a glass of that Chablis in the back of the refrigerator, she'll probably cooperate, too. When she finally gets back." I glanced over at her, but she was miles away.

Within five minutes, my shoes were off, my purse was perched on the naugahyde hassock, my phone was on the coffee table, and I was nestled into a corner of the couch with a cup of Andrew's daily special. Three parts coffee, one part scotch. Bixie, who appeared to be back on the earth plane, was holding an oversized glass of Chablis and trying to make herself comfortable in the rocker. Andrew had refreshed his own drink and surprised me by taking up residence on the other end of the couch rather than his usual choice of the La-Z-Boy.

Suddenly, the couch seemed smaller. Much smaller. I inched back further into my corner nook. Why, I couldn't say. Maybe it was all those awkward memories of high school make-out sessions on the family sofa. Or maybe it

187

was something else I preferred not to think about.

Bixie and I were halfway through our story—which included an account of her ridiculously expensive bouquet—when my phone sounded and a familiar number appeared on the screen. I stood up. "Gotta get this. Paul promised to do some digging for me." I headed for the back door. "And, yes, I'll tell you what he's found."

Paul was exultant. "I am so, so good at getting people to dish. Although," he admitted, "it wasn't all that hard. Ben's death is pretty much the talk of the town. It was the most natural thing in the world for me to be asking questions about him and his nearest and dearest. No one suspected a thing."

I hoped he was right about that.

Without waiting for a response, he powered on. "So, who shall we start with? Ben, we already know about. The man was filthy rich."

I took a fortifying sip of scotch-enhanced coffee before answering. Why had I never thought of this combination? "Devon, I think, since he's at the top of my suspect list." I neglected to mention that he was there because I disliked him and was hoping that whatever Paul had uncovered would keep him in the number one spot.

"Right." I could hear the sound of notebook pages being turned. "Here we are. My main source was an investment banker, guy named Doug Phillips. He's a client of mine who also happens to be a frat brother of Devon's. Delt Sig, I think." As if it mattered to anyone but Paul. "They tend to attract poor little rich boys. For instance…"

"Paul, could you stay on topic, please? I really want to know what you learned."

After letting out a snort, he continued. "So anyway, Doug was very careful about what he said. Cryptic. Kept throwing around vague terms like 'major reversals' and 'negative assets.' But the net result is that although Devon isn't on his uppers, he's got money problems. He sustained some big losses, and it sounds like he's living beyond his means. I got the sense that he'd managed to get himself into some serious debt. And he'd been counting on Ben to let him into the Sand Point condo project, and maybe even *give* him shares. Which, of course, would be way out of character for his father."

Interesting. In my mind, the whodunit meter edged closer to Devon. Much closer. Then I realized that Paul was still talking. "On the other hand, he's got a six-figure job with some real estate investment firm in South Carolina. Or maybe it's North Carolina. Oh, and I nearly forgot, although it may not be important, his wife is getting pretty close to calling it quits."

"It could matter," I said, mentally filing that entry, "depending on how much alimony she wants. So what about Audrey? Did you turn up anything on her?"

"Oh yes." More page-flipping noises. "Audrey is a cipher. I talked with Anna Sommerstadt. She teaches at the U of M art school and was Audrey's mentor or advisor or whatever they're called these days. She's one of the people who helped Audrey land that cushy job at the Art Institute."

I shook my head in amazement tinged ever so slightly with admiration. "Is there anyone in Ann Arbor you don't know?"

Paul had the grace to think for a moment before answering, "No one of any consequence. Now, where was I? Oh yes. Anna told me that Audrey really loves her work as a curator. Feels that she's found her, let's see, what did Anna call it? Ah, yes, her place and her purpose. Nicely put, don't you think? Also, during all the years they've known each other, Anna said the subject of money has never come up. Ever."

The plebe in me couldn't resist such a perfect opportunity for snarkiness. "Don't you think that might have a little something to do with the fact that if things ever got tough, she could always tap into daddy's bank account?"

"Maybe," Paul admitted. "But Anna seemed to think that despite her upbringing, Audrey really isn't driven by money."

My brain started clicking. "Alright, let's say money wasn't a motive for her. What about loyalty? Love? In this case, for her brother. Audrey and Devon have always been close. She's very protective of him. You have to wonder how far that might go."

"Oh, Karin." I hated it when Paul used his brush-off voice on me. "I think that's highly unlikely, and so do you. But you haven't asked about Meredith."

"I thought we agreed she didn't belong on the suspect list," I bristled. The lake breeze had temporarily disappeared, and the rising heat seemed to activate my temper. "And what's her motive? Ever since I've known her, she's given the impression of having a fairytale life. Big swanky house. Vacations to die for. And I'm guessing Ben gave her money from time to time."

On the other end of the line, Paul made a lip-smacking sound. "Well, hon, it turns out that fairytale life of hers really is a fairytale. It's all done with smoke and mirrors. The house was part of her divorce settlement years ago. And the exotic vacations are just her tagging along with well-endowed friends. She's always been a kind of status-symbol socialite, someone people like to say they know. So there's never a shortage of rich folks who are delighted to host her at their lodge in Snowbird or loan her their condo in Puerto Vallarta. According to my sources, she spends every dollar she makes and then some." He made that irritating, self-satisfied smacking sound again.

"But she could always rely on Ben," I felt compelled to point out. "Which would make keeping him alive one of her top priorities."

"But could she rely on Ben?" Paul challenged. "He was a notorious bully. And everyone knows that when it came to women, his cock was like a weathervane."

"Paul!"

"Sor-ry," he said in a singsong voice. "I always forget about your Midwestern modesty. I love you dearly, Karin, but that prudish streak of yours does get tiresome." He took a breath. "Look, I'm just laying out the facts. And the fact is that Meredith's life with Ben was about as stable as Jello. If she's really close to the edge financially, she might have decided that Ben was worth more to her dead. She's bound to be in his will. Even Ben wasn't enough of a bastard to cut off his mistress of more than twenty-five years."

I wasn't buying it. "Look, I know grief. And from what I've seen, hers is the real thing."

"Is it?" I didn't like the smug tone in his voice. "Don't forget, she has a graduate degree in theater. And she spent several years doing summer stock and trekking around the hinterlands, starring in second-rung productions of Broadway hits. The woman knows how to put on an act."

My brain reversed course. If true, that last bit of information cast a new and troubling light on the scene in Meredith's suite. Had Bixie and I been a gullible audience of two, watching a performance meant to convince us that Meredith was a victim and not a murderer? Had she staged a fake suicide attempt to cast blame on Devon?

"Brilliant job, thanks so much," I said, eager to end the conversation and go off by myself to puzzle over all these new facts. "Just one more question. How is Albert doing?"

Paul gave a giggle. "Absolutely fine, of course. He ambles around the house as if he owns the place, regal as all get-out, allowing everyone to adore him. The only thing missing is a little cape and crown. He's pretty much taken over as the alpha pet. And of course, Marlowe is only too glad to oblige. He follows Al around like, well, like a dog."

"Which he is," I pointed out.

Paul released one of his trademark drama queen sighs. "Yes, but it's so pathetic, the way Marlowe will traipse after Al from room to room, keeping his distance, never giving up, waiting humbly for a glance, desperate for a crumb of affection. Which never comes."

In the background, a door slammed shut. I heard David's voice followed by a joyous bark. "Actually," Paul went on in a sly tone, "the situation reminds me of you and Andrew. With you being Albert, of course, and Andrew, well…"

In response to my gasp, he added. "Do you really think no one notices all that sexual tension? And don't deny it." Before I could protest, he galloped on. "A word of advice. Several words, actually. First, although Andrew is definitely not my type, I can see that he might have a kind of Daniel Craig appeal. You know. Good looking without being pretty. Vulnerable and dangerous at the same time. I suppose one could do worse."

I began to fidget.

"Second," he went on, "you deserve to be happy. Third, Terry would agree. You should ask him." He stopped to take a quick breath. "And now I really have to go. Bye. Love you."

Chapter Forty-Two

As I stood there, motionless, staring at the lake without seeing it, phone still at my ear, the back door gave its signature creak. A hand landed gently on my shoulder, and Andrew reached around me with a coffee mug. "I thought you might be ready for a refill."

I took the cup, held it with both hands, and inhaled the scent of coffee and scotch. "Good timing. Thanks."

His hand stayed where it was, resting on my right shoulder. A harmless, probably absent-minded gesture. Nothing more. But it made me realize how much I missed being touched. I thought about women I know, women who live alone and who, in rare moments of self-disclosure, have admitted that they sometimes schedule massages, chiropractic sessions, haircuts, even dental exams simply because they crave the touch of another human being. They're that desperate for physical contact.

I used to pity them. Now I was one of them.

Thankfully, Andrew was not a mind reader. "Bixie called the Brownstone Inn," he informed me.

"For dinner reservations? Tonight?" I sipped gratefully at the coffee. "Good luck with that."

"That's what she thought. But it turns out somebody had just cancelled, so she snapped up that time slot. We've got a table for three."

I love the Brownstone Inn. The cozy atmosphere, the fireplace, the solid, vintage look and feel of the place, the generous drinks, the made-from-scratch food that never disappoints. Even so, I resisted. "Thanks, but I think I'll pass." Damn, but that coffee went down easily. "It's been a long, strange day, and I need time to think. Or maybe not think."

"Too bad." With elaborate casualness, Andrew stepped around me, and we stood side by side on the tiny porch, almost touching. "A couple of hours ago, I got a call from my friend Paul."

That snapped me out of my reverie. "The friend on the Marquette Police force?"

"The very same." Andrew gazed at the lake as if he were barely aware of my presence. "They've turned up some new evidence. I thought you and Bixie might like to buy me dinner, ply me with liquor, and see how much you can get me to tell you."

I thought about the forty-two dollars and change I'd blown on flowers for Meredith. This was clearly a better investment. "Bribing an officer? Count me in."

"Good. We should leave in about twenty minutes." He swiveled around, opened the door and then, almost as an afterthought, leaned over and whispered into my ear, "And don't forget, you promised us a full replay of the conversation with *your* Paul."

Right. My Paul and his words of advice. For the next ten minutes, as I repaired my makeup, combed the wind-snarls out of my hair, and swapped my polo shirt and blue jeans for a blouse and dress slacks, I indulged in what my twelve-year-old nephew would call a pity party. Why were people so presumptuous? So parental? So directive? So intrusive? Why were they always throwing advice at me? Always so certain of what I needed to do? Was it just one of those unavoidable widow things? One of the many penalties of being a woman alone? Had Terry's death shoved me automatically into the category of Poor Lost Souls? Even worse, did I belong there?

Fortunately, my lousy mood evaporated when Andrew pulled into the inn's crammed parking lot. As we arranged ourselves at a table near the fireplace, opened our menus, and placed our drink orders in voices loud enough to be heard over the cheerful, hungry crowd, the tensions of the day began to fade.

When my mineral water with lime arrived—I needed a clear head—I launched into an edited version of my conversation with Paul. By the time our dinners were being served, Andrew and Bixie had a fairly detailed account of the phone call. Minus the last bits, of course.

"I can't believe Paul is so hot on the idea of Meredith as the murderer," I said, dipping my fork into a mound of mashed potatoes.

Andrew unfurled his napkin. "Oh, I don't know. I can see her doing it, if she was desperate enough for money and certain enough of getting a decent legacy from Ben. But money is just one possible motive. There's also love. Or jealousy. Which is in the same neighborhood."

"Right," Bixie chimed in, and I realized how unusual it was to hear her agreeing with her brother. About anything. "Marriage was never part of Meredith's arrangement with Ben, and she always seemed okay with that. But who knows? Maybe Ben was seeing someone else. He often was. And maybe he liked this new someone else enough that Meredith felt threatened."

I turned to Andrew. "Okay. You know what *my* Paul discovered. Now tell us what *your* Paul had to say."

"I'll tell you what I can." Andrew sampled the schooner of beer next to his plate. "Starting with heated arguments between Devon and his father, some public, some in the context of meetings with Ben's fellow investors. According to reports, Devon was frustrated to the point of rage at being left out of the Sand Point condo project. Believe it or not, he also objected, strongly, to the way Indian relics were being treated on the work site. He and Ben used to go at it hammer and tong."

Abandoning her salad, Bixie leaned forward, eyes glimmering. "And that wasn't the only major source of tension between them. About a year ago, Meredith hired me to design some signage for her. During one of our meetings, we got to talking about Ben and the agency. She told me how upset he was that neither Audrey nor Devon was interested in taking over his share of the business. He and Devon had huge blow-ups about it. I also remember her saying that when Devon is upset, he can be ferocious. That he has his father's temper, and you never know what he's going to do."

For the first time that evening, Andrew looked directly into my eyes. "Well, that should make Karin happy. She's not a big fan of Devon's. In fact, I have a feeling she's got a vested interest in proving that he was the murderer."

I slammed down my fork with a clatter, exasperated. The thirty-something couple at the next table, upscale tourists from the look of them, interrupted their moon-eyed, hand-holding conversation to stare at me. I leaned in and lowered my voice.

"So, basically, we now know pretty much what we already knew or suspected. Ben was probably killed over money. Devon has a bad temper. Meredith might have a motive for murder. Might. The rest is pure guesswork. We know nothing about Ben's investors. Or the dozens of people who hated him for all kinds of reasons." I leaned back in my chair and stared up at the ceiling beams.

In that moment, I was not only frustrated by all the dead ends and circular arguments and lack of facts and baseless suspicions. I was bored. Weary. Tired of maybe's and what-ifs. Tired of guesses that went nowhere. Tired of knowing too little to really know anything.

"This is useless." I shoved my empty plate away. "We might as well be running on a gerbil wheel."

If I hadn't deserved it so much, I would have resented the I-told-you-so expression on Andrew's face. Head cocked to one side, arms crossed, he couldn't resist saying, "You just now realized this?"

For a few seconds, I studied our server, Louise, who was on the other side of the room next to the long mahogany bar, joking with the bartender. Louise. A bottle blonde in her fifties with beautiful eyes, time-worn skin, and a perpetual smile. The owner's sister-in-law, who'd been a fixture on the wait staff here for years. She had a passel of kids, a ramshackle house, and a husband with so-so health and a spotty job history. Yet she was always cheerful, always radiating homespun serenity, always glad to see you, whoever you were. How did she manage to be so happy with her lot in life? Maybe someday I'd ask her.

"I think we all need a break from this case. At least for a while." Brother and sister stared at me. "Really," I added for emphasis. "I'm serious."

My phone, lying forgotten next to plate, went off. I glanced at it and wished I hadn't. Roger. I tossed it into my purse.

On the screen above the bar, the Marquette weather woman was back, flashing that perfect smile of hers and waving long, tapered fingers at a blue line labeled "cold front" just to the west. A click of her remote control and she was pointing to a list of temperatures for the week. Tomorrow. Overcast. High of fifty-five. We were about to experience one of northern Michigan's weather whiplash events.

"It's supposed to be cool tomorrow," I said without moving my eyes from the screen. "Highs in the mid-fifties. Not great tourist weather." I turned back to my companions. "I'm thinking it might be a good day to visit some lighthouses and maybe stop at Ilsa and Jalo's for a sauna."

I looked at Bixie. "Interested?"

Instantly, a blush spread across that flawless Dante-Rossetti face of hers. "I can't," she said, avoiding my eyes. "Charles has the day off, and he plans to work on his house. He just finished re-flooring the downstairs, and I promised to help him pick out paint and new window treatments. And we might drive to Marquette to look at living room furniture."

Andrew gaped at his sister, and I realized I was doing the same. Sleeping with a man is one thing. But redecorating his house for him? That elevated the relationship to a whole new level of intimacy. Clearly, things were far more serious than I'd realized.

"Sounds like fun," I said carefully before turning to Andrew. "What about you? Ready to pick up our tour?"

"Sorry," he shook his head. " I promised to help Tim and his army of cousins make some repairs to the cottage roof tomorrow morning. No idea of how long it's going to take."

"Okay." I drummed my fingers and took a few seconds to recalibrate. Louise was clearing the table next to us. She must have felt my gaze because she turned toward me and winked, as if we shared a secret. It gave me a good feeling.

Andrew broke into my thoughts. "So what are you going to do?"

"I don't know yet," I admitted. Louise's smile was contagious. "But whatever it is, I'm going to enjoy it."

Chapter Forty-Three

I t had been quite a while since I entered a room and walked in on a naked man. Or, as my grandmother would say, as near to naked as makes no difference.

Of course, I shouldn't have been entirely surprised. Andrew's jeep was in the parking area, so I knew he was back from the cottage disaster site. And it would be reasonable to assume that, after a morning of dirty, sweaty work, he'd head directly for the nearest shower.

Even so, it was a shock to nudge open the door, peer over the top of the grocery bag I was clutching, and see him stroll leisurely across the living room holding one of Evelyn's skimpy towels around his waist, more or less. Well, less actually, since the towel had slipped down a considerable distance.

I'm not a prude. Honestly. Despite what Paul may think. I like men. Back in my single days, I dated what sometimes seemed like too many of them. Or at least my mother and her sisters saw it that way.

When Terry came into my life, I was smitten. We both were. And during our eighteen years together, the romance never ended.

So there's nothing shocking to me about men's bodies, clothed or otherwise. But still, it was a jolt, returning from a mundane errand just before noon and being greeted by all that bare male skin. Besides, as Edmund Burke famously observed, it's upsetting when "all the decent drapery of life is rudely torn off." If I'm not mistaken, he also said that the age of chivalry is gone. Too true.

Unfortunately, Mr. Burke's eloquence eluded me at that moment. Struggling to keep a grip on the bulky, lopsided bag of groceries in my arms, the best I could manage was a startled "Oh!"

In contrast, Andrew registered nothing more than mild surprise and amusement. In fact, if I didn't know better, I'd say he was enjoying the moment and my obvious discomfort. He stopped, hiked up his towel a few inches, and said simply, "I didn't expect you back so soon." Then he settled in for a chat. "You know, I'd forgotten what it's like to do heavy construction for hours. I got to the cottage before seven, and we worked like stevedores all morning. I can't remember the last time I sweated that much. But we did finish most of the repairs."

The towel slipped again, and he tweaked it up. Hard as it was, I managed to keep my eyes on his face, for the most part.

Showing no interest whatever in getting dressed, he came close and peered into the grocery bag. "I hope there's more beer somewhere in there. I finished off the last one before I got into the shower."

"I did," I stammered, readjusting the bag in my tired arms. "I mean, I do. Have more beer." Grateful for an excuse to turn away, I lugged the bag across the room and deposited it with a thud on the kitchen counter. "It's in the car, with the rest of the groceries."

"Need any help?" Even without turning around, I could tell from the tone of his voice that he was enjoying this.

Okay, if that's the way we were going to play this scene, so be it. "No, I'm fine," I turned to face him. "I can handle it." Slowly and deliberately, I let my eyes scan his body, inch by inch, top to bottom, then back up again. "Besides, you'd probably be more comfortable if you put on some clothes."

He grinned. "Well, I think one of us would be more comfortable anyway." Still grinning, he moved toward the bedroom. "I'll help you unpack the groceries after I'm decent. And we can discuss our plans for the afternoon."

"Our plans?" I echoed.

"Our plans." He spoke in that in-charge tone I hadn't heard for a while. What I thought of as his cop voice. "After that escapade with Meredith, you and my sister are on a short leash. Letting you two go off by yourselves was a tactical error on my part," he shook his head. "And it won't happen again. Charles is keeping Bixie out of trouble today. But you..." His grey eyes focused on me in an unsettling way. "I'm not letting you out of my sight. Consider yourself on probation."

Ten minutes later, a fully dressed Andrew was in the kitchen, helping me put away the groceries. When that was done, we sat down with some of the snacks I'd bought. The hummus, lentil chips, and organic salsa were for Bixie. The cashews, cheese curls, pretzels, potato chips, and sour cream dip were for those of us with more normal appetites.

After downing a handful of cashews followed by a beer chaser, Andrew was ready to work out the afternoon's schedule. "So, what are we doing for the rest of the day?"

It was an awkward question, considering that I'd agreed to meet Roger at the new coffee shop in town at one-thirty, just a little over an hour from now. He promised to tell me what he'd discovered in the last day and a half. I also wanted to call Sandy and see what the Channel Six news team had churned up.

But now here I was, sitting at a kitchen table, trying to stare down my self-described parole officer. "Well," I began, "considering the weather, I hadn't planned on doing much of anything." Thick grey clouds and a stiff northerly wind made it feel more like October than June. "I need to stop at the ATM to get some cash. Then I thought I'd pick out a novel at Falling Rock, head over to the new coffee boutique, check my emails, and settle in with my book and some lunch."

I helped myself to more potato chips and pulled the dip a little closer. "So I won't be doing anything that requires a chaperone. You'll just be bored."

Andrew tossed back the last of his beer. "Bored sounds good right about now. And I need to get some cash too. Let's go. I'm ready for a small-town afternoon." He put down his glass and pointed at my left shoulder. "What's that?"

Damn. A wayward hot flash had swept over me, so, without thinking, I'd peeled off my sweater and was now sitting across from Andrew in a tank top. I looked at my upper arm and the ugly purple and yellow-grey smears Roger had put there.

"It's nothing," I mumbled. "Just a small accident. I was clumsy."

Andrew came over to my side of the table and touched the bruises gently. "And who gave you this accident?" He traced each of the finger marks, fading but still visible. "One of the things you learn in my line of work is how to read injuries. I've seen this kind of bruising too often in domestic abuse cases. It must have hurt like hell. So…I repeat…who gave you this accident?"

He seemed to tower over me. From where I sat, I had a clear view of his clenched jaw. Without waiting for an answer that he knew would be a lie, he went on. "Never mind. I can guess. The flowers. The profuse apologies. The begging for another chance. It was Roger, wasn't it? That sonofabitch."

"He was just tired." I twitched my shoulder out from under Andrew's hand, hating myself for defending indefensible behavior. "He didn't realize what he was doing."

From the grim look on Andrew's face, I guessed that his next encounter with Roger was likely to be a memorable one. Especially for Roger. At first, I wondered if it might be best to bring Andrew with me to the coffee shop and get that inevitable, messy encounter over and done. With me there as mediator, explainer, umpire, and—I glanced up at Andrew's tensed jaw line again—possibly bailiff as well.

But watching him as he cleared the table, studying the cold fury of his face, I realized what a terrible idea it was, bringing those two together today. If there was one thing this so-called vacation didn't need, it was another disaster, another incident that ginned up gossip and drew the attention of the police. Grabbing my phone, I went outside to call Roger and reschedule.

After the fourth ring, with me rocking foot-to-foot and willing Roger to pick up, I left a lengthy voicemail. I counted to ten, then called again and left another message, not bothering to hide the rising panic in my voice this time. Finally, after sending a text by way of back-up, I told myself that, even if Roger didn't get the messages, or even if for some crazy reason he chose to ignore them and pursue a secret death wish he'd been harboring, even if he showed up as planned, all I needed to do was keep Andrew away from the café.

And how hard could that be? No problem, I told myself firmly, sidestepping the sense of foreboding that was making itself at home in a shadowy corner of my mind. No problem whatsoever.

Chapter Forty-Four

The thing about small-town afternoons is that they tend to be filled with chance encounters. Pleasant and otherwise. This particular afternoon was no exception.

For starters, if I hadn't been standing at the ATM waiting for Andrew to finish his banking business, I wouldn't have heard Bob Worthington call out my name in his booming, jovial voice. In addition to being president of the credit union and director of half a dozen civic organizations, he also happened to be a sort-of family friend and, when I was a kid, a sort-of uncle to my brother and me.

In his navy suit, blazing white shirt, and burgundy-and-blue-striped banker's tie, he was easy to spot among all the tourists. Except for the addition of maybe ten pounds, he looked—and sounded—the same as always.

"Karin, nice to see you." I shook the hand he held out and was oddly comforted by the strong, warm grip that time hadn't altered. "Home for a visit? Or home for good? I know your aunts would love to have you back up here."

"Just a vacation, unfortunately," I said before introducing Andrew.

"Well, you certainly picked an exciting time to come back. What with Ben Roberts getting himself killed." He spoke in a matter-of-fact way. No titillation. But then he'd never been a gossip. Of course, he didn't have to be, since he knew just about everyone in town and most of their secrets. "You worked for Ben for a while, didn't you? In that ad agency of his? And I'm sure I saw you at his open house last summer."

"That's right, I was there." What a memory. "I remember Ben kept wanting to talk about the new condo development on Sand Point. He was fixated on it. I'd never seen him that excited about anything. What do you think of the project?"

Bob straightened his already straight tie. "I'm all for it. And the chamber of commerce is behind the development one hundred percent. It's exactly the sort of thing this town needs."

Before I could launch into my elevator speech on the importance of preserving the quality of life in small towns and how all those millions would be far better spent on affordable housing for locals, Andrew jumped in. "So then, the project is going forward without Ben."

"Oh, absolutely," Bob assured us. "There's a strong, committed team of investors behind it. In fact, I happen to be part of that group." Of course, he was. The Worthington clan had been involved in local real estate since there *was* local real estate. There's never been a commercial project of any importance that didn't include at least one member of the family. Bob's smile widened. "And as these things go, it's been smooth sailing. Generally."

His face clouded over, and his gaze strayed across the downtown landscape. "There were a few issues recently, but nothing we couldn't handle. And they've all been resolved now." The look of professional serenity returned. "Things are proceeding as planned. In fact, the site prep is completed, and we're hoping to break ground early this fall."

"Resolved…now," I repeated. "Are you saying that Ben's death put an end to whatever problems there were?" Hearing myself ask the question, I was slightly appalled at my audacity.

Bob had a sudden urge to clear his throat several times. Finally, being careful to avoid eye contact, he dismissed my question with a curt, "Of course not. Why would you assume that?"

Snapping back into his convivial businessman mode, he looked over at Andrew and winked. "I've known Karin since she was a little girl. I was just starting out back then. Her father and I were friends. She was always getting into mischief. Cute as a bug, but a real troublemaker. You just never knew what she'd say or do next."

Andrew gave a knowing nod. "Interesting, isn't it, how some things never change?"

After tugging at his tie one last time, Bob put out his hand. "Well, I've got to get back to the office. Good to see you, Karin. Pleasure to meet you, Mr. Murray."

Andrew's face took on a thoughtful expression as we watched Bob stride away with his usual dignified swagger. "Right out of central casting, isn't he?" It wasn't a question. "Tough as hardtack beneath that friendly exterior, and nearly impossible to tip over. Although, true to form, you managed to upset his equilibrium."

Before I could answer, a tall figure moved into my peripheral view and came to a stop next to me. I turned slightly and found myself face to face with none other than Bill Harris. Two encounters in two days. Mere coincidence? Or was the guy keeping tabs on me?

"Good afternoon, Ms. Niemi," he touched his hat. "Lieutenant Murray. Getting some cash before you head out of town for the afternoon?"

"Actually, we aren't planning to go anywhere today," I said, sounding more defensive than I'd intended.

"Oh, but there's so much to see and do up here. No sense in limiting yourself to Munising. I'm sure the lieutenant would enjoy Tahquamenon Falls. Or the Soo Locks. And then there's Iron County. Plenty to explore there, including that big indoor-outdoor museum of theirs. And he really shouldn't leave without seeing the Keweenaw Peninsula."

His voice sounded mild enough, but the aviator sunglasses made it impossible to gauge his real feelings. Although, I could make a good guess.

"Why, Officer Harris, if I didn't know better, I'd say you were encouraging me to spend as little time in Munising as possible."

"Just pointing out a few of the UP's many attractions, Ms. Niemi. All of which your guest would enjoy. Well, have a good day." He touched his hat again in a parting gesture, took a few steps, then stopped, did an about-face, and walked back.

"I almost forgot to tell you." He took another step toward me, darted a glance right and left as if to make sure we wouldn't be overheard, and pitched his voice to a stage whisper. "Khoury did it."

I blanked out. Total synapse failure. For a couple of seconds, I experienced the weird sensation of momentary amnesia that occurs when you think you've just heard something you should understand, but don't. "Khoury? I…I don't know any Khoury."

The lieutenant shook his head. "Of course you do. Khoury is the one who killed Barry Hazen."

Light dawned. Fugue state ended. Synapse restored. "You mean… You're talking about the characters in *Death of a Demon*. The Nero Wolfe novel I'm reading."

"That's right."

A small, outraged sound escaped from my throat. "But I haven't finished the book yet. And you just ruined the ending."

Bill Harris gave that cold smile he specializes in. "Think of it as a little reminder, Ms. Niemi." The smile disappeared. "A friendly warning not to ruin the ending for me and my colleagues." He seemed to grow larger as he spoke. "I've told you before, and I'm telling you again. For the last time. In the presence of a witness. Stay out of this case."

The chilly smile returned. He nodded at me and then at Andrew, who—was it possible?—seemed to be struggling mightily not to burst out laughing.

One more tip of the hat. "You have a good day now."

The lieutenant was halfway down the block when Andrew gave up trying to contain himself and let out an explosion of laughter that nearly doubled him over.

"It's not funny…" I began.

"Oh…yes…it…is," he said, gasping for air. "My God, that was perfect. Caldwell is going to love this when I tell him."

That would be Detective Sergeant Moses B. Caldwell of the Ann Arbor Police. My nemesis, although he'd tell you that he nearly saved my life once. Of course, I only have his word for that, since Paul beat him to it.

"And now," Andrew said, wiping his eyes with the tissue I handed him, "where's that new café you were talking about? I could murder a cup of coffee and a sandwich."

Chapter Forty-Five

I was still fuming and Andrew was still chortling when we arrived at Café du Lac. The word chortle, in case you're interested, was invented by Lewis Carroll and is assumed to be a cross between a chuckle and snort, which is exactly the sound Andrew was making at the moment. What finally silenced him was the sight of Roger across the street, about to enter the town's Chinese-Thai restaurant. Ignoring Andrew's death ray stare, Roger made an "okay" hand gesture, pointed to his phone, and then at me. Which explained the text message alert that had pinged in my back pocket a minute earlier.

Before I walked through the door Andrew held open for me, I made a guess as to what was waiting for us inside.

In my experience, Up North coffee shops and cafés tend to fall into three basic categories. In category number one are the franchises, convenient and predictable. Category two includes the vintage restaurants that have been in business longer than anyone still drawing breath can remember, whose owners somehow never got around to that long-promised sprucing up, and whose virtually unchanged interiors—always with knotty pine paneling—have now taken on a nostalgic appeal. In category three are what I call the IKEA cafés: pared-down decor, light oak furniture, supersized windows, and pale walls lined with photographs of lighthouses, forests, agate-lined beaches, waterfalls, and the occasional doe with fawn. Even if they're sitting in a mall parking lot, these places make you feel as if you're drawing in deep breaths of crystalline lake air.

Café du Lac was a category three.

Once we'd settled on a table with a view of the marina and Andrew had walked over to the counter to place our orders, I pulled out my phone. There it was. A long, luxuriant text message from Roger. Despite his many failings—too many to count, really—that man writes the best, most entertaining texts of anyone I know. He gives free rein to his writerly impulses, never uses one word when two will do, never stints on verbal flourishes, never tosses in irritating acronyms or abbreviations, and never passes up an opportunity to slip in the occasional literary reference. Brilliant texting could very well be Roger's one redeeming quality.

I tapped the "open" key, eager to learn what he'd uncovered in the last... I did a quick calculation. Was it really just two days since the police interrogations? After checking to make sure Andrew's attention was fully focused on the woman behind the counter, I began reading:

Thanks for letting me know Sir Galahad is on his high horse yet again. The man must have saddle sores by now. In return for alerting me to present dangers, here's a juicy morsel or two for you to think about, proof of my remarkable journalistic skills and dogged determination. Meredith was—and likely still is—having an affair with one of Ben's fellow Sand Point condo investors, Jerry Rhinegold by name. Actually, he's the developer, and Ben was the lead equity investor. Rumors abound. Evidently, there was a constant battle of wills. Clash of the Titans. I'm looking into his background now, also scavenging for answers to all the obvious questions: Did Ben know about the affair? Was the midnight hot-tub rendezvous Meredith's attempt to patch things up, stay in Ben's good graces, and salvage her chunk of his estate? Was the situation desperate enough that she was prepared to take more drastic measures? For whatever reason, you seem to be willing to grant her a pass. I'm not. All for now. Vive la Vérité!

There was a second text as well:

When you get bored with that overgrown Boy Scout, as you most certainly will, you know how to reach me.

I was rereading Roger's text for the third time and pondering the questions he'd posed when Andrew arrived carrying a tray loaded down with two bowls of fish chowder, sides of coleslaw, home fries, a steaming mug of coffee, and a café latte with—could it be?—extra foam. He began transferring all the items from tray to table with the practiced skill of someone who had worked as a server during his high school summers.

"Omigod," I burst out. "I think I'm in love."

Lifting the last side dish from the tray, Andrew placed it next to my plate. "I've always been amazed at the intensity of your relationship with food." He stowed the empty tray on the adjoining table before sitting down. "Makes me wish I was a turkey sandwich."

By the time half of my meal had disappeared, I felt strong enough to converse. "I'm guessing you're not interested in discussing Ben's murder." I picked up my last lonely fry and pointed it at his plate. "Are you planning to eat the rest of your coleslaw?"

"Good guess about Ben's murder," he said, and pushed his half-finished plate of slaw to my side of the table.

"Thanks." I picked up my fork. "So then you probably wouldn't be interested in knowing that Meredith was having an affair with one of the investors in the condo project. I mean, one of the investors other than Ben."

"Well, that should give Harris and his team another set of motives to untangle. I don't envy them." Dead end.

While I finished the coleslaw and considered my next conversational gambit, Andrew sipped his coffee and studied the other customers. Only then did I realize that the table he'd chosen had a view of every table in the restaurant as well as the kitchen door.

"Anyway," he continued, "as intriguing as that rumor may be, there's nothing we can do about it except speculate. So why don't we give Bill Harris a break and get out of town?" I waited. "The sun doesn't even think about setting up here until nearly ten. We have plenty of day left."

"And exactly what destination did you have in mind?" I asked.

He refolded his napkin and toyed with his empty coffee cup. "Well, for years I've been hearing stories from you and Bixie about that aunt and uncle of yours in Marquette. It seems as if they've practically adopted her." He did some more staring into his cup. "I'd like to meet them. So, unless you think they'd object, maybe we could pay them a visit." He studied my face. "What's wrong?"

"Just a little surprised, that's all."

Time for some quick thinking. I had to do something with him this afternoon. A quiet session at the library, catching up on emails, could only last so long. And I didn't relish the prospect of hanging around the cottage all afternoon, just the two of us. I wasn't in the mood to fight off mobs of tourists for a glimpse of Miner's Castle. Aunt Ilsa and Uncle Jalo liked company and always enjoyed meeting my friends. The more I thought about it, the better it sounded.

"Okay, fine." I reached for my phone. "I'll see if they've got anything planned for this afternoon."

Andrew put down his napkin and glanced at his watch. "Great." He stood up. "While you do that, there's something I need to take care of. Just a quick errand. I won't be long."

As I expected, Aunt Ilsa was delighted at the prospect of finally meeting Bixie's brother. "Although," she added, "I have to warn you. Jalo had two cords of wood delivered this morning, and that Wiltanen boy is so lazy he just dumped the whole load in the front yard. You know how Jalo is. He hates mess, so he's determined to get all the wood moved out back and piled up in the racks by the end of the day."

Perfect. I was ready for a little payback. "Tell Uncle Jalo to hold off on that. Help is on the way." I smiled contentedly at the thought of Andrew hauling and stacking damp, fresh hardwood after a morning of heavy labor on his friend's cottage. It would serve him right for his general high-handedness, the way he'd ambushed my day. And who knows? I might even pitch in myself. I've always loved the smell of fresh-cut wood.

"Well," Ilsa said doubtfully, "we'll see. In the meantime, I'll tell Jalo to fire up the sauna."

After calling Bixie to let her know where her brother and I were heading, and leaving a message for Sandy with the passive-aggressive receptionist at the news desk, I treated myself to more coffee and theorized as to Andrew's whereabouts. A few minutes later, he walked back into the café wearing the face of a very satisfied man. "Well, that's handled," he announced.

Handled? A tiny alarm went off in my brain. I looked up at him, hoping he hadn't created too much of a scene with Roger.

"Ilsa and Jalo are looking forward to seeing us," I told him. "In fact, they even invited you to try out their sauna. You should feel honored."

"That's great." He hesitated. "But tell me. Just out of curiosity, why are you wearing your evil twin smile?"

"Oh, puh-leeze." I busied myself with my purse and jacket. "You're on vacation, remember? You really need to let go of that professional paranoia you carry around." I stood up. "This is going to be fun."

Chapter Forty-Six

When we pulled up to the grey clapboard house I knew so well, it was evident that Ilsa had not exaggerated the laziness of young Wiltanen. The haphazard pile of wood was a blight on the otherwise immaculate yard. After Andrew had been introduced and received his requisite hug from my aunt—because, after all, his sister was practically a member of the family and that made him a near-relative as well—he volunteered to move and stack the wood.

After a few cursory rounds of Jalo protesting and Andrew insisting, my uncle gave in and agreed he could use the extra muscle. I offered to be part of the work detail, but Jalo dispatched me to the kitchen to help Ilsa finish her latest batch of raspberry jam and cut up vegetables for the mojakka. Given the fact that my uncle enjoys having me as his DIY sidekick, and given the fact that he knows I can heft wood as well as most men and better than most women, I could only assume he wanted some time alone with his guest.

Half an hour later, twelve jars of raspberry jam had been liberated from their boiling water bath and were resting on a wooden rack, and I had moved on to washing and peeling vegetables for the stew. My solace was the garden window above the sink, which offered a panoramic view of the backyard. From what I could see, Andrew was doing the lion's share of the work, shifting logs into the large cart Jalo had attached to his riding mower and then loading the wood into racks behind the garage while Jalo supervised and made sure each piece was stacked in precise alignment.

It could have been the onions, but as I watched Andrew take on the brunt of the labor and somehow manage to spare my uncle's ego while doing it, my eyes started burning, and one tiny tear escaped. As I said, probably just the onions.

Finally, when every stick of wood had been stacked to Jalo's satisfaction and they were back inside swigging down well-deserved beers at the kitchen table, Ilsa went out to check on the bathhouse stove. She returned a few minutes later, stood in the doorway, and announced that the sauna was ready. For the men.

It's hard to describe the look on Andrew's face when it became clear that he'd be steaming and sweating with Jalo rather than Jalo's niece. Actually, it was a lot like the look men get when they open a gift envelope for what they think are, say, tickets to an NFL game and then discover the tickets are actually for the ballet or, worse, the opera.

Taking pity on his bafflement, I tried to explain. "It's a long tradition. Men always go first, women and children afterwards. Think of it as the reverse of what's supposed to happen on a sinking ship or a downed aircraft. It's been that way as long as I can remember." Truth is, that ridiculous men-first thing always rankled me, even when I was a tyke.

"So then," Andrew wondered out loud, "men and women never take saunas together?"

Ilsa's hazel eyes had a distinct twinkle as she answered, "Oh no. Not unless they're married. That changes everything."

Thirty minutes later, Andrew and Jalo reappeared in the kitchen looking rosy and relaxed. By then, the mojakka was simmering on a back burner, and a rhubarb-strawberry pie was cooling on the kitchen counter, so Ilsa and I grabbed a couple of bath towels and went out to enjoy our own long, languorous sauna. Sitting in the steamy heat and sluicing my back with a birch bough soaked in cold water, I could feel the tensions of the past week melt away.

By the time dinner had ended, the kitchen had been picked up, Ilsa had filled the back seat with two weeks' worth of home baking, and she and Jalo had waved us off in the deepening twilight, I felt calmer than I had in weeks.

The sound of my phone a few minutes later was jarring, as if someone had banged a gong next to my ear. I assumed it was Bixie, calling to see how the visit went or when we planned to be back at the cottage. Instead, I found myself looking down at Meredith's number. I let it go to voicemail, tapped the speaker button, and upped the volume.

"Karin. It's Meredith. I'm calling to apologize for the awful scene I made in my hotel room the other day." Her voice was slightly breathless, with undertones of desperate sincerity. "This past week has been a non-stop nightmare, what with Ben's death and the police and the hospital and the reporters. Even so, I was way out of line, tossing you out the way I did." There was a brief silence. "To tell you the truth, I'm beginning to wonder if you were right about Devon. It's a horrible thought, but..." Another pause. "I know you and Bixie were just trying to help. Can you forgive me? I feel I need to apologize in person. How about getting together sometime tomorrow? Lunch. Dinner. Drinks. Whatever works for you. Give me a call. P..." My phone cut off at what I assumed was a "Please."

Authentic remorse? Or a first-rate performance? I looked down at the screen and remembered Paul's comment about Meredith's stint with summer stock and off-off-Broadway. "Why do I have the feeling that something very unfortunate could happen if I met with Meredith?"

"Probably because you're finally letting common sense and survival instincts win out over that crazy idea you and Bixie had about tracking down the murderer." Andrew kept his eyes on the road as he spoke. "Or murderers."

Normally, I would have bristled. Instead, I let myself fall back into stillness and watched in silence as the darkening landscape slipped past under a purple-tinged sky. But gradually, insidiously, that so-called crazy idea—to get to the truth about Ben's death—tiptoed back into my brain. I began to wonder, would it be worth the risk, whatever that risk might be, to meet with Meredith and learn what I could about Jerry Rhinegold?

I was still considering the question when we drove into the cottage parking lot twenty minutes later. Charles' SUV was parked next to Bixie's car. Despite their obvious romance, Bixie spent her nights at the cottage. Of course, she never was one to bunk in overnight with whatever man she happened to be dating. Regardless of how late in the evening or how early in the morning it might be, she always insisted on getting home for at least part of the night, as if to separate herself from any sticky, permanent, public commitment. The fact that she'd kept the habit going with Charles surprised me. But then, that was Bixie. Predictably unpredictable.

It took us a while to collect all the items from the back seat—jackets, hats, my purse, grocery bags packed with Ilsa's baking, plastic totes stuffed with bathing suits still damp from the sauna. As we approached the cottage door, I expected to walk in on a relaxed end-of-day conversation. Instead, Bixie and Charles were huddled on the sofa. She was clutching a tumbler filled with what looked like watered-down brandy, an afghan around her lap, and Charles' arm around her shoulder. On the table was a half-empty cup of coffee. Both of them looked grim.

While Andrew assessed the situation from the doorway, I dropped my bags on the nearest chair, rushed over to the couch, and sat down next to Bixie, book-ending her between Charles and myself. "What's wrong?" Through the afghan, I could feel her shaking. "What happened? Tell us."

Bixie stared down at the glass she held in both hands and released a sigh. "On the way back to the cottage, I had one of my intuition attacks. That's what you always call them. It was this overwhelming sense, a feeling of absolute certainty that we needed to go to Ben's house. That something was happening there, something that wasn't right." The glass vibrated slightly, setting off a tinkle of ice cubes. "So we did."

The silence that followed seemed to last a long time. Too long for Andrew. "Well?" he demanded. "*Was* something going on there?"

Bixie lifted her head and met her brother's eyes. "Oh yes," she said in a monotone. "Yes, there definitely was."

Chapter Forty-Seven

Gradually, the full story came out. The story of how, when Charles was driving her back to the cottage, Bixie had an overpowering impulse to check on Ben's place. An intuitive compulsion was how she described it. According to Charles, she was so definite—his polite way of saying "hysterical," which, knowing Bixie, was probably closer to the truth—that rather than argue, he drove up Sand Point Road. Approaching the house, they saw lights on inside and an SUV parked in the driveway.

Charles had shrugged it off. "I thought it was probably someone from the FBI or maybe the local police. But Bixie insisted that we should take a look, in case something illegal was going on." Exactly what she shouldn't have done, exactly what Bixie would do. "So I doused my headlights. We parked at the entrance and then walked to the house, to see what we could through the windows."

For one crazy moment, I felt envious. "Did you see who it was?"

Bixie stared at me with glassy eyes. "Yes. It was Devon."

Charles chimed in. "We must have made some noise, moving around outside the house, because he disappeared. Next thing we knew, the flood lights were on and he was walking toward us." Charles took a quick breath. "With a gun in his hand."

I studied Bixie's blonde hair, white canvas jacket, and tan-colored jeans. "Well, you weren't exactly dressed for a raid. You would have been easy to spot, day or night."

Ignoring my comment, Charles continued. "We explained how we'd seen the lights and got concerned that someone had broken in."

Under his breath, Andrew muttered something that included the words damn and stupid. "Then what?" he demanded. "Did Devon tell you what he was doing there? Why he was rooting around his father's house while it was still officially off limits?"

"Sort of," Bixie said. "He said he was looking for some important legal documents. I assumed it had to do with Ben's will or maybe the condo development. Anyway, that's when he apologized for pulling the gun on us."

Andrew squeezed his eyes shut for a few seconds, his equivalent of counting to ten. "Okay, so just to be clear. You two barged into an official crime scene, leaving footprints and God knows what else in the way of evidence, and then you confronted the murdered man's son, who had much more of a right to be there than you did, and who was armed with a pistol."

"From where I stood, it looked like a Glock," Charles added, almost as an afterthought. He reached for his coffee cup and went into the kitchen for a refill, no doubt relieved to have even a temporary reprieve from Andrew's relentless grilling.

"Technically, we didn't confront him," Bixie insisted. "We were just observing him."

"Wrong," Andrew countered. "Technically, legally, you were trespassing, interfering with a police investigation, compromising evidence, and stalking Devon."

Always prone to dramatic gestures, and forgetting that she held a full glass in one hand, Bixie threw open her arms in protest. I felt a cold spray on my legs, even through the jeans. She didn't seem to notice that her hands were wet. "That's not fair. At the time, it seemed like the right thing to do. We were conscientious passers-by, concerned that a crime might be taking place."

"So you illegally crossed a crime scene barrier in order to…what? Make a citizen's arrest? Is that what you're going to tell the police?"

"Tell the police?" Bixie echoed. Clearly, that particular course of action had not crossed her mind until this moment.

"Of course." By now, Andrew's voice was rising dangerously. "Are you saying it hasn't occurred to you?" For a split second, I had a weird flash. In

216

my mind's eye, I saw Bixie and Andrew as teenagers, staging a major fracas with their mother as referee. Only their mother had my face.

Before Andrew could toss any more verbal grenades, I cut in. "Okay, enough." I made my voice as strong and loud as I could from a sitting position while sopping up Bixie's wine spatters with a napkin. "Let's ratchet this down a little."

"Fine, I need some air anyway." Andrew threw the words over his shoulder as he stalked out the back door. After a few seconds, I took Bixie's glass into the kitchen, wiped it down with a paper towel, filled it with a judicious mixture of brandy and water, and followed Andrew outside. For a while, we stood in silence, breathing in the night, listening to the hypnotic sound of waves lapping at the shore. I took a sip, handed the glass to him, and gave words to the unspoken question that hung in the air.

"Are you going to tell Bill Harris what happened?"

"Legally and professionally, not to mention ethically, I am bound to do that." He lifted the glass. "Besides, someone has to."

"I know. But is that someone going to be you?"

He took a swallow and let out a ragged sigh. "Hell if I know."

"If you do, what will happen to Charles and Bixie? Will they be charged with all the offenses you rattled off?"

"Probably not." He put the glass on the railing, rubbed the back of his neck, then dropped his head back and stared up at the night sky. I did the same and let myself be awed and amazed, as I always am, at how many more stars are visible in these clear, far northern skies. "I laid it on pretty thick, to put the fear of God in them. Fact is, the police have a lot of discretion in cases like this, when citizens trespass on crime scenes. If they press charges at all, which is doubtful, it will be for a misdemeanor. Most likely, they'll both get off with a warning."

He turned toward me with the beginning of a smile. "Although maybe not. You and Bixie have made such a royal nuisance of yourselves that the sheriff will probably be tempted to lock my sister up and throw away the key. At least until the case is solved. And I wouldn't blame him."

In the seconds that followed, I experienced what Margaret would call a minor epiphany. Bixie would refer to it as a shift in consciousness. Evelyn would say I was seeing, in the true sense of the word. Seeing with more than just my eyes, seeing with my heart. No filters. No defenses. No expectations or suspicions.

What I saw was a genuinely good man. In some ways, a beautiful man. Well-intentioned. Overconfident. Sometimes overbearing. Weary. Frustrated. Secretly worried. I saw a man dealing with a personal crisis and a high-pressure job who dropped everything and drove four hundred miles to keep his sister and her friend from being wrongly accused of murder. And he did it knowing full well it would be a thankless task.

Without thinking, I moved closer to him, put my hand on the side of his face, and kissed his cheek. And then, in a voice as soft as I could make it, I whispered, "Thank you."

"For what?" We were so close I could feel his breath on my face.

"For coming all this way to rescue two women who refuse to cooperate in being rescued. For not giving up. For sleeping on an army cot. For putting out all the fires that Bixie and I keep accidentally lighting." I moved my hand from his cheek to his chest, just over the heart. "And for other things, too. For being so kind to everyone I care about. For helping Jalo and making sure he didn't take on more work than he should. For charming Ilsa. For liking Evelyn. For all of it. Thank you."

Whatever irresistible impulses Andrew or I might have followed in the next few seconds will remain forever a mystery. Just then, the back door burst open, and Bixie came out in a rush. "Alright," she announced, sounding strong and determined. "Here's what Charles and I have decided..." She paused and took in the scene. "...to do."

Andrew and I moved apart like two guilty teenagers. I was grateful that the light from the cottage was dim enough to camouflage my face, which at the moment seemed to be burning.

"Sorry for interrupting whatever it was I interrupted," Bixie went on. "But I wanted to tell you. Tomorrow morning, first thing, I'm going to call the Munising police and tell them what happened. How we were taking a late-night drive up to Sand Point Beach when we noticed that the lights were on in Ben's house and decided to check it out and then, well, all the rest of it."

Andrew cleared his throat. "Good. That's exactly the right thing to do." He steered her back through the open door. "There are just a couple of things I want to coach you on, both you and Charles, so you know what to expect." Except for a slight hoarseness in his voice, he sounded like his normal, bossy, brotherly self.

I stayed on the back porch until the door closed. Then I walked down to the beach and took refuge in my old friend, the unreliable but intrepid Adirondack chair. The night air carried a hint of autumn, a warning of what was to come, making me grateful for the fleece jacket I wore.

I pulled up the hood, crossed my arms to conserve body heat, and settled in for what could be a long session. After searching the sky for a minute or so, I located the Summer Triangle. Vega, Deneb and Altair. Three bright, burning stars from three different constellations.

"Terry," I whispered into the chilled night air. "It's me, hon. Have you got a few minutes? We need to talk."

Chapter Forty-Eight

Being an early riser has definite advantages, especially when cohabiting in close quarters. Usually, I have the coffee pot and television to myself for at least half an hour. I like it. I like the solitude. I like savoring that brief, blissful transition between waking and doing, when time is temporarily suspended. I like not having to be "on." But when I padded out of my bedroom, bleary-eyed and bare-footed, I discovered that the day had already started without me.

Andrew was standing near the TV set, decked out in chinos and a T-shirt, coffee mug in hand, watching with rapt attention as Sandy delivered the morning's news. Bixie stood next to him, dressed in an elegant summer pantsuit, intent on wrangling her mass of hair into something resembling a French twist.

According to the cockeyed clock in the kitchen, it was six fifty-one, give or take, and the room was drenched with sunlight. When I emerged from the bathroom a few minutes later, face scrubbed and teeth brushed, Andrew handed me a cup of coffee. Strong, no sugar, lots of cream. Exactly the way I like it. I inhaled the fumes and exhaled a thank you.

Glancing up at him over the rim, I contemplated what kind of super-genes he and his sister must have inherited. At a time of day when normal human beings are dazed and disheveled, those two were glossy, groomed, and primed for a photo shoot. "Any late-breaking news on Ben's murder?" I asked.

"Not much," Bixie answered while checking the contents of her purse. "Except a quick mention that the police have started looking into various business dealings of the Sand Point Development Group." She closed the zipper, stepped into a pair of two-inch heels—she really was dressing to intimidate this morning—and adjusted the purse strap on her shoulder. Like a female gladiator preparing for a match in the forum, I thought. Or a female Sherpa—are there female Sherpas?—adjusting her backpack before scaling mountainous heights.

"I phoned the police station around six this morning and left a message for Bill Harris. The call-back came about ten minutes later." She glanced at her watch. "They want me to come by at nine to make a statement. I assume they'll call Charles in separately. So I'm heading out now to meet him for breakfast and make sure we're both on message. Wish me luck." She gave me a quick hug, leaving the scent of lavender in her wake.

Andrew and I listened expectantly. Within a matter of seconds, the parking lot echoed with the sound of an engine struggling to turn over. Andrew grinned at me. "Care to wager how many times she has to crank the starter before that rattletrap fires up?" I bet a quarter on five tries and won.

Feeling a need to fill the quiet, I cast around for something to say. "So, did you manage to get any decent sleep on Eleanor's army cot?" Lame, but better than silence.

"I did. In fact, I slept better than I have for weeks," he said. "Except I had the weirdest dream." Not being fond of dream talk, I tensed. Andrew looked out the picture window at the lake. "I dreamed about Terry." He glanced at me half apologetically. "That doesn't upset you, does it?"

Of course it did, a little. "No, not at all," I shrugged. "So what happened in the dream? Did Terry say anything?"

"Not a word. He just stared at me for a long time. It was really intense. Almost as if he were trying to read me. Probe my thoughts. Then…" Andrew shook his head. "You sure you want to hear this? It's hardly worth telling." He took my silence for a yes. "Finally, he nodded. Just once. Very slowly. And then he disappeared." He gave a short, almost nervous laugh and stopped when he saw my face. "I told you it was weird. What do you think it means? What was he trying to tell me?"

I held my cup in both hands to keep it steady. "I think you'll figure it out.

It can take dreams a while to reveal themselves. Anyway, you should be asking Bixie, not me. She's the resident authority on dream interpretation."

"Right. Well, enough of this." He put his coffee mug on the counter. "I've got to finish dressing and get myself to Marquette. I'm meeting Paul for breakfast, and then he wants to show me some of the local sights. He mentioned the lighthouse at Whitefish Point."

"Ah, yes, the oldest light on Lake Superior." I gently pried the TV remote out of his hand. "Also known as the graveyard of the Great Lakes." I punched up the volume. "Wear comfortable shoes. And make sure to bring plenty of insect repellent."

He stopped at his bedroom door and turned back to me. "Can I trust you to stay out of trouble while I'm gone? And stay off the case?"

"Do you even have to ask?" I headed toward the refrigerator and the organic eggs that Bixie had bought at the local farm market. Two of those with a couple of slices of Aunt Ilsa's rye bread would see me through the morning nicely.

I yanked open the drawer underneath the stove, which always sticks, and pulled out a cast-iron frying pan. "If you must know, after breakfast I'm driving into town where I plan to find a quiet corner table at Falling Rock, order myself the most decadent latte they make, and catch up on emails. There must be dozens clogging up my In Box by now. Then at ten, I need to call a client at the Michigan Business School."

"New project?"

"You could say that."

The fact is, this particular client happened to be an expert in real estate development, and I planned to pick her brains in the hope of discovering some possible links between Ben's death and the condo development. I told myself it was purely an intellectual exercise, nothing more than mental gymnastics, something that couldn't possibly get me into any trouble. Or, rather, any additional trouble.

Three hours later, with all emails read, answered or trashed, with a second supersized latte in easy reach, and with a fresh legal pad and two pens at the ready, I dialed the office number of Professor Roberta Wang.

I'd met Bobbi a few years back. She was one of the featured faculty in a series of profiles I was writing for the Business School's alumni magazine. The idea was to inspire donors to give big by showing them the amazing things their dollars could achieve. And in Bobbi's case, they achieved a lot.

She was a trophy hire for the school. Before entering the rarefied realm of academe, Bobbi was an enfant terrible, a major player in the world of real estate development. Her specialty was high-end residential and commercial projects in urban centers. Miami. Chicago. Manhattan.

During the course of my work, we'd become friendly—in an arm's-length sort of way. These days, we get together every month or so for coffee and conversation.

I'd texted her late the night before and hadn't expected to hear back until this morning. But being one of those super-high achievers for whom sleep is optional, she was awake and intrigued enough that she agreed to give me half an hour of her time this morning.

"Hey, Karin." Her voice was as bracing as ever. Bobbi always has energy to spare and, when she's speaking, every sentence seems to end with an exclamation point. As a result, conversations with her often leave me a little breathless. "Before we start, tell me. Why this sudden interest in real estate development? Did you win the lottery? Or did a rich uncle die and leave you a fortune?"

I played my ace. "Neither. It has to do with Ben Roberts' death. Or I should say murder." I sneaked a quick sip of my latte.

"But I thought you swore off sleuthing after that last, uh..."

"Fiasco?" I finished the thought for her. "I did. But then two days after I arrived up here, Ben had the misfortune to get himself killed less than a mile from where I'm staying. For a while, I was a minor suspect. Now I'm just an interested bystander. Very interested."

"A suspect." Bobbi gave a long whistle. "That couldn't have been fun."

I continued. "It seems Ben was the lead equity investor in a major real estate development here in Munising. Luxury condos on Lake Superior. There was supposedly some friction between him and the developer, and I'm thinking there may be a connection between that friction and his death.

I need to try to figure this out, just for my personal satisfaction. No other reason." Except maybe to show up the local police in general and one aggravating lieutenant in particular. To solve the case before they did, at least in my head. "Problem is, I don't know anything about the inner workings of real estate developments and what could make a developer feel threatened enough—or furious enough—to commit murder."

Silence, followed by a burst of Bobbi energy. "Okay, I'm in. Buckle up. You're about to get a thirty-minute graduate seminar in the bloodthirsty art of putting together a real estate deal. Including some killer strategies that would make Machiavelli swoon."

Chapter Forty-Nine

If there's anything more frustrating than solving a murder case and having no one to tell, I can't imagine what it would be.

As Bobbi talked me through structures and stratagems, all the vagrant facts and bits of truth that had surfaced over the past week fell into place—in a completely unexpected way. Paradigm shift. By the time our conversation ended, I knew the why of Ben's murder. And the who. Or, rather, the who's.

I knew. But what of it? Being persona non grata with the local constabulary, I could hardly race over to the police station, blurt out my discovery, and expect to be taken seriously. Or even be allowed on the premises. I couldn't tell Bixie, since she was tucked away in one of their cozy interrogation rooms. Same for Charles. By now, Andrew was probably somewhere north of Paradise and likely in one of the UP's famous dead zones. Evelyn was in the midst of a busy morning at the Ojibwe Community Service Center and wouldn't appreciate being interrupted for what she'd probably dismiss as a hunch. And telling Paul was out of the question, since anything I said would be fodder for his vast gossip mill.

Of course, there was always Roger. Assuming he hadn't been mortally wounded by Andrew and assuming he was willing to take my calls.

Leaving my briefcase and jacket where they were—trust runs deep in small-town girls, even when their small towns are flooded with strangers—I walked out the door and made my way to the side of the building, which functions as a combination parking lot and unofficial walkway.

It took a few rings before Roger picked up. "What do you want, Karin?" Instead of his usual boisterous brogue, he spoke in the wary tones of a chastened man. "You're a dangerous woman to be talking to."

Even though no one was within earshot, I lowered my voice. "Andrew said he had an errand to run. I had no idea it involved you. He didn't hurt you, did he?"

"Let's just say I took an unexpected fall. And my nose now has a great deal more character than it used to. Think Marlon Brando or Al Pacino."

Worse than I thought. "Well, this will make you feel better. I'm pretty sure I know who murdered Ben."

"Wait. Let me take a wild guess. Meredith and Jerry Rhinegold."

"How...?"

"As usual, I'm way ahead of you. Good thing you're a copywriter and not a reporter." I scoured my brain for a snappy retort and came up empty. "Here's some more for you. Meredith and her new love began their fling way, way back, during the early discussions about the Sand Point condos. Ben only learned about it after the project was underway. By then, he'd already decided that Rhinegold was the wrong person to be heading up the project, and that he himself was the right one. According to Devon, he was furious. Are you taking notes? For starters, he planned to write Meredith out of his will."

There was a slurping sound on Roger's end, as if he were drinking out of a straw. I didn't want to know why.

"But," he continued, "in keeping with his usual nasty tendencies—Ben could be such a bastard, couldn't he?—he didn't let on that he knew Meredith was sleeping with the enemy. So he kept enjoying her occasional favors even while he was planning to cut her out of his will and dirty-deal her new boyfriend. As the lead equity investor, with more shares than anyone else..."

I pounced. "Ben had the power to get Rhinegold fired and take over the project himself."

Two middle-aged women wearing rainbow-colored saris under their windbreakers slowed down and gave me a quizzical glance as they walked across the parking lot. Probably wondering who Rhinegold was. I lowered my voice. "And I'm betting that Ben had insisted on all kinds of clauses in the contract. For instance, penalizing Rhinegold for cost overruns. Maybe withholding his fees for services if he lost the confidence of investors. And it wouldn't surprise me if there was also a clause that limited Jerry's share of the profits if the investors soured on him."

Roger grunted. "Sounds like someone has been doing her homework."

"You think the police know all this?"

"I'd say that's a safe assumption." Another slurp. "And speaking of safe, my advice to you is to steer clear of Meredith. She knows the police are closing in. They've had Rhinegold in for questioning at least twice that I'm aware of. By now, she must be feeling desperate. She's erratic under the best of circumstances and, as we know, capable of just about anything."

A middle-aged couple, weighed down with camera equipment and a fancy cooler bag, looked at me in a worried way. Was my anxiety that evident?

Roger went on. "Also, she's probably deluded herself into believing that you and Bixie are the reason the police are on to her. That if it weren't for you two..."

"Okay, enough," I blurted out. "I get it." Despite the warmth of the day, a shiver made its way from my toes to the base of my skull. "Bixie and I will stay out of Meredith's reach for the next couple of days."

After Roger signed off, I stood there, lost in thought and barely noticing the tourists and locals passing by. When I finally glanced at my watch, it read eleven-thirty. Time to head back to the relative safety of my funky little beach rental.

I'd only been in the cottage for fifteen or twenty minutes when Bixie arrived. She was agitated, talkative, and hungry. While I raided the refrigerator, harvested tidbits from the cupboards, and laid out a lunch buffet, she vented. Still feeling pensive after my conversation with Roger, I listened closely and—unusual for me—without comment.

According to Bixie, the interview was aggressive but with no serious consequences beyond a warning. She told me that Charles planned to go back to work immediately after his session with the police. His bosses at the casino were not at all pleased with his recent extracurricular activities, and he'd be putting in long hours for the next several weeks to redeem himself. I could tell she was relieved. I'd seen the same process play out many times before. A sudden need to separate herself, to distance the man in her life, to back away from the Red Zone of relationships.

Finally, she ran out of words. My turn. I shoved my plate aside, retrieved my briefcase from the couch, took out my notebook, and placed it in front of me with a ceremonial flourish. "I spent part of my morning talking with an expert in commercial real estate," I flipped through my notes. "And the rest of it, talking with Roger."

I folded my hands on top of the notebook, schoolmarm style, and asked, "Would you like to know who killed Ben and why?"

The startled look on Bixie's face was hugely satisfying. Elbows on the table, head cupped in her hands, she looked like a child waiting for a story.

"Okay," I continued. "It all starts with the basics of real estate development." I thumbed through my notes until I found the page with an inky lasso around the key facts.

"The first thing you need to know—and something I didn't know until I talked with Bobbi—is that developers don't own the projects they work on, in this case, the condos. The real owners are the equity investors." My phone rang. I ignored it. "A commercial lender, usually a bank, typically puts up anywhere from sixty to eighty percent of the total construction cost. Let's say sixty. As the developer, Jerry probably funded five or ten percent. That's standard. The remaining thirty or thirty-five percent would come from a group of private equity investors. In this case, Ben was the lead equity investor. Which means he had more shares than anyone else, including Jerry Rhinegold."

"Right, I get it." Bixie reached toward the plate of gluten-free cookies I'd put out. "Ben had a lot of financial clout."

"More than that." I nabbed one of the cookies and took a bite. Almond shortbread. Not bad for a fake pastry. "Equity investors have a lot of power and all kinds of rights." I ticked off a few from my notes. "The right to elect a board of directors. The right to vote on all major business decisions. And here's the corker. The right to sue the company if their rights aren't being honored." I helped myself to another cookie.

"So what does all that rights stuff mean in practical terms?" Bixie was still

228

working on cookie number one. A model of restraint.

I swiped a napkin across the crumbs decorating my upper lip. "It means that, technically, Ben and his cohorts—but Ben especially—had control over every major decision. Normally, private equity investors try to get along and go along with the developer. But that was not Ben's intention. He had a super majority of stock, so he could stir up problems and create a lot of obstacles. Ultimately, he had the power to take over the project and fire Rhinegold. Which is what he planned to do."

Bixie reached for another cookie. "How do you know that?"

"Because of what I learned from Roger," I explained, and proceeded to summarize what he'd told me.

By the end of my recitation, Bixie was wide-eyed. "My God, what an amazing series of betrayals all around." She chewed for a few seconds. "If Meredith really did cast her lot with Jerry Rhinegold, there was a huge amount at stake for both of them."

For the next minute or so, the only sounds to be heard were the lake breeze rattling a loose windowpane and the kitchen clock ticking away steadily. I noticed, with a small but definite feeling of alarm, that Bixie's eyes had started to glitter. That meant an idea was percolating, probably not a good one.

"Wouldn't it be great to be able to prove your theory? Now? Without waiting?" She leaned back in her chair. "Oh, I know it wouldn't be safe or smart. But part of me would love to sit down with Meredith and get the real story."

"Let's not." I stood up. "Let's go with safe and smart and leave it to the police to handle the dangerous part." I slapped the notebook shut, walked it back to my briefcase, and glanced out the window just in time to see a white BMW pull into the parking lot.

Holy mother of God.

Keeping my eyes on the car and the brunette at the wheel, I spoke as fast as I could. "It's too late for safe and smart. Meredith is here. With a bouquet of flowers. And probably a basket of poisoned apples."

Chapter Fifty

The adrenal gland is a wonderful thing. In the moments that followed, I took multitasking to a whole new level—surveilling Meredith from behind a curtain, texting Andrew on the off chance that his phone was working, praying fervently that it did, and issuing instructions to Bixie at warp speed.

"We need to get out of here if we can. Grab your purse. Pretend you're getting ready to leave. We both are, that's the story. We're going to Marquette to visit Sandy. She's expecting us at three, an hour from now. She'll be worried if we don't turn up." I took in a shaky breath. "And if we can't manage to get rid of Meredith, we'll just have to hope Roger's wrong. That she hasn't come here on some crazy vendetta against us for setting the police on her."

Meredith was just a few steps from the door now. I picked up my bag from the chair next to the door, slung it over my shoulder, and half-whispered, "Let me take the lead."

There was a knock. I gave Bixie one last worried look. Purse in hand, face a bloodless white, she stood up. I pulled open the door.

"Meredith." I seemed to be short of breath. Did she notice? "What a surprise. We were just on our way out."

"Sorry to drop by unannounced, but I did call a few minutes ago." Meredith held out an elaborate bouquet with what she probably thought was a winsome smile, but what at that moment reminded me of the leering grin of the deranged housekeeper in *Rebecca,* just before she tries to kill Joan Fontaine. Even so, I had no choice but to take the flowers.

Meredith stepped through the doorway. "I got worried when you didn't return my calls or voicemails. And I just had to make amends. Can I come in?" A moot question, since she already was in.

Stay in character, I reminded myself. Don't let on that you suspect anything. What would you normally say right now? "We're meeting a friend of mine in Marquette at three," I began. "But, of course, come in." I took a step backwards. "We don't need to leave for a few minutes yet. By the way, how did you know where to find us?"

Meredith flicked her fingers in an offhand way. "Oh, Roger mentioned it days ago." Without being invited, she sat down in the armchair closest to the door and placed her purse on her lap.

I walked the flowers over to the kitchen counter, trying to quiet my breath as I moved. "These are so lovely, they deserve to be put in water right away. I'm sure I can find a vase somewhere." My hands were damp against the waxy tissue paper, and I held the bouquet at arm's length to avoid the heavy hothouse perfume they exhaled. Odd, the things you notice in a crisis situation. I opened the door of a cupboard that faced the living room and started moving kitchen paraphernalia around in a noisy, random way.

Meredith gave the room a quick once-over. "What a sweet little place. So rustic. It has that authentic up north feel, doesn't it?"

Bixie finally found her voice, or at least enough of it to answer. "Yes, we all like it, being right on the lake. Andrew especially. He's staying with us. In fact," she glanced at her watch, "he should be back anytime now."

At the news that Andrew might be on his way, Meredith's spine jerked upright. Then, as if willing herself to appear calm and unconcerned, she crossed her legs and readjusted the purse, settling it more firmly on her lap. "As I said, I just wanted to tell you how sorry I am for the way I acted the other day, when you suggested that Devon... that Devon might have been involved in my so-called overdose. I've always considered myself a second mother to him, and the idea that he would harm me, deliberately, or cast suspicion on me, well, I just couldn't take it in."

She twisted her head and shoulders to get me into her sightline. "Karin, aren't you going to sit down? It's hard to apologize properly when I can't see one of the people I'm apologizing to."

By now, I had unearthed an old mason jar and was trying to keep my hands from trembling as I arranged the stalks of peonies and dahlias into a clumsy display. "Oh no," I assured her. "I still need a couple of minutes to get this right. Besides, sometimes standing feels so much better than sitting." And so much safer.

Bixie's cadaverous pallor had been replaced with a bright red flush, and her voice was stronger. "There's really no need to apologize, Meredith. In fact, we should be the ones asking your forgiveness for springing our theories on you while you were still recovering from that terrible ordeal."

"Exactly," I added from my off-stage position in the kitchen. "We're the ones at fault, not you." I pushed the lopsided flower arrangement to the far end of the counter, now strewn with chunks of stems and cast-off greenery. It felt good to have the scissors still in my hand, even if it was a false comfort.

"That's very sweet of you both. Apology accepted." Purse in hand, Mercedes stood up as she spoke, which I took as a hopeful sign. Mistakenly, as it turned out. "And now…" she looked around the cottage, "I really need to use your bathroom."

"Right behind you," I said, and watched her enter the tiny room. Grasping wildly at straws, I wondered if we dared prop a chair under the doorknob. It always worked in movies. But if it didn't work now, and I guessed it probably wouldn't, what then? What desperate reaction would it provoke?

"Bixie," I whispered as I yanked the cell phone out of my back pocket. "Check for calls or texts from Andrew. Maybe he got my message and copied you on his response." Nothing on my phone. Bixie looked over at me and shook her head. God help us.

At the sound of the bathroom door creaking, I forced myself to smile. "So…" I looked down at my watch. "Not to be rude, but now that we've all apologized and we're friends again, Bixie and I really have to get going. My friend Sandy will start worrying if we delay much longer. And being a reporter, Sandy doesn't just worry, she acts. You never know what she's going to do."

The look of alarm on Meredith's face morphed almost instantly into artificial friendliness, strained eyes, tight smile. "Oh, but I was hoping we could spend a little time together this afternoon." Something in the way she said those words made my skin crawl. "Now that we're on good terms again, I thought it might be fun to take in some of the sights. Starting with Miner's Castle. I've never been to the overlook and the walkway."

The overlook and the walkway? It took a couple of seconds before I realized that she was referring to the upper viewing platform and the trail that led to the lower platform. The trail where a murder once took place. The trail where dozens of ill-fated tourists in pursuit of the perfect photo have taken one step too many toward the cliff's edge. Have stood on the brittle and untrustworthy sandstone. And have fallen to their deaths, into a lake that never forgives an error in judgment.

I struggled and failed to keep the fear out of my eyes. Glancing at Bixie, I saw that her eyes had also glazed over and were now staring at Meredith in unblinking terror.

Whether or not she guessed what I was thinking, Meredith kept talking in that same syrupy voice she'd been using since our conversation started. "You can be so persuasive when you want to be, Karin. I'm sure your friend will understand if you call her and reschedule for another day."

She gave a smile-that-wasn't-a-smile. "But before you do that, there's something important I need to talk to you both about." She began unzipping her purse. Her very large, very bulky purse. I held my breath. "And something I want to show you."

Chapter Fifty-One

What that something was, we would never know. At that moment, there was a series of heavy knocks on the door. Pounding, really.

Before I could even think about moving, a male voice yelled out "Police!" and the door seemed to fly open, revealing Rob Ketola in uniform, both arms straight in front of him, both hands gripping his gun.

Meredith was just about to pull whatever it was out of her purse when Bill Harris stepped through the door behind Rob. Hand on his holstered gun, he barked, "Stop right where you are, Ms. Wood. Then I want you to stand up and raise your hands. Slowly."

Meredith froze. Even in profile, I could see that she was struggling with herself over her next move. Unsure as to whether or not we were included in the raid, if that's what it was, Bixie and I raised our hands.

After five or six seconds that seemed like an eternity, Meredith slowly released her bag, letting it fall to the floor with a loud thud, and Rob boomed out words that I never expected to hear anywhere except in movies and TV crime dramas. "Meredith Wood, I am placing you under arrest for the murder of Benjamin Roberts. You have the right to remain silent. Anything you say can and will be used against you in a court of law. You have the right to an attorney. If you cannot..."

So my text message must have reached Andrew after all, and he alerted the local police. Somehow, I lost track of reality after that. It was as if I had walked into a dream, a chaotic, room-spinning dream. The scene playing out in front of me seemed to recede. The voices were distorted. I gripped the kitchen counter to steady myself.

Bill Harris was the first to notice my wonky state. Keeping his hand on the butt of his gun and not taking his eyes off Meredith, he barked out another order, this time at Bixie. "Better get over to the counter and grab Ms. Niemi. She seems to be in a rough state. After all this, we wouldn't want anything to happen to her." Even under duress, the man was a master of irony.

He turned toward us as Rob escorted Meredith, hands cuffed behind her back, out the door and down the steps. "We'll be in touch."

Forty-five minutes later, Bixie and I were sitting on the couch shoulder to shoulder, two glasses of wine within easy reach on the nearest end table, when a car pulled into the drive. A few seconds after that, Andrew raced up the steps and stood just inside the front door. Which we'd somehow neglected to close.

Bixie and I had been hashing over the events of the afternoon. Trying to make sense out of what happened. Puzzling over what *might* have happened. Working through our shock and disbelief. Theorizing as to what Meredith had stashed in that mysterious purse of hers. At the sight of Andrew, we fell silent.

For a few seconds, hands braced against the door frame, he stood statue-still, taking in the scene as if he were committing every detail to memory. Then he did something that was completely out of character. Completely unexpected.

He walked over to the couch until he stood directly in front of us, dropped to his knees, and pulled us both toward him in a rough, bruising bear hug. It was like being in a three-person football huddle, only a lot closer than the players ever get.

He didn't speak. Just held us.

Finally, in a voice muffled by his shoulder, I asked what seemed to be the obvious question, based on past experience. "Are you going to yell at us? Because if you are, you should know..."

Without releasing his hold on us, he let out a sound that could have been a laugh, but wasn't.

"No." He tightened his grip. "No yelling. Not now."

After maybe half a minute, I began to fidget, knowing that we didn't have the luxury of extended hugs and long conversations. Word travels fast on the Munising grapevine. Sometimes, when something really big happens, something like this, it moved at close to the speed of light. We didn't need warm fuzzies right now. What we needed was a communications strategy.

The public interest tsunami started about twenty minutes later, with Evelyn knocking persistently on the front door, demanding to know if we were all right. Her arrival coincided with a near-hysterical call from my Aunt Saimi, just back in town. Saimi, naturally, had already phoned Ilsa and Jalo, who were so worried when they couldn't reach me—due to Saimi asking so many questions and demanding so many details—that they phoned Bixie. Who would have answered their call except that Charles had pre-empted them, after first being bounced to Bixie's voicemail eight or nine times while she explained to her parents why they might be hearing her name and mine on the evening news.

The first half dozen text alerts that beeped out from my phone were—no surprise—from Roger, who would normally have turned up in person were it not for his latest run-in with Andrew.

As I was attempting to answer at least a few of Roger's messages, a fresh batch of texts came through, this time from Sandy warning us to prepare ourselves for a deluge of calls and unannounced visits from her colleagues at Channel Six News and broadcasters further afield, plus journalists from every news outlet in the state. In the hours that followed, many of them did in fact call the cottage landline and were told by Andrew that, on the advice of the Munising Police and their own legal counsel, Ms. Niemi and Ms. Murray would be making no comments and granting no interviews.

Our legal counsel? Now there was a thought. I made a mental note to contact Bob Worthington for recommendations. Although, as a Sand Point condo investor and thus a person of interest in the case, it was likely he'd already corralled the best legal talent for himself.

After ordering Bixie and me to screen all incoming contacts and ignore any unfamiliar numbers—as if we weren't already doing that—Andrew got a call from his friend Paul, who wanted to share status updates. Among those updates was the surprising news that Devon had been cooperating with the police for some time and had been providing them with documented evidence of the blood feud between Ben and Rhinegold, as well as Ben's plans to axe the developer from his own project. So that explained Devon's late-night prowl at his father's house.

By five o'clock, feeling frayed and edgy, we made a pact to ignore all incoming calls and texts, except those from the police. Fortunately, Evelyn staged a return visit around six, bringing with her a Turkey á la King casserole she'd whipped up—or more likely pulled out of her massive freezer and defrosted—along with biscuits from the Munising Bakery, a tossed salad made with fresh-picked greens, and a dozen oatmeal raisin cookies. If I haven't mentioned it before, Evelyn has a genius for comfort food.

Around seven, I microwaved Evelyn's casserole, tossed the salad, and uncorked a bottle of Pinot Noir that had been waiting in the refrigerator for a memorable occasion—and this night certainly seemed to qualify. As we ate, we conducted a verbal post-mortem of the whole crazy afternoon. Of course, there were a lot of unknowns, so we focused on the few facts we had. Andrew did most of the talking.

"When your text came through," he explained, "Paul and I contacted the Munising Police as well as the Marquette force. Turns out they already had warrants for Meredith and Jerry, and had planned to make arrests once they located the two of them. They'd been staking out the Holiday Inn in Munising and Jerry's home and office in Marquette. My call just accelerated their timeline."

Halfway through dinner, Bixie—who had been unusually quiet and tense—pushed her chair away from the table. "Sorry, but I've got a terrible headache. It must be all the tension. I need some gelsemium."

"You stay put, I'll get it," Andrew waved her back into her seat. "It's in the medicine cabinet, right?" Bixie nodded.

The table talk had barely restarted when Andrew called out from the bathroom in a loud voice. "Have either of you been taking amoxicillin for anything and forgot to mention it?" He moved to stand in the doorway. "Because there's a vial of it in the medicine cabinet, just behind the Tylenol."

Chapter Fifty-Two

It took Rob Ketola less than fifteen minutes to arrive on the scene with a plastic box that contained, among other things, latex gloves and small evidence bags. After Andrew had explained how he found the amoxicillin, Rob took some photos of the open cabinet and then, very carefully and methodically, collected the bottle. He left, after also collecting our assurances that we'd be at the station bright and early the next day to make detailed statements.

After dinner, when our energy reserves were finally tapped out and exhaustion had set in, we locked both doors, pulled the shades, and drew the curtains. Bixie and I muted our phones, took early showers, and collapsed into our respective beds, leaving Andrew to the tender mercies of local and regional news hounds. That included one Lester Holt wannabe who turned up around ten p.m., unannounced, in a broadcast van fully equipped with portable satellite dish, lights and camera crew.

Don't ask me how, but I managed to sleep like a child.

Luckily, and predictably, by the time we dragged ourselves out of bed the next morning, our celebrityhood was waning. We'd been eclipsed by the far brighter luster of Meredith, Jerry Rhinegold, and every investor and contractor involved with the Sand Point condo development.

Even so, it was bizarre and more than a little disturbing to watch Sandy deliver a lead story in which I figured as one of the major actors. After all, this was the woman I roomed with in college. The woman who held my head while I threw up my first and only bottle of Boone's Farm Apple Wine. The woman who made me her sole confidante when she fell in love and into bed with a married professor.

This was one of my forever friends. And there she was, on screen, telling the public about me and my role in a murder investigation in her cool, polished newscaster voice. Referring to me in the third person, as if I were a stranger. "Karin Niemi, a Munising native now living in Ann Arbor and a former employee of Ben Roberts, whose murder…" Draining all the drama out of our rescue by describing how "the incident ended when two Munising police officers entered the premises and apprehended the suspect." She wrapped up her report with the chilling revelation that "although the exact motives of the suspect are still under investigation, police believe that she may have intended to harm or kill both women."

To harm or kill both women.

Listening to Sandy, I had an overwhelming urge to crawl into one of the caves along the Lake Superior shoreline and hole up there until this whole mess blew over.

Of course, there were a few positive outcomes. One being the fact that Bixie and I were no longer the target of Rob Ketola's unrelenting hostility, animosity, call it what you will. This time the interrogation was mild and included courtesies like a cup of herbal tea for Bixie—don't ask me how they managed that—and a decent cup of coffee for me.

Pig-headed as ever, Rob at first refused to answer my perfectly reasonable questions and to share facts that Bixie and I deserved to know. Topping the list: What was the mysterious object that Meredith had stashed in her purse? What was she about to pull out when she was so fortuitously interrupted by Officers Ketola and Harris?

Eventually, though, his better angels won out. He grudgingly told me it could have been any one of numerous items. As he explained, "She had lots of options. It could have been the tube of lipstick. The compact. The latex gloves that she probably used to plant the amoxicillin in your bathroom. The photos of you and Ben and some other people at what looked like a company party. It could have been the scrap of notepaper with the addresses of hotels in Toronto and Mexico City. Or it could have been the loaded Derringer."

When I pointed out that none of her actions made sense and wondered out loud what she could have possibly been thinking, Rob replied in a patronizing voice, "Desperate is as desperate does. I seriously doubt if Meredith herself knew what she was going to do. By that point, she wasn't thinking, just reacting blindly to circumstances. Spinning the roulette wheel. Crazy as it sounds, maybe she believed she could make it look like you two killed Ben and then committed suicide rather than face a trial." The only reassurance he offered was that, eventually, they'd get to the truth. As he reminded me, "It will all come out in the courtroom."

The courtroom. What a stomach-churning prospect that was.

Around noon, when our statements had been signed and the three of us were free again, we stood together on the sidewalk outside the station. We didn't say a word, just let the July sun beat down on us while we took in deep lungfuls of Lake Superior air. It was almost like an impromptu group meditation. Gradually, I noticed that the tension and anxiety I'd been carrying around all morning were being edged out by feelings of calm and relief and gratitude. All of which tend to be rare visitors in my life.

Sad to say, they didn't hang around very long.

Before we disappeared into our respective vehicles, Bixie spoke. "I'm heading to the casino right now. Charles and I need to have a talk." Her tone wasn't exactly ominous, but close enough that neither Andrew nor I said a word. Instead, we waited as if expecting a shoe to drop.

Bixie slipped on her sunglasses and tossed her purse into the passenger seat. Then, settling herself behind the wheel, key in the ignition, she looked up at us through the open window. And dropped the shoe.

"I'll be heading back to Ann Arbor tomorrow morning."

Feeling a sudden need for lakeside solitude, I white-lied about having a long list of errands to run. Within a few minutes, I was driving the familiar miles along M-28. My destination was a tiny spit of land, popular with locals in search of a picnic or barbecue spot but generally overlooked by tourists seeking the broad white driftwood-strewn beaches further west.

Sitting at a picnic table under a cluster of towering White Pines, I gave myself up to the unusually warm wind and felt my heart slow with every wave that broke gently on the beach. But even after an hour of lakeside reverie, I still wasn't ready to spend the remnants of the day in the company of others. So I drove to the casino, bought a copy of the *Marquette Mining Journal,* and then parked across the highway at Foggy's.

The lunch crowd had dwindled to a handful of tourists and four women of a certain age, all locals, so I had no problem finding a small corner table. Once the women, two of whom I knew slightly, stopped giving me sideways glances and talking in excited whispers about me being "one of the girls who nearly got herself killed yesterday by that suspect in the Ben Roberts' murder case," I was able to enjoy my meal in relative peace.

While dawdling over dessert, I scanned my accumulated texts and voicemails, none of which I bothered to answer, and then gave my full attention to the paper's lead story detailing the investigation. After that, I idled away another few hours driving aimlessly from one local waterfall to another—ten in all—walking the trails, climbing the steps, and dodging tourists posing for selfies.

When I drove into the cottage parking area just before seven o'clock, it was still empty. Bixie arrived about thirty minutes later, muttered a quick hello, and began packing with fierce concentration. Andrew showed up around nine with the same leave-me-alone attitude, offering no explanation of where he'd been. After a quick shower and a terse "See you both in the morning," he took himself off to bed. I was next in the shower queue, after which I tucked myself in with an Agatha Raisin mystery and fell asleep with the bedside light on.

Chapter Fifty-Three

Knowing Bixie's late-riser tendencies, I was surprised to hear her shuttling luggage through the living room at seven a.m., the screen door slamming behind her periodically. After a quick cup of coffee, I helped her finish hauling out her totes and cooler.

When the car was loaded and we were making minor adjustments, she seemed to relax and become more like herself again. Shading her eyes against the strong morning sun, she launched into a half-explanation-half-apology for her sudden departure.

"My client at TriState Health moved up the completion date for their annual report by a month." She sighed. "So all of a sudden, we're in crisis mode. The first creative session is just three days from now."

I nodded. "Why is it always the big projects that get a rush deadline?" I asked, rhetorically. "Why is it never the little stuff?"

She leaned against the car door and looked at me straight on. "But I'd be leaving in any case." Was that sheen on her eyes from the sun? "This whole thing with Charles has me feeling... I don't even know what I'm feeling. I don't know if this is love or just some out-of-control summer crush. Hormones run wild." She pushed the hair away from her face. "I've never felt this way about a man before. So...connected. As if we belong together. As if we've known each other forever, even though it seems like such a crazy mismatch of cultures and backgrounds and personalities and..." She dredged up a deep sigh. "I need time and space to sort this all out."

Overhead, a wedge of wild geese made their usual clamoring calls. I resisted the urge to count them.

How do you comfort someone in a situation that defies comforting? If you're me, you change the subject. "You're doing what you need to," I assured her. "And I plan to do the same thing. I've still got ten days left on my rental agreement, and I'll be damned if this mess is going to ruin the rest of my time up here. But I need to lower my profile, so I'm thinking day trips are the best strategy. I'm going to take Bill Harris' advice and tour around Iron County and the Copper Country. Then I'll disappear for a day into the Keweenaw Peninsula. Who knows, I might even make my first trek ever to the upper falls at Tahquamenon."

I wondered if any of these jaunts would appeal to Andrew.

As if that thought had summoned him, I heard his voice a few paces behind me. "Sounds like a good plan. And I won't tell a soul that you've never seen one of the UP's premier tourist attractions."

His appearance was Bixie's cue for mood-switch. She pushed herself away from the hood. Hands on her hips, she stood motionless for a few seconds, staring at each of us in turn.

"Before I go, there are some things you both need to hear. I'm through tiptoeing around the truth." My shoulders tensed. As a dedicated tiptoeer myself, I knew I wasn't going to like this. "You two have some serious work to do. For one thing, you need to stop pretending that no one else notices this…this thing between you. We all see it. And now that you have time and space and privacy, you need to face it. Figure out what you want and what you mean to each other."

"Bixie, this isn't…" Andrew began, but she cut him off.

"Stop it." She snapped. "Stop trying to ignore the elephant in the room. Stop denying your feelings." By now, Andrew and I were both shifting foot to foot and finding new and creative ways to fidget in place.

Without warning, the shimmer in Bixie's eyes turned into frustrated, exasperated tears.

She sniffed, rummaged in the back pocket of her jeans, and pulled out a wad of tissues.

"Just one more thing." Her wet eyes slid back and forth between Andrew and me. "Despite those shells you carry around, you're both vulnerable.

Promise me that, whatever happens, you won't hurt each other. You won't do any permanent damage, either one of you."

I sent out a message at the top of my telepathic voice. Stop. Stop. Stop. But it was useless. I flitted a glance at Andrew and took comfort in the fact that he looked as mortified as I was at that moment.

"I love you both." Bixie's tears were coming fast now, and she seemed to have forgotten all those tissues clutched in her left hand. "So don't make me choose between you. Because I can't. And I won't."

Before I could respond, she gave me a fast, ferocious hug and did the same to her brother. Then, wiping at her face, she got into the car, started the engine after just two tries, and promised to call us when she arrived home.

Watching her drive away, I realized I had no idea what to say.

It was Andrew who broke the silence. "One thing about my sister, she really knows how to make a dramatic exit. But today she outdid herself." He kicked at a small rock just in front of him and turned his face to the lake. "Well, now that my mission is over, I guess it's time for me to follow her example and head back to Ann Arbor."

Something in the general region of my heart clenched. "You're leaving?" I tried to keep my face under control. "But there's so much you haven't seen. And you still have, what, another week of vacation time?"

"Nine days," he answered. I glanced up in time to see yet another line of wild geese make their way inland. What was it with all the birds this morning? Andrew continued, "If I start getting my things together now, I can be on the road by ten."

I stared at him. Wordless.

It was now or never.

My heart was banging in my chest. My hand—was it my hand? Was I really doing this?—reached out and touched his arm. "Before you go, I have a favor to ask."

"A favor?" He smiled in spite of himself. "Coming from you, that's hard to believe. Okay." Another smile. Something inside of me was melting. "What is it?"

I swallowed, but the lump in my throat refused to budge. "Do you remember when I told you that if I ever needed any protection, I'd let you know?" What was it about those grey eyes of his that managed to look so fierce and so inviting at the same time? I could get lost in those eyes. Maybe I already was.

"Of course," he shook his head at the memory. "How could I forget?"

"Well." I took a step towards him and then another until we were just a few inches apart. "The fact is…" Deep breath. "I could use some protecting right about now."

Silence. Then, slowly, he closed the distance between us. "Are you sure?" He spoke in a low whisper. His face was so close, I began feeling swoony.

"Mmmm…" I nodded.

He touched his forehead to mine. "You know," he said, "protecting someone can take a while."

"Then you should probably start now." Did I really say that?

In Munising, public displays of affection are rare and generally limited to out-of-the-way nooks, dim bars, dark corners, and appropriate evening hours. But for the next couple of minutes, drivers on Sand Point Road were treated to a highly unusual sight. There, early on a July morning, in the middle of Eleanor Donahue's gravel parking lot, a man and a woman were wrapped in each other's arms, engaged in some serious kissing.

I could hear cars and even a few heavy-duty trucks slow down as they passed. At one point, I heard young male voices whooping and whistling against the backdrop of a souped-up engine. But somehow it all seemed far away and unimportant.

Finally, I came up for air. "So then. How long do you think it will take, all this protecting?" I asked. "Maybe a week?"

"Oh, at least a week." Andrew drew me closer and brushed his lips against my cheek. "Probably longer."

From somewhere in the distance, a car horn blared approvingly and then faded.

"Yeah," his voice was a husky whisper next to my ear. "I'm guessing a lot longer than a week."

A Note from the Author

This story takes place in Munising, Michigan, on the northernmost coast of the Upper Peninsula, also known as The Yoop or the UP. There are numerous references to Ojibwe language and culture throughout the book, and the plot itself centers on land and artifacts related to the area's original "settlers."

The Upper Peninsula itself came into being as a result of the Toledo War, otherwise known as the Michigan-Ohio War of 1835-36. Both Wikipedia and Michiganology (https://michiganology.org/stories/toledo-michigan-2/) offer detailed accounts of the border dispute and the eventual land swaps that resulted in what is now the UP.

The region has been home to various groups of native peoples for over 3,000 years. (https://npshistory.com). Members of the Sioux/Ojibwe tribe migrated to this area during the early 1600's, following a war with eastern tribes, and lived on what is now known as Grand Island and along Munising bay. It was these original residents who gave the town its name: Kitchi-Minissing ("place of the island").

The first whites to arrive were primarily fur traders. They were followed by miners, lumberjacks and determined, stoic farmers, many of them from Scandinavian and Eastern European countries. Munising was incorporated as a village in 1896 and officially became a city in 1915.

For well over a century, downstate residents regarded the land north of the Mackinac Bridge as relatively useless and a financial burden on the rest of the state. This view changed dramatically over time, as the Michigan Chamber of Commerce came to realize that the Upper Peninsula was a treasure trove of natural wonders...waiting to be discovered by vacationers. These days, the once-quiet town of Munising hosts approximately one million tourists annually, who are drawn to the Pictured Rocks National Lakeshore, the waterfalls, the hiking trails, the nearby Porcupine Mountains, the forests, the beaches, and the magic of Lake Superior.

This is the setting for Karin Niemi and her downstate friends as they try to unravel a mysterious death, the equally mysterious disappearance of Ojibwe artifacts, and the even more mysterious workings of the human heart.

For those interested in learning more about the UP and its Ojibwe heritage, here are a few "starter" suggestions:

Pictured Rocks National Lakeshore
(https://www.uptravel.com)

Bemidji State University's Anishinaabe timeline and other resources
(https://bemidjistate.edu)

The University of Minnesota's Ojibwe People's Dictionary
(https://ojibwe.lib.umn.edu)

The history of Alger County (Munising)
(https://www.algercounty.gov)

The Sault Tribe of Chippewa Indians
(https://saulttribe.com)

The Inter-Tribal Council of Michigan
(https://www.itcmi.org)

A Face in the Rock: The Tale of a Grand Island Chippewa by Loren R. Graham
(https://islandpress.org/books/face-rock#desc)

The Hiawatha Legends by Henry R. Schoolcraft
(https://www.amazon.com/Hiawatha-Legends-Henry-R-Schoolcraft/dp/0932212352)

Acknowledgments

This book couldn't have been written without the support and expert knowledge of others.

Topping the list are Sheriff Todd Brock and Under Sheriff Steve Blank of the Alger County Sheriff's Office as well as Detective Captain Mike Kohler, now retired, of the Marquette City Police Department, all of whom were extremely generous with their time and expertise, and all of whom showed remarkable patience and professionalism in answering my many questions. Any factual or technical errors relating to law enforcement that appear in this book are mine alone and in no way reflect on any of them.

A special shout-out to ethicist and friend Jeanine DeLay for setting this entire project in motion by insisting that Karin Niemi's first adventure left her in a state of ambiguity, and that it was my responsibility "to fix Karin's life." I'm grateful that all my attempts to ignore her suggestion failed miserably.

Heartfelt appreciation to Doris ("Sis") and Mari LeVeque for sharing their deep knowledge of Ojibwe culture and history, for providing so much useful background information on the Sault Tribe of Chippewa Indians (https://saulttribe.com), for inviting me to a pow-wow, and for answering what probably seemed like odd and endless questions during the writing of this book. It's a delight and an honor to be part of this generations-long friendship between two families.

Gratitude to all the friends, relatives and readers who encouraged me at every step. Thank you to Munising insider Vicki Sowa for useful facts and to Kathleen Elavsky Brinton for sharing her knowledge of life on Lost Lake. Sincere thanks as well to my alpha and beta readers—Deborah Crosby, Ann Neiswander, Terri Devall, Frederick Fischer, Judalyn Seling, Grace

Shackman, Sharon Brown, Christine Koskimaki-Attalai, Jason Coleman and Bernadette Quist—for their intelligent, insightful and helpfully critical readings of the manuscript.

Particular thanks to my late and much-missed friend Nancy Rupprecht for handing me a copy of Dorothy Sayers' *Murder Must Advertise* more than four decades ago and telling me to read it. (I never stopped.) A grateful hug to Pauline Elavsky, aunt extraordinaire and resident expert and advisor on all things relating to our hometown of Munising. And gratitude as well to Terri Devall and Jane Delancey for moving the cover art forward.

Finally, and most importantly, thank you to Tom for all those amazing years together, for making our marriage an endless adventure, and for making me believe I could do just about anything. Wherever you are now, however near or far, this book is for you.

About the Author

A native of Michigan's Upper Peninsula, Linda Wirtanen Fitzgerald migrated to Ann Arbor for graduate school and, like so many others, never left. After brief stints as a magazine editor, newspaper reporter, and scriptwriter for sales seminars, she found her professional niche as senior copywriter in an ad agency and later launched her own one-woman firm. In 2023, she realized her longtime ambition of authoring a mystery novel with the publication of *Death at the Doorstep*, the debut adventure of Ann Arbor freelance writer and amateur sleuth Karin Niemi. The second novel in the series, *A Superior Way to Die*, is set in her hometown of Munising.

AUTHOR WEBSITE:
  https://DeathattheDoorstep.com

SOCIAL MEDIA HANDLES:
  https://www.instagram.com/lindafitzmysteries
  https://www.facebook.com/DeathattheDoorstep/

Also by Linda W. Fitzgerald

Death at the Doorstep, Level Best Books